FLEE

A CURVY GIRL ROMANTIC SUSPENSE

F-BOMB: CURVY VIGILANTES
BOOK 7

MARY E THOMPSON

F-BOMB: CURVY VIGILANTES

Say hello to the Curvy Vigilantes, a group of plus-size women who protect their city. They have no training, but they don't need it. All they need is the desire to right wrongs and to protect the ones they love... and maybe some help from the men strong (and smart) enough to fall for these kick-ass curvy women.

F-BOMB: CURVY VIGILANTES

Forsaken (subscriber exclusive)

Fury

Framed

Feign

Fierce

Fatal

Fear

Flee

Fracture

Faith

SUBSCRIBE NOW AT MARYETHOMPSON.COM

To being brave enough to accept what is yours... and to know you deserve every last bit of it, so matter what anyone else says.

1

Dawn Patterson blinked away tears as she read the latest text from her ex-husband.

> Savannah doesn't want to go to dinner
> Friday night.

Her first instinct was to threaten Owen with a call from her lawyer, reminding him of the custody agreement they had and that she was entitled to one dinner a month alone with their daughter, but Dawn was trying to be better. It wasn't easy, but she was trying.

> Okay.

Dawn shoved the phone back into her pocket and drew a deep breath. Making a fourteen-year-old to do something she didn't want to do would only create bigger problems. Dawn needed to be patient.

And she needed to focus on work. She always saved her favorite patient for last, and today, she needed the confidence and joy from the man more than most days.

Dawn waved her hand beneath the automatic hand sanitizer dispenser and rubbed her hands together as she walked into the room.

Robert Davis laid in his bed, his head propped up with too many pillows as he struggled to breathe. His pale skin was wrinkled and weathered, but his light brown eyes were still bright and full of life. It was like his body was trying to drag his mind out of the world and into the afterlife.

"Jeez, what did they do to you?" Dawn asked, hurrying to Mr. Davis. She pulled one of the pillows from behind his head and lowered the head of his hospital bed.

"You just take my breath away," Mr. Davis said with a wheeze and a smile.

Dawn chuckled with him and shook her head. "You're good for my ego."

"If only I were five decades younger..."

Dawn laughed at the old joke. It had become his favorite line with her over the last year. A year where Dawn had fought with everything she had to begin to rebuild her life.

A life where her daughter still wanted nothing to do with her and her ex-husband was the eternal good guy.

"How are you feeling now that you can breathe again?" Dawn unwound the stethoscope from around her neck and checked his heart and lungs. Still okay, but slower. Every day they were getting slower.

"Like I'm fifty years old again."

Dawn grinned. She knew he didn't feel fifty again, but he never complained. She sat on the edge of his bed. "How do you really feel?"

He sighed, the sound pulling his eternal grin down just a touch. "I'm tired, honey."

"I know." Dawn patted the man's hand. She loved the work she did. What started as a penance enacted on herself became work she had a passion for. A part of her felt guilty for enjoying the job when she went into the work to atone for her many, many sins, but she knew what she was doing was helping people.

"How come you're still here? I thought you got off at five."

Dawn shrugged. "No reason to rush home."

"That'll change one day. Owen and Savannah will realize what they're missing by keeping you at arm's length."

The kind words brought tears back to Dawn's eyes. Not because she wished Mr. Davis was right, but because he had such faith in her, even though he knew everything she'd done. "I don't think that's going to happen. Savannah just canceled dinner for Friday night."

"I thought that was court ordered," Mr. Davis barked. He tried to push himself upright, indignant that her life wasn't going as planned.

Dawn pushed his shoulders so he'd lie down again. "It is, but I can't force her to have a relationship with me."

Mr. Davis shook his head. "You can't give up on her. I gave up on my sons. Both of them became people I didn't recognize. I put all of myself into work and didn't pay enough attention to them. I wish I'd made different choices. It's my biggest regret. I don't want you to have the same one when you're on your deathbed."

"You're not on your deathbed just yet," Dawn told him, not wanting to think about the man not being around.

"Dawn," he said, gripping her hand with far more strength than she expected from the frail man. "I know you think I'm a crazy old man, but please listen to me. Do whatever it takes to fix your relationship with Savannah. If you're not interested in getting back together with Owen, don't think twice about that, but Savannah matters."

Dawn nodded, knowing the man was speaking from experience and not just offering bland advice.

"When my wife died, I let myself get lost in work. I let myself ignore my sons. If I could go back, I would, but I lost them both a long time ago. By the time I tried, it was too late to reach them."

"I will. I promise."

Mr. Davis nodded, relaxing once more, his grip failing as he sank against the bed. His face relaxed, sleep coming for him. "I apologize. I hate to see you repeating my mistakes."

"Thank you. I know. I'm not sure Savannah will ever forgive me, but you're right. I need to try. I need to make sure she knows I've changed."

Mr. Davis nodded. "Good. I apologize for fading on you, but I know I'm not going to be awake much longer."

"You never have to apologize to me for anything. Rest. We'll talk tomorrow."

Mr. Davis nodded, his eyes falling closed as he fell asleep just that quickly.

Dawn finished her work for the day and headed home. Her apartment was empty and lonely and depressing, but it was one more piece of her penance. One more thing to remind her she owed her life to others. To the nine-one-one operator who kept Savannah calm that night, and to the fire-fighters and paramedics who saved Dawn's life.

Rock bottom hurt. But it worked. Dawn turned her life around after that night, but she couldn't erase all the pain she caused. All she could hope for was forgiveness one day.

Clearly, not today.

GAGE STEVENS REACHED for the phone as he keyed in his password to unlock his computer. He'd barely made it into his office and had just spoken to his assistant, Betsy.

"Yeah?" Gage asked into the phone.

"You have a call, Mr. Stevens." It didn't matter how many times Gage told her to call him by his first name, the older woman refused. Said she'd never called a boss by his first name and didn't intend to start now, even though she claimed to be old enough to be his mother.

"Can you take a message?"

"It's Mr. Davis."

Gage sighed. Mr. Davis was a longtime client, and he was nearing the end of his life. Gage knew it, and Mr. Davis knew it. Gage never refused the man's calls. Not when any of them could be the last one.

"Line two," Betsy said, knowing Gage was going to take the call.

"Good morning," Gage said into the phone.

"I woke up, so I guess I'll agree with you for now," Mr. Davis said. Robert was a friendly man, and a wealthy man. Over the years, Gage had grown to respect him.

But Mr. Davis had secrets. Secrets Gage had never been able to get out of him.

"What can I do for you today?" Gage asked, knowing Mr. Davis didn't tolerate small talk or beating around the bush.

"I need to make an amendment."

"Excuse me?"

"I want to change my beneficiary."

"You can't possibly be serious," Gage said. As much as Gage hated it, Mr. Davis's only son was his heir and would inherit a seven-figure company. They'd spoken many times about it, and Mr. Davis was reluctant to hand that kind of money over to his son, but with no other family, he had few choices, and had eliminated all of them.

"We both know the end is coming for me, Gage. And Trevor is getting more and more erratic. I can't. I have no proof, but we both know what he's doing isn't good. I can't sit back and know my company is going to be used for criminal activity. My name will be tarnished, and my employees will be out on the streets. If they survive."

"He's going to be furious," Gage whispered. Trevor Davis was a crazy son-of-a-bitch. The man was unhinged and deadly. Gage had no proof either, but he had every reason to believe Trevor was involved in some of the events happening in Niagara Falls recently.

And attorney-client privilege kept him from sharing his worries with the police department because everything Gage suspected was based on conversations Gage had with Robert.

"Yeah, he is. But with my money, he's going to burn the city. It won't be safe for anyone."

Gage sighed. Robert was right. Gage knew he was right. But it was going to be hell when Trevor found out. "Okay. Who do you want to leave everything to?"

"Dawn Patterson."

"Who is that?"

"She's a nurse here. She's had a lot of shit happen in her life, and she's a good person. She deserves this more than Trevor. She will honor my company."

"Trevor is going to go after her."

"That's why you're not going to let him know about her."

Gage sucked in a breath. "I'll draw up the paperwork and come by in an hour." There was no time to waste when the client was so close to the end. "I need witnesses."

"I'll have the doctor here," Mr. Davis said. He understood. Someone had to be there to confirm Mr. Davis was of sound mind when he was making a decision like the one he proposed. Otherwise, it would all be for nothing.

"See you then." Gage hung up the phone and dropped his head into his hands. Dealing with clients at the end of their lives was always tough, but this was pushing it.

Gage pushed aside his thoughts and started on the new paperwork. He made all the changes that needed to be made and printed out everything Mr. Davis needed to sign.

An hour after their call, Gage walked into Mr. Davis's room. Both a doctor and a nurse were in the room, talking to Mr. Davis.

"Mr. Stevens?" the doctor asked.

Gage nodded and shook her hand.

"Dr. Walden. Mandy and I were doing the cognitive exam, and I can certify that Mr. Davis is of sound mind and capable of making this change of his own free will."

"Thank you, Dr. Walden. And Mandy."

The nurse nodded.

"Will you both be willing to sign as witnesses to Mr. Davis?" Gage asked them.

"Of course," they said at the same time.

Gage went through the changes he made, including the name of the woman Mr. Davis had chosen as his new beneficiary. At her name, the doctor and nurse both gasped.

Gage spared them a glance, but Mr. Davis didn't flinch.

"Sign here, sir," Gage told Mr. Davis. They'd been through this before. Every few years, Mr. Davis updated his will with his current assets, ensuring nothing was left out. He signed his name with the familiar care he always used, his hand moving slowly so there was no mistaking his signature.

Gage took the paperwork from him when he was

finished and set it on the table in front of Dr. Walden and Mandy. "If you would both sign beneath his as witnesses to his signature."

Dr. Walden signed first, then slid the paperwork in front of Mandy. When both were done, Gage confirmed their signatures and names, then stamped it as the notary of record.

"I will file this with the court today and keep the originals, as always."

Mr. Davis nodded, understanding what Gage wasn't saying. If it was only in his office, and Trevor got to it, he could destroy the updated will and claim he was the sole heir.

"Do you need anything else from us?" Dr. Walden asked.

Gage shook his head. "Thank you both for your time."

They nodded and excused themselves from the room, their whispered voices disappearing when they were outside.

"I take it they know Ms. Patterson?"

Mr. Davis nodded.

"Is there something I should know about her?"

Mr. Davis shook his head. "All you need to know is she's the best person to do this. It won't be easy for her, but Dawn deserves a break."

Gage sighed. Mr. Davis had a big heart. He was always giving back, donating his entire salary to local charities for the last decade he worked. With no major expenses and plenty of savings, he insisted on helping others. He was generous with his bonus structure and rewarded loyalty and exceptional work.

Gage took his answer to mean Dawn Patterson had some trouble, and Mr. Davis decided she was his latest charity project.

Maybe he'd change his mind. Maybe she'd never know about the lottery ticket he would be handing her.

But like any lottery ticket, it came with strings. Ones that could either set a person free or kill them.

Gage hoped the woman knew how to free herself.

TREVOR DAVIS WALKED down the hallway toward his father's room. He hated the place, but it was the only way he could see his father anymore. And the only way the grumpy bastard would give Trevor money.

Trevor stepped into the room, spotting a fat nurse sitting on the edge of the bed.

"It'll get better," his father said, patting the woman's hand like she was important. Like she mattered. Instead of like she was the damn help.

"Dad," Trevor growled, letting them know he was there.

The fat nurse jumped, spinning to face him with a guilty look on her face. She smoothed the purple scrubs over her chunky stomach and pressed her hands into wide hips.

Trevor let his gaze trail over her. He liked the big ones. Once they got hooked on drugs, they lost weight, forgetting to care about food and choosing drugs only. She'd be a good fuck. Fat bitches had tight pussies because no one else liked to fuck them.

"Trevor," his father said, the encouraging tone he'd used with the fat chick replaced by one of disdain. "What are you doing here?"

"I'll just let you two talk," the nurse said. She made her way around Trevor, giving him space like she couldn't bear the thought of touching him.

Trevor stepped in her path and ran a hand down her cheek.

She swallowed roughly. "Excuse me."

"Let her be," his father barked.

Trevor smiled, letting his gaze run down her chunky body again. Yeah, he'd enjoy a go at her. It had definitely been a while since a man put his hands on her. Trevor would pound her into submission.

She stepped around Trevor and hurried out of the room, closing the door behind her.

Trevor sneered. He delighted in making others uncomfortable. Made him hard. If his dad wasn't glaring at him, Trevor would have stroked one out right then and there, but the miserable bastard was watching him. "What?"

"You're the one who showed up at my home. What do you want?"

"Money. I'm almost out. I need ten grand."

"I gave you ten grand last week."

"And I spent it. Now, I need more."

"What are you doing with all this money, Trevor?"

"What the fuck do you care? You haven't worried about me since I was nine and mom died. Fuck, you probably didn't worry about me then. She did."

"I always worried about you."

"Could have fucking fooled me," Trevor spat. He hated his father. All he'd ever done was disappear. Trevor and his older brother, Clyde, had to learn to take care of themselves. And they did. By taking what they wanted.

Their father never gave a shit. Not until Trevor no longer needed a father.

"One day you're not going to be able to get my money," his father said, almost sounding sad at the admission.

"Because you'll be dead? Yeah, I'm counting the days, old man."

His father grimaced. He swung his legs over the side of the bed and eased himself upright. He walked across the small room to the dresser where he kept his cash. He unlocked the safe and retrieved rolls of bills. He counted it quickly, then locked the box again and turned to Trevor.

"I'm sorry I was such a horrible father."

"Whatever. When I inherit all your money, I'll appreciate the fact that you only cared about your company and never about me." Trevor turned to leave.

"You're not going to inherit my money," his father whispered.

Trevor stopped halfway to the door. He had to have heard him wrong. "What did you say?"

His father straightened when Trevor turned back to him. He held himself upright, but the exhaustion on his face betrayed the false bravado of his posture. "I said you're not going to inherit my money. I changed my will."

"The fuck you did."

"It's already done, Trevor. I can't have you destroying my company. You'll—"

Trevor was on his father so quickly he didn't even remember moving. He wrapped a hand around the man's throat and guided him to the bed. "You never cared about me. That company was all that ever mattered to you."

His father shook his head, the movement just enough to break Trevor's hold. His father sank to the bed, knocking a pillow onto the floor. "That's not true. I loved you and your brother. I would have done anything for you two."

"Except give me your company. You are treating me no better than a dog in the street, rejecting me and refusing to give me what I've earned."

"How did you earn it? You've never worked there a day in your life!"

"I earned it by being born. I earned it by surviving. I earned it by sharing your blood. And I will have what I earned."

Trevor picked up the pillow from the floor. He held it between his hands and pressed it over his father's face.

The old man's feet kicked. He fought against the pillow. He tried to scream, but the pillow drowned out the sound. He grabbed at Trevor's hands, but Trevor held still.

Until his father stopped fighting.

Trevor removed the pillow from his father's face. Terrified eyes stared up at him. Vacant. Hollow. Dead.

It was the most loving look his father had ever given him. The one Trevor would remember for the rest of his life.

He fluffed the pillow and put it behind his father's head. He positioned him so it looked like he was sleeping. Then Trevor left the room with his money and a promise to himself that he would get what he deserved. Every last penny.

2

———————

Gage fell to his chair and put his head in his hand. "I was just there two days ago. I just saw him."

"I know, Mr. Stevens. And I am sorry. It's clear you cared about Mr. Davis," the care facility administrator said. Gage had already forgotten her name. It wasn't as important as the news of Mr. Davis's passing. "The doctor said he went peacefully, likely when he was sleeping."

"Have you notified his son?"

"Yes, sir, we have."

"Okay. Thank you. When can I make arrangements to collect his belongings?"

"Um, well, his family—"

"I am the executor of the estate, and I will need to collect Mr. Davis's belongings."

"I wasn't aware of that."

"Has his son already come to collect items?"

"Uh, no, not to my knowledge, but when I spoke to him, I asked him to let me know when he would like to."

"Did he give you a time?"

"No. He just said he'd be in touch."

"Okay, good. I will come this afternoon. I will also claim Mr. Davis's body and take care of the funeral arrangements."

"We will need to see a copy of the will naming you as executor, Mr. Stevens."

"I'd expect nothing less. I'll be there at one."

"Okay. Thank you."

Gage hung up the phone and immediately pulled up another number. He needed help. Now.

"Patrick," the captain of the police department said.

"Marcus, I need a favor."

"That's not like you. What can I do for you, Gage?"

"I have a client who just passed away. His son was written out of his will two days ago."

Marcus whistled. "Cutting it close."

"He was. And he had his reasons." Gage's tone didn't hide his opinion, and Marcus picked up on it.

"Reasons I should be aware of?"

"Reasons I would assume you're already aware of."

"Um, okay. So, what do you need from me?" Marcus's tone was no longer friendly. The police captain was in charge.

"As the executor of Mr. Davis's estate, I need to collect his belongings. I am going to Angel's Grove at one today. Is there a way you could send me an officer or two to help me collect the man's things and take them to his home?"

"Mr. Davis? As in Robert Davis? Owner of Davis Developments?"

"The same."

"And Mr. Davis's son is Trevor Davis. His son Clyde died years ago."

"Yes," Gage said, knowing he was giving Marcus just enough information without violating attorney-client privilege.

"Okay. I will be there myself, and I'll bring another officer with me. Maybe two. Do we need to secure Mr. Davis's home?"

"I'm not sure as of yet."

"Well, you sure know how to make for an interesting day." Marcus chuckled mirthlessly.

"Don't I know it," Gage said wryly.

"I'll see you in a few hours, Gage."

"Thanks, Marcus."

Gage hung up and called the moving company he always used when he had to relocate a client. Andy agreed to be there at one when Marcus and Gage would arrive. Everything was set.

Gage just hoped Trevor Davis didn't show up and try to get something that didn't belong to him.

"PRETTY EASY ASSIGNMENT," Marcus said to Gage as they watched the last of Robert Davis's belongings get loaded onto the small moving truck.

"Cross your fingers it stays that way," Gage told him.

Andy closed up the truck and confirmed the address with Gage, then climbed into the van with his employee. Gage and Marcus watched as the truck pulled out of the lot, a police car following them.

"No Trevor Davis today," Marcus said.

Gage shook his head. "No, but he'll show up. He's not going to be happy Robert wrote him out of the will when he finds out. He's probably going to be angry when he shows up here and finds his father's things are gone."

"I'll keep an officer stationed here until after the funeral."

Gage nodded. "Probably a good idea. Especially since the new beneficiary is an employee."

"Of this place?" Marcus hitched his thumb toward the one-story brick structure. The sprawling campus it was on made for a peaceful environment, but it wasn't exactly a happy place. The people who lived there were at the end of their lives. They were well cared for, but they were still dying. And they all knew it.

"Robert was a very generous man, and he made it seem as though this nurse was someone who would do well with his company and fortune."

"Do you know the nurse?"

Gage shook his head. "Dawn Patterson. I've never met her."

Marcus's brows went up.

"I take it you know her?"

Marcus shook his head. "Common enough name that it might not be her, but about eighteen months ago, we responded to an overdose. Woman's daughter called. Found her mom passed out and blue. Saved her mother's life, but can't imagine at what cost."

"What do you mean?"

"The kid was only twelve. Couldn't have been easy."

"Shit." Gage scrubbed his face. "Do you know what happened to her after that?"

Marcus shook his head. "I hope she turned her life around and came here to work, but I'm not sure. Why would Davis have given everything to someone he didn't know that well? I thought he was only here a year?"

Gage shrugged. "He was. And no clue, but it sounds like something he would have done. He gave back more than anyone knows. And he would have seen someone with a past like that, especially if she turned her life around, as someone he wanted to help."

"I hope she did turn her life around. And I hope Trevor Davis doesn't find out who she is."

"Will is already filed at the courthouse. Original is safe, too. There's no way he can contest it. No way he'll win."

"Doesn't mean he won't try something."

"Hopefully, he's smarter than that."

Marcus gave Gage a look that said he clearly didn't think that was possible.

Gage chuckled. "Okay, well, hopefully she can take care of herself. Or is married to someone who can."

Marcus nodded. "We can hope. Ready to follow that truck?"

"Yep. Let's go."

Gage went to his SUV and followed Marcus out of the parking lot. Mr. Davis's house wasn't too far from Angel's Grove, and when they arrived, the truck was parked and open, and the two officers were walking out of the house.

"Everything good?" Marcus asked the officers.

They exchanged a glance. "Front door was unlocked when we got here. We went through the house. It looks clear, but big houses like this could have all kinds of places for people to hide."

"You agree with Murphy?" Marcus asked the other cop.

The second one nodded. "I do. We checked the garage, and the vehicles are cool to the touch, but that doesn't mean someone hasn't been here for a while."

Marcus turned to Gage. "Do you know who has access to the property?"

"Employees and his son, to my knowledge. Mr. Davis hasn't lived here for a year, but he kept up the property.

There's a caretaker who lives here. He could be out some-where, though."

"Can you give him a call?" Marcus asked.

Gage nodded. He called Cole, the caretaker, who answered on the first ring.

"Mr. Stevens. Is everything okay?"

"Yes, Cole. I'm at the estate with Mr. Davis's belongings. The front door was unlocked when we arrived. The police officers I'm with asked me to confirm everything is okay."

"Oh, no. I apologize, sir. A package was delivered this morning, and I went out the front to retrieve it. Phone rang when I was on the porch, and I rushed back inside. I must have forgotten to check the door."

"But everything is okay?"

"Yes, Mr. Stevens. Absolutely. I'm at the grocery store at the moment, but I will be back in about thirty minutes if you'd like to wait. Or I can leave now and be back in ten minutes."

"No, I think we're okay. Just wanted to double check. Have you seen Mr. Davis's son?"

"No," Cole breathed. "Thankfully. I worried that was why you were calling."

"Are you aware of the change in the will?"

"Yes, sir. Mr. Davis called me to let me know. It's still hard to believe he's gone. We just spoke a few days ago. He sounded good."

"I agree. Thank you, Cole. I know I'll see you soon."

"Yes, sir. Thank you."

Cole hung up, and Gage looked at his phone. Something was off, but Gage couldn't put his finger on what it was.

"Are we good?" Marcus asked quietly.

Gage looked up and smiled. "Yes. Sorry. The caretaker

said he grabbed a package this morning and must have forgotten to lock the door."

"Let's get this stuff inside," Marcus told the others.

Gage watched the activity as Mr. Davis's life for the last year was returned to the home he'd lived in for the decades before. When Robert made the choice to leave his home, he knew he wouldn't ever see it again. But he also felt staying there wasn't an option for him. His health had been declining for years, and after a fall a little over a year ago, he accepted that he needed more regular care.

He considered hiring someone to come to his home, but he didn't want to put that on Cole and the other staff. Instead, he made the decision to move to a long-term care facility that was staffed with people who would be able to help him.

Gage spoke to Mr. Davis at least once a week for the last year. He genuinely liked the man. Gage knew Robert had regrets, but he was trying to make up for what he considered his failures. He ran out of time to do more.

"All set, Gage," Andy said, bringing Gage paperwork to sign that everything had been delivered.

Gage signed and shook Andy's hand. He handed Andy a check for twice the quoted amount, something Gage knew Robert would have done if he were there. "Thank you. It means a lot that you were able to jump on this today."

"Happy to help."

Andy and his guys loaded up their truck and left. Gage turned his attention to Marcus and the two officers he was speaking to.

"Thank you all for being here," Gage said. "It appears as though it was an unnecessary precaution."

"No such thing," one of the officers said.

"Officer Pryce Murphy is studying to be a detective. His girlfriend is Edie Warren," Marcus said.

Gage knew the name from the papers and the story of what she'd been through. "Edie Warren? It's good to know she's found some happiness."

"Thank you," Pryce said. "She is still haunted by what she went through. What Trevor put her through."

"Trevor?" Gage barked. "Did you say Trevor?" Gage looked between Pryce and Marcus.

"Edie doesn't know Trevor's last name, but she said that's the name of the man who had her," Marcus provided.

Gage rocked back on his heels. "What are the odds?"

Marcus pressed his lips into a smile. "Not a very common name, is it?" Marcus looked up at the house they were all standing in front of. "Strange that a very wealthy man, who just died, has a son named Trevor."

"And that he just changed his will," Gage said.

Pryce and the other officer both raised their brows.

"What are the odds?" Marcus repeated Gage's words.

A vehicle coming up the driveway stopped the conversation. They all watched as the car crept toward them and the garage opened. Gage waved when he recognized Cole behind the wheel.

"That's the caretaker," he told the others.

The three police officers relaxed.

"We might need a patrol," Marcus told the other cops.

"On it," the one whose name Gage didn't know said.

"Thanks, Foster. I'll see you two back at the station," Marcus said, dismissing them before the caretaker came out of the garage.

Foster and Pryce went to their vehicle and waved before heading back down the driveway and out of sight.

"Foster and Murphy are two I know I can trust. Invaluable. And involved with all of this."

Gage nodded, understanding what Marcus meant. They would look into Trevor Davis and find what Gage didn't have proof of.

"Mr. Stevens, I apologize for the oversight. Was anything taken?" Cole asked, approaching them with a quick step.

"All good, Cole. Just a concern. We've moved the furniture back into Mr. Davis's rooms. I am hoping to get the funeral set for Saturday."

"That quickly?" Cole asked.

Gage nodded. "Mr. Davis already prepaid for everything and has it all set up. I just need to confirm it can be done in two days. He didn't want things to linger. I'll be in touch with funeral arrangements once I have confirmation, if you'd like to attend."

"Of course. Mr. Davis was a very kind man. I wish he'd felt like he could stay here. I always felt guilty enjoying this large home when he wasn't able to." Cole looked up at the house wistfully. "Do you know what's going to happen to the home?"

Gage shook his head. "No, I don't. The beneficiary of the estate will have that choice."

"And do you know who that is?"

Gage exchanged a glance with Marcus. Marcus raised his brows, indicating it was up to Gage what he shared.

"I do, but until I've had a chance to speak with them, nothing is confirmed."

"Understandable. Hopefully it's someone who will honor this home and Mr. Davis in the way he deserves."

"I'm sure it is. Mr. Davis wouldn't have selected the person if not."

Cole smiled. "True."

Gage and Marcus spoke to Cole a few more minutes before Cole excused himself to bring in the groceries. Marcus and Gage said their goodbyes and left the estate.

Gage had work to do. And so did Marcus.

"He's dead?" Dawn squeaked. Her voice wobbled and rose sharply. "When?"

"Wednesday. Night shift found him," Ali said. "He was nice. We're all upset."

Dawn nodded, unable to stop the emotions from welling up. Mr. Davis wasn't just her favorite patient, he was someone she thought of as a friend. Someone she trusted and liked speaking to. And he was gone. She was alone.

Dawn's throat was tight. She tried to remember the last time she spoke to Mr. Davis. When the memory came to her, she shivered. It was the day his son showed up. "Wait, night shift found Mr. Davis?"

Ali looked up from her paperwork. "Yeah, why?"

"When I left, he was with his son."

"Okay?"

"Just... don't you find it strange his son was here, and then Mr. Davis dies?"

"I hope you're not saying you think his son killed him. Dr. Tacker said it appeared to be natural causes. The guy was old, Dawn. And sick."

"Yeah, I guess."

Ali glared at her. "I wouldn't tell anyone else what you just told me."

"Why not?"

"That could get his son into a lot of trouble. An accusation like that. It could get Dr. Tacker into trouble, too. Unless you have some kind of proof, you don't need to say things like that."

Dawn looked at the other nurse. Ali was young and cute. Compared to most of her coworkers, Dawn felt like she was the old lady of the group at forty-one. Ali was smart, but she was innocent and inexperienced.

The way Trevor looked at Dawn and touched her cheek still made her skin crawl. She wouldn't be surprised if he killed his father. The look in his eyes said he was capable of it. He was capable of anything.

Ali would have giggled if Trevor had treated her the way he did Dawn. Ali would have thought it was flattering. She made no secret of her goal to find a husband and have a family.

It wasn't the goal that was the issue. It was the way Ali would throw herself at any single man in her vicinity. She didn't care who fathered her children as long as he also supported her.

Trevor Davis was not the kind of man who should have children. There was evil in him. Darkness that made Dawn shiver.

"Promise me you're not going to say anything to anyone about Mr. Davis's son," Ali said. She had been working at Angel's Grove for three years and outranked Dawn, which meant Dawn answered to the younger woman. And she respected the tentative authority.

"I promise, Ali. I was just—"

"You weren't doing anything. We never had this conversation."

Dawn nodded. "One thing. Do you know when the funeral is?"

"Two o'clock, I think. Why?"

"Today?" Dawn gasped.

Ali nodded. "Yeah. There was no reason to do an autopsy, and the lawyer who's in charge of everything said it was all set up and paid for a while ago, so he made it happen on a Saturday when it was easier for people to get there."

Dawn looked at the clock. She'd only been there an hour, and asking to leave four hours early so she could make it to the funeral of one of their residents was not likely to be approved. Especially the day of when she hadn't lined up someone else to cover for her.

"Do you—?"

"No," Ali said before Dawn could finish her question. "I know you liked Mr. Davis, but there's no way you can leave to go to the funeral. You're already filling in for vacation. On top of that, Megan called in, and Becca is sick. We're beyond shorthanded as it is."

"Yeah, you're right," Dawn said, knowing Ali was looking out for her.

"Stop by the cemetery after work tonight. I'm off tomorrow and was going to go then. Say goodbye."

Dawn nodded. "Yeah, I will. Thanks, Ali."

"Yep."

The younger woman walked off, a tablet in her hand. She stuck the tablet on the cart outside one room and knocked before walking in.

Dawn needed to do the same. Start her day and focus on the patients who were still there. She had a job to do. She could grieve Mr. Davis later.

3

———

FOR DAYS, GAGE WAS ON EDGE. HE KEPT WAITING FOR TREVOR to go off on someone. For him to lash out when he learned he wasn't going to be getting everything of his father's.

But things were quiet.

Quiet made Gage anxious.

All the arrangements were made for the funeral. Gage had followed Robert's detailed instructions. Gage stood at the entrance to the church, greeting visitors and thanking them for coming.

What Trevor should have done, but Trevor wasn't there.

Gage called the man the day after Robert died to let Trevor know Gage was handling things. Trevor didn't argue and dismissed Gage as quickly as he could. Gage debated telling Trevor he was no longer the heir to his father's fortune, but he decided not to do that over the phone. Telling Trevor Davis in person was a risky move, but it was what Gage would have done in any other situation and he wasn't going to change things just because Trevor was dangerous.

That one conversation was the last time Gage spoke to

Trevor. Trevor didn't show up at the viewing the night before. And with the funeral starting in ten minutes, Gage had his doubts about Trevor showing up for that, either.

Another noticeable absence was Dawn Patterson. After his conversation with Marcus, Gage looked the woman up. The story Marcus told him was definitely about the woman who was about to inherit billions. From what Gage read, she'd indeed turned her life around. She was an exemplary employee and well-respected by staff and patients. There had been no rumors or concerns about drug use since her time in rehab.

But there was a notice of divorce. And a custody agreement that said she did not have custody of her fourteen-year-old daughter.

With the funeral almost behind him, Gage knew he needed to contact Dawn Patterson. Even though she didn't know she was the beneficiary of the Davis Estate, Gage still half-expected her to attend the funeral.

The minister approached Gage and asked if they were ready to get started. Gage agreed and took his seat. Gage invited Cole and the other staff to sit with him, but they all said they didn't feel right doing so, leaving Gage alone in the front row. He tried not to think about the last time he sat alone in the front row at a funeral.

The minister performed a nice ceremony. He was an old friend of Robert's and shared stories about the man that Gage had never heard. Robert was praised for his generosity and kindness and for the overall way he treated his employees.

When the funeral was over, Gage drove himself to the cemetery. Robert didn't want his money spent on things he believed were a waste. The number one thing was a limousine no one would ride in since his wife and oldest son were gone and Robert possibly knew his younger son wouldn't attend.

Gage parked behind the hearse and followed the small crowd to the gravesite. A few more words were said, and Robert Davis was lowered into the ground.

One by one, the guests who came to the cemetery drifted away. Gage assumed some were people hoping for a reception and a chance to see the man's home. Others were employees from Davis Developments who felt they were doing right by their boss. Some others appeared to have been medical personnel from the care facility.

None were Trevor Davis or Dawn Patterson.

"Is there anything I can do for you, sir?" Cole asked, approaching Gage from the side.

Gage shook his head. "No, thank you, Cole. I'm sure Mr. Davis would have appreciated you being here."

Cole nodded. "We all enjoyed working for him. He was a kind and generous man. He will be missed."

Gage nodded his agreement, letting Cole go knowing he had fulfilled his obligation to his boss.

Gage looked back at the hole in the ground and tried not to imagine his own funeral and what it might look like. Much the same, he assumed. People who felt obligated to attend, even though none of them had a real connection with him. Mr. Davis was alone. He had more money than he could spend in a lifetime, and when the end arrived, he didn't have a single relative to honor him.

Would Gage be the same? No family, no connections, no one to even keep his bed warm. Was he really living his life?

Gage's phone rang in his pocket, the vibration pulling him out of his melancholy. He hated funerals. He'd attended more than his fair share, and they never got easier. But this one was getting to him more than most.

"Hello?" Gage said, not recognizing the number calling him.

"Mr. Stevens?"

"Yes. Who is this?"

"This is Detective Drake Foster. We met the other day with Captain Patrick."

"Yes, of course. How can I help you, Detective?"

"Unfortunately, I'm calling to let you know someone broke into your home."

"Excuse me?"

"One of your neighbors called in that they saw a man walking around your property and then he disappeared into your backyard. They believed the man broke into your house through your back door. I'm at your home now, and unfortunately, your neighbor was correct. Are you available to come home?"

Gage sighed and looked at the empty cemetery. "Yeah, I'll be there in ten minutes. Thank you, Detective."

Gage pocketed his phone and hurried to his SUV. There was nothing he could do about an intruder after the fact, but if he had to guess, he knew exactly who it was and what he was looking for.

Hopefully Trevor didn't find the will. But Gage still had to check. Then he had to find out how Trevor knew it had been changed.

THREE POLICE CARS were in front of Gage's house when he got home. He pulled into his short driveway and was met by Detective Drake Foster.

"Sorry to see you again under these circumstances," Foster said as he reached to shake Gage's hand.

"Me, too, Detective. What am I walking into?"

"Call me Drake. And unfortunately, a bit of a mess. It appears as though someone was looking for something. The worse news is I asked a car to head to your office after I showed up here, and that was hit, too."

Gage sighed. "Which means he didn't find what he was looking for at one of them and came to the other. Any idea where he started?"

Drake shook his head. "Not yet, but it sounds like you know who did this."

"My guess would be Trevor Davis."

Drake sucked in a breath. "I was afraid you were going to say that."

Gage exchanged a look with the man. They both knew what it meant. "Today was his father's funeral. He knew I'd be there. It was a perfect opportunity to look for Robert's will, which was changed this week, although I'm not sure how Trevor knows that. My guess is he started at my office, and he came here when he didn't find it in my files."

"Is it here?"

Gage shrugged. "It was. I guess I'll see if it still is."

"I'll go in with you. Make sure no one else follows you to wherever you need to go. If that's okay with you."

Gage nodded. "Yeah. Marcus brought you in on this so I know I can trust you."

Drake nodded, letting Gage lead the way.

Gage went in through the front door. He was proud of his home. It wasn't in the best neighborhood, and it wasn't the fanciest house, but it was his. He grew up in the two-story house with his mother. It was the best she could afford, and something she worked hard to provide for him.

Until she was taken from him in a robbery gone wrong that was still unsolved almost thirty years later. When Gage saw the house was on the market four years ago, he was willing to pay whatever it took to make sure it was his.

His home was a refuge for Gage. A safe place, even though the neighborhood had its trouble. Gage knew his neighbors and could count on them to watch out for him, and he did the same. He loved where he lived, and his home. Seeing what Trevor did to it...

"Do you know which neighbor called it in?" Gage asked Drake.

Drake tapped something on his phone and said, "Mrs. Gerty Wilson. Do you know her?"

Gage nodded and pointed to the right. "Next door. She was a friend of my mother's."

"I didn't realize you lived here that long."

Gage shook his head. "I left when I was young. Just bought the house a few years ago."

Drake nodded, looking around at the destruction. There was no judgment or question in his gaze. Some cops came to Gage's neighborhood and assumed whoever lived there deserved what they got because it was a bad section of town. Gage knew that was bullshit, and he was relieved to see Drake wasn't one of those cops.

Gage moved past the living room at the front of the house, trying to keep his emotions in check. The couch was upended, the TV smashed. The drawers in the sideboard were open and tossed on the floor, some broken. Pictures and artwork were dropped from their previous hanging spots on the walls. It could all be replaced, but it pissed Gage off that he had to.

Gage wanted to go upstairs and check the will, but he needed to see the rest of the first floor first. Detective Foster followed Gage down the hallway to the coat closet under the stairs. The door was open, all the shoes and coats thrown out. One hanger was left on the rod. Mocking Gage. Across from the stairs was a half bathroom that was relatively untouched.

The kitchen was as much of a mess as the living room with drawers yanked out and tossed all over. Dishes and glasses were smashed and in pieces. The small dining room attached to the kitchen only held a table and chairs and appeared okay. Gage was thankful Trevor didn't leave gas or water running. The damage so far was limited to stuff.

Gage went back to the front of the house and turned to climb the stairs. Two bedrooms were separated by a bathroom. Gage glanced into his room before going to the one in the front. He used it as a home office and added a bed that had never been used. Files were everywhere, and the mattress was off the bed. The hall bathroom was relatively untouched.

Gage used the bedroom at the back of the house, his childhood bedroom, as his room. Clothes were tossed from the closet, the mattress flipped, dresser drawers all yanked from their resting places to be emptied.

"He obviously was searching," Drake said softly. "I'm sorry."

Gage shook his head. There was nothing any of them could do. "He was quick if Mrs. Wilson called the police when she saw him in the backyard."

"Hopefully that means he didn't get what he was looking for."

"It doesn't really matter because I filed it last week when Mr. Davis signed it, but I'd rather Trevor not know who the recipient is for all of his father's wealth."

"Definitely puts a target on them."

Gage nodded. "Yep." Gage looked over at Detective

Drake Foster and blew out a breath. "Are you staying in here?"

"It's here?"

Gage nodded.

"Your call. It makes no difference to me as long as no one else knows what's going on. I think I can trust everyone, but if they know something, they're a target, too."

"So are you," Gage said.

"I'm not worried about me."

"We should all be worried. If Trevor is who we all think he is, we should all be worried."

Drake inhaled sharply, the reality hitting him visibly. Drake nodded and took a step toward the door. He closed it behind him, putting himself in the hallway while Gage searched.

Gage lifted the edge of the rug under his bed. The loose floorboard didn't appear to have been moved. Gage stuck his finger in the tiny notch he found when he was a teenager and pulled the loose board up.

Gage let out a breath. The vinyl envelope was still there.

He retrieved it from the hiding spot and checked that everything was still inside. When he was sure Trevor hadn't seen any of it, Gage replaced the board and the rug and picked up a messenger bag from the floor.

Trevor wouldn't stop. Eventually, news would break about Dawn Patterson, but Gage couldn't be the one who let it out. Not until he had a chance to speak to the woman herself and make sure she was willing to fulfill the obligation she never asked for.

"All set?" Drake asked when Gage opened the door.

Gage patted the bag and nodded. "All good."

"Let's take a look around and you can see if anything is missing."

"We both know nothing is going to be missing."

"Yeah, but I still need a report. We're going to talk to Mrs. Wilson and see if she can identify Trevor as the man who broke in. If he took something, we can add on charges."

Gage shook his head. "Never thought I'd hope someone stole something from me."

Drake snorted. "Right? Messed up isn't it?"

Gage nodded and followed Drake down the stairs to take inventory of all his possessions.

DAWN STOOD at the edge of the dirt and stared at it. She was the only one at the cemetery. The sun was setting and darkness was following her, but Dawn wanted to say goodbye to the man who'd become a friend.

"I'm sorry I wasn't there," she whispered into the air. "I'm sorry you were alone."

The wind around her whipped up her hair. She smiled, imagining it was Mr. Davis telling her he didn't blame her. That was the kind of man he was. One who always wanted the best for the people around him. Even those who didn't deserve it.

Dawn was definitely one who didn't deserve his kindness. But he offered it freely. He was quick to encourage her to keep trying with Savannah and Owen, and quick to boost her spirits.

Dawn remembered the first time she met Mr. Davis. It was her first day of work, and he'd been at Angel's Grove for two weeks. He was bored, and he tried to talk her into playing hooky with him and going outside.

Not wanting to get fired on her first day, Dawn asked her supervisor if she could take Mr. Davis outside. Her supervisor told her residents were allowed to go wherever they wanted and that it wasn't breaking any rules for him to go outside.

When Dawn relayed the message, Mr. Davis told her she was no fun. That everything is better when you think you're breaking the rules.

Dawn confessed that she'd broken too many rules and it had almost cost her her life and wasn't going to break more. Mr. Davis forgot all about going outside and made her sit and tell him everything.

By the time Dawn finished her sob story, she was in tears, and Mr. Davis was telling her she deserved better. Something Dawn still didn't believe, but something Mr. Davis never stopped telling her.

He always believed in her. All the way to the end, he encouraged her to go after the things she wanted. And what she wanted more than anything was a relationship with her daughter.

"Maybe you can whisper into Savannah's ear to give me a chance," Dawn said out loud. "Maybe she'll listen to you."

The snap of a twig not far from Dawn brought her head up. She looked around the cemetery, but no one was there.

She gazed back at the dirt mound that hid Mr. Davis. "I miss you."

The dirt didn't answer, of course. But something else whispered. A tingle up her spine. Like someone was watching her.

Dawn glanced around again, once more not finding anyone. But the feeling didn't go away.

She said her goodbyes and promised to visit Mr. Davis again, in the daylight, and made her way to her car.

Dawn locked the doors and started the engine. She pulled away from the edge of the drive and slowly worked toward the exit. She watched her rearview mirror as much as the road in front of her, not seeing anyone behind her.

She made it to the main road and shook her head at herself. She was being silly. No one was there. No one was watching her. She was letting her imagination get the best of her.

But she still watched her mirror as she drove home. She still circled the block before she pulled into her apartment complex. And she still locked the door as soon as she was inside her studio apartment.

Trevor sat outside the apartment and stared at the window. The glow behind the blinds told him the fat nurse was still up. The flickering light a TV she watched.

He wondered if she was the one his father left everything to. If she was the person who would try to stop him from taking what he earned by a lifetime of bowing down to his miserable fucking excuse for a father.

Breaking into the lawyer's office was the only way Trevor could find out the name on the will. Instead, there was a gap in the asshole's files.

His home didn't help. But if Trevor had more time, he might have found something. Nosy fucking neighbors. Next time, he'd have to take care of the neighbors first. Make sure none of them would try to do the right thing and call the cops.

Trevor's phone lit up with a call from the boss. He thought about ignoring it, but he knew that would only make things worse.

"Yeah?"

"Where the fuck are you?"

"I'm following a lead."

"What lead? We have people for that. And if you're going to do what you promised you would do, you need to stay the fuck out of it."

"My fucking father screwed me."

"What did you expect? I told you this was a risk."

"I didn't think he would cut me out."

"Family is messy."

Trevor snorted. If anyone knew that, it was definitely the boss.

"Put someone on whatever the hell you're chasing and get over here."

Her tone dropped, and his dick rose. "Yeah?"

"Yeah. I had a good day, and I need a good fuck. Unless you're not up to the task."

"Always. I'm always up to the task."

"Then get your ass over here, or I'll find someone else who won't let me down."

Trevor knew she wasn't lying. The boss was ruthless. She'd proven that time and again over the years. Which was why Trevor was smart enough to make sure he was in the position he was in. One that meant she would call him when she needed something. Anything.

And he was more than happy to deliver.

He slammed the car into gear and growled, "Don't you fucking dare. I'm on my way."

"Five minutes or I start without you."

"I'll be there in three."

4

Gage didn't sleep. Two fucking nights and no sleep. Every time he drifted off, something woke him, and he jumped up. Listening. Waiting. Ready.

Gage never thought of himself as a violent man, but he didn't take well to being threatened. Trevor might not have said the words, but the implication was clear. He was going to do whatever it took to get what he felt belonged to him. Including breaking into Gage's house and office.

Even knowing something was coming didn't prepare Gage for how it felt to know someone was in his space uninvited. Trevor could have planted anything in Gage's home or office when he was there. As far as the police could tell, he hadn't, but Gage still called a security company first thing Monday morning when he got to his office. He couldn't take the chance any of his conversations with his clients were overheard by anyone, but especially Trevor.

"Good morning, Mr. Stevens," Betsy said cautiously when she walked in. It wasn't usual for Gage to be there before her, but he didn't want her there alone, at least until Trevor was put away.

"We had a break-in over the weekend," Gage said in greeting.

Betsy gasped. Her gaze swept the waiting room, the one room in the place mostly untouched.

"He was looking for something in particular and didn't find it, so he broke into my home as well."

"Are you okay?" Betsy asked. Her face went pale. She clutched her purse in both hands, wringing them tight around the strap.

Gage nodded. "I wasn't home. Which he knew."

"You know who it was?"

"Mr. Davis's son."

Betsy's fear morphed to outrage. "What did he think finding the will would do? It's already been filed."

"I'm guessing he doesn't know that. I'm also unsure how he knows he's been written out of it. I haven't spoken to him about that."

"Well, I certainly haven't told anyone."

"I know, Betsy. I would never suspect you. But it gives us very few suspects."

"Well, who knows? Obviously, Mr. Davis didn't tell him. The witnesses are the only other ones who knew, and whoever they told."

Gage swiped a hand down his face. Betsy was right. But her words made him wonder. "I need to make a few calls. I've tried to put things back to right, but I know you have a system. I'm sure I didn't keep to it well enough."

Betsy smiled wryly. "I will take care of it, Mr. Stevens." She walked closer and patted Gage on the cheek. "You look like you didn't sleep all weekend."

Gage shook his head. "I didn't."

"I'm sorry, Gage. No one should be this way."

Gage's brows shot up at her use of his first name.

Betsy noticed and grinned. "Don't get all excited on me. I'm speaking to you as a person and not my boss. I worry about you more than you know. I told Albert this weekend you need a good woman to take care of you."

"I have you," Gage said without missing a beat.

Betsy chuckled and shook her head. "Yes, well, there are limits to my employment requirements."

Gage laughed at her proper words. "I hope you'll be at my funeral."

Betsy gasped. "You better not be planning to have one anytime soon. You have a lot more people to help."

Gage nodded, knowing she was right. "I hope I have a few more years in me."

Betsy looked at him closely. "This Trevor Davis has you worried, doesn't he?"

"Yeah. He does. There's a reason Robert cut him out of his will. I don't know all the details of what it is, but Robert was never very complimentary about his son."

"Should I be worried?"

Gage didn't want to lie to the woman, but he didn't know how to answer the question. "I don't know. I don't know what he's capable of or what he's willing to do to get what he wants. What I do know is I have a security company coming in this morning to outfit this whole place with an alarm system. I don't want you here alone, if at all possible. And when you leave, I will walk you to your vehicle."

Betsy shivered. "I don't like this, Mr. Stevens."

"I don't either, Betsy. If you would rather take a leave of absence, I will cover your full salary until you feel comfortable coming back."

"Then you'll be here alone."

Gage shrugged. "I don't have anyone, Betsy. I don't have a spouse or kids and grandkids. I don't have anyone counting on me and looking for me. You do. If something happens to me, other lawyers will take over my cases and life will go on."

"Don't speak that way about my friend. You have people who care about you, Gage."

Gage took a moment to appreciate Betsy's words. "Thank you. But we both know you have a lot more at stake. My offer always stands if you feel better not being here for a while."

"Let me think about it. For now, what can I do?"

"Get your office back to how you like it. The security company should be here in thirty minutes. Then I need to set up an appointment with the new beneficiary. And I need to check in with Marcus."

"You go make your calls. I'll handle the security company. Who is it?"

"Rose Protection Agency. A guy named Zeke Donovan will be the one coming here."

Betsy scribbled the information on a sticky note and shooed Gage away. "I'll check his ID before I let him in the door."

Gage nodded and sucked in a breath. "Thank you, Betsy. And I'm sorry you've been dragged into this."

"We'll take care of it, Mr. Stevens. Go get your day started. I'll make the coffee."

"Extra strong?"

"No sense in drinking it if it's not," Betsy said. She believed that to her soul and chastised anyone who tried to argue with her that her coffee was too strong.

Gage went to his office. He'd picked up everything on the floor, but the files were still a mess. It would take far too long to get everything back to where it was supposed to be, but he had to start with one.

After he made his first call of the day.

"Patrick," Marcus answered.

"Did you get the report on Robert Davis's death?" Gage asked, knowing Marcus knew he was the one calling.

"Can't say I've seen one. Why?"

"How does Trevor know the will has been changed?"

"Huh." Marcus was quiet for a few seconds. "I'm guessing you haven't told him."

"I have not. Part of the stipulation is Ms. Patterson has to agree. Robert didn't even want his son to know anything, but if she agrees, it'll be obvious when she shows up at Davis Developments and his house that she's the beneficiary."

"Really? She gets to choose?"

"Robert knew he was going to be asking her to do something outside her skills. He intended to speak to her, but that didn't happen. I intended to speak to her before I notified his son of the change."

"But if he's breaking into your home and office, you're assuming he's looking for the will because he knows it's been changed."

"Yes. But how does he know?"

"What are you getting at?"

"I have nothing to back this up, and it's only speculation, but what if Robert told his son he'd made the change? What if Trevor came looking for something and Robert told him he wouldn't be getting anything when he died?"

"You think he killed his father?" Marcus was clearly surprised at the suggestion.

"Can you honestly tell me you don't think he's capable? If he is who you think he is."

Marcus sucked in a breath. The creak of a chair said he leaned back. "Shit. That's a whole different can of worms."

"There was no autopsy because someone said he

appeared to go in his sleep. He was old and not well. No one bothered to consider other options. But what if something else happened?"

"Jesus, Gage, this is a fucking mess," Marcus breathed.

"Yeah, it is."

"Shit. Okay, so say you're right. Say Robert told Trevor, Trevor killed him and made it look like natural causes. Now what?"

"That's your department. I'm just trying to figure out how Trevor knew the will was changed. I haven't heard anything about the witnesses getting hurt, so I'm assuming Trevor doesn't know who they are. But once he has the will, he doesn't need them, anyway. All he needs is Dawn Patterson's name."

"Which he'll have once the will is public."

"If she agrees to take over."

Marcus exhaled slowly. "When are you going to speak to her?"

"I was going to call her this morning. Rose Protection Agency is sending someone over soon to put in a full system. If I get a chance, I'll call her before they arrive. If not, first thing after."

"Call her now. Let me know when she's coming. I'll make sure I'm there. No matter what. I won't come in because that's private, but I'll sit outside in case anyone shows up uninvited."

"Okay. Thanks, Marcus. I appreciate the help."

"You're sure calling in all those favors I owe you in a hurry."

Gage snorted. "Yeah. I was planning to save them for something really good. Instead, I'm trying to stay alive and keep others the same way."

"We'll take him down. He's not going to get away with all of this."

"I hope not."

"You have my word."

"Thanks, Marcus. I'll let you know when the meeting is."

"Sounds good."

Gage didn't hear voices outside his office, so he made his next call to Dawn Patterson.

She answered on the third ring with a cautious, "Hello?"

"Is this Dawn Patterson?"

"Yes, it is. Who is this?"

"My name is Gage Stevens, Ms. Patterson. I am a lawyer representing Mr. Robert Davis's estate. I need you to come in for a meeting at your earliest convenience."

"Mr. Davis? Why?"

"We will discuss all of that when you are able to come to the office. Is there a time today or tomorrow that will work for you?"

She inhaled softly, the confusion evident in her hesitation. "Um, yeah. I work both days, but I can make come by after my shift. I'm assuming you're local."

"Yes, we are. I invite you to look up my name online and get the address from our website. I will give it to you, but I understand this request is not something you expected."

"No, not at all. I'm still heartbroken he's gone."

"I understand. Is four this afternoon okay with you?"

"Yes, that works. Thank you, Mr..."

"Stevens. Gage Stevens. I'll see you at four, Ms. Patterson."

"See you then."

Gage hung up just as he heard a male voice outside his office. Betsy replied, and Gage breathed a little easier. He assumed it was the security company Marcus recommended and wanted to meet the man.

Gage walked out of his office and stopped short at the man the size of a small car in the waiting area. He was tall and wide with muscles for days. He wore a pair of pressed pants that looked custom made for a man of his size and a black button-down shirt with Rose Protection Agency on his left pec.

"Mr. Stevens, this is Zeke Donovan. He's going to be installing our system."

Gage moved forward and shook the man's hand. It was clear Zeke was well capable of crushing anyone he came into contact with and held back when it wasn't necessary to use such force.

"Nice to meet you, sir."

"You as well. Thank you for coming so quickly."

"We know when someone calls, it's usually for a reason. Betsy was just telling me you've had some issues with a client's family. Sorry to hear about that."

"Thank you. It's... A lot."

"I'll get you all set up and our team will monitor your properties around the clock. We contract with a company that provides twenty-four-seven monitoring if we are unavailable for any reason, but most of the time, someone in our local company will be watching your properties."

"Thank you. That's perfect. Captain Marcus Patrick recommended your company."

Zeke smiled, and his entire face transformed. "Captain Patrick has been singing our praises lately. Friend of a friend, but a good man to know. And a good man, now that I've had the pleasure of meeting him myself."

"Marcus is a good man. His recommendation was enough for me."

"Thank you, sir. I'll be sure to tell my boss."

Gage nodded. "I'll let you get started."

Zeke nodded and took in the room. He moved through the space like he could see things Gage couldn't. Which was why Gage hired him. He wouldn't know where to start, but Zeke clearly did.

An hour later, Zeke had installed a full system. He offered to meet Gage at his home that evening so Betsy wasn't alone. Gage agreed gratefully and thanked Zeke for his time at the office.

When Zeke left, Gage sent Marcus a text thanking him for the recommendation and letting him know when Dawn Patterson would be there for their meeting. Marcus said he'd be there.

All Gage had to do was convince the woman to accept a few billion dollars and the price it would put on her head.

Dawn stared at the man across the desk from her, sure she heard him wrong. "Mr. Davis left me his company?"

The lawyer, Mr. Stevens, nodded. "Yes. And his home, and all his money. You're the beneficiary of all of his wealth."

"And he's a billionaire," Dawn said, repeating the words Mr. Stevens told her when he read the will.

"Mr. Davis has been a client of mine for years. He was very clear when he made the changes to his will. He left you a letter, if you'd like it."

Dawn nodded, feeling exposed and overwhelmed and maybe a tiny bit giddy. It could all be a big joke. Hire a lawyer to tell her she was rich, then leave her a letter saying just kidding. It didn't sound like the man Dawn knew, but neither did billionaire.

She reached for the envelope Mr. Stevens held out with a shaky hand. Everything was shaky. She didn't know what to expect.

Dawn tore open the envelope and retrieved the single sheet of paper. She flipped it open and saw the letterhead for Angel's Grove. She smiled, thinking of the day Mr. Davis asked if she had any paper with the fancy title on it.

Dawn smiled and began to read.

Dearest Dawn,

I know leaving you in this position is a poor thing to do to you. I'm hoping the money eases some of the pain this is going to put you through. Not losing me, though. I know I was more of a pain above ground for you. No, the pain I'm talking about is my son.

Trevor has gotten involved with people he shouldn't. He always wanted to be like his big brother, and I'd hoped when Clyde was killed, Trevor would realize that life wasn't a good one. For a while, I thought he had.

I was wrong, Dawn. So very wrong.

Trevor is going to be angry that he didn't inherit everything I'm giving you. Legally, there's nothing he can do about it. But Trevor hasn't cared much about the law, so I have no doubt he'll try something. I hope you are safe. I know Gage will do everything he can to keep Trevor from finding out who you are, but eventually, the truth will come out. Please know I never intended any harm to come to you or Savannah. Trevor has never heard your name from me, so you should have time to figure out what you want to do.

Gage has the paperwork to set up a trust fund for Savannah. I needed approval from you and Owen to do it so it isn't complete, but it's all ready. She won't have to worry about a thing. And I hope you won't either. If you want to run my company, they will be lucky to have such a caring and capable person in charge. If it's not for you, Gage will handle that. You will maintain ownership regardless. If you agree. You can say no to all of this.

I trust you, Dawn. I know you will do what's right. I know you will help. I'm sorry for laying all this on you, but I didn't know who else I could trust.

Thank you for all the talks. For sitting with me and treating me like a human. For being kind and sympathetic. For your smile. If we'd met in a different lifetime, I'd like to think I would have had a chance with you. But alas, it wasn't meant to be. I hope you will find someone who makes you smile as you made me smile the last year of my life. It was a blessing I hadn't realized I was missing until I met you.

With love,
Robert

Dawn wiped her falling tears as she tucked the letter back into the envelope. Mr. Davis had actually left her his fortune. He trusted her.

"What is he talking about? What is his son involved in?" Dawn asked.

"Mr. Davis believed his son was involved in illegal activity. He didn't want everything he worked his whole life to build to end up funding things he didn't believe in. That's why he changed his will just before he died. Less than two days before."

"Two days?" Dawn breathed. "Why me?"

"Unfortunately, I don't know the whole answer to that. He told me he trusted you. And he believed you would help. There are stipulations. Ones that include giving you time to think about your options, including the option to say no. If you'd like."

Dawn considered the words Mr. Davis wrote and knew she couldn't say no to him. It didn't matter that they'd only known each other for a year, he trusted her, so she was going to trust him.

"I don't need time to think about it. I'll do what he asked."

Mr. Stevens regarded her carefully before nodding once. "I'll need you to sign this paperwork, then we can get started on adding you to all of his accounts and giving you access to his property and company."

"Thank you. That's great."

Mr. Stevens held her gaze for a long moment before tearing his away and focusing on the job ahead of him.

Dawn was grateful for the reprieve from his assessing stare, one that made her feel more than a little warm.

He was an attractive man, and if she hadn't promised herself she'd be single forever, she might be interested. But Dawn learned her lesson before. Gorgeous men were her kryptonite, and she knew better than to get involved with another one.

Especially one who was about to give her billions of dollars in an inheritance she never knew was coming.

It was her lucky day.

5

———

GAGE REMINDED HIMSELF AGAIN THAT THE WOMAN ACROSS THE desk from him was not available. Just because she was divorced didn't mean she was available. Or interested. She was in danger, and she was a client, which meant she was off-limits.

He watched her hand as she signed her name in a loopy signature. It was soft and sweet, like the woman herself. The articles he read about her didn't include a picture. He'd found a few online, but he wasn't prepared for the gut punch he'd feel when she shook his hand. Or the overwhelming sense of rightness at having her in his space.

"This is all just so strange," she whispered.

"What is?"

She stared at the paper in front of her for another minute before she looked up. There were tears shimmering in her eyes. She blinked and pressed her red lips into a smile. "That Mr. Davis would leave all this to me. I'm very appreciative of it, and I will do my best to live up to his expectations, but I guess it makes me sad."

"Sad?"

She nodded, her blonde hair swinging over her shoulders. The ends hit her collarbones and pointed the way down to her necklace. A silver phoenix. "Mr. Davis said he lost one of his sons and his wife, but I met his other son. I assumed he would be the one getting everything."

"You met Trevor Davis?"

Her nod was jilted, stiff, like the memory was not one she wanted to relive. "He is nothing like his father."

"What did he do?" His hands tightened into fists. His heart raced. He was ready to fight, something he hadn't felt in a very long time.

"He was just kind of creepy. He looked at me like he... Was interested in more than his father's care."

"When did you see him?"

"The day Mr. Davis died, actually. I left when his son arrived. I found out he'd died that night when I came back for my next shift."

Gage nearly fell over with that information. It supported his theory that Trevor might have had something to do with his father's death. And told Gage Dawn was definitely in danger if Trevor already knew who she was.

"He's a dangerous man," Gage said.

"That's what this says, too." She tapped the letter from Mr. Davis. "I'm not surprised."

"Do you know something?"

"Something like what?" Her tone hinted at a wary fear.

Gage backed off and shook his head. "Nothing. I just... Mr. Davis chose you instead of his son for a reason. He believed Trevor was going to use Davis Developments for illegal activity. Mr. Davis wanted to protect his employees and stop his son from hurting others."

"I have a daughter, Mr. Stevens. She lives with her father,

but I need to know if I should be worried about her safety. If Trevor is going to come after me, she's the way to get to me."

Gage shook his head. "As of now, I don't think Trevor knows you're the one his father chose. I haven't spoken to him about the change in the will, but I have reason to believe he's aware it's been changed."

"What will he do to me?"

Gage looked closely at Dawn. She was beautiful. She was kind and compassionate. She'd spent the last year caring for people most forgot about. People with no family willing to take them in. People who couldn't do much for themselves. A person didn't choose that life unless they were patient and understanding and giving.

"I believe Trevor Davis is dangerous. He will do anything to get what he wants. But I don't think hurting you will do anything for him."

"You don't think?" she squeaked.

"Ms. Patterson, I'm not going to lie to you. You are taking a risk by agreeing to this. You are accepting that you could become a target. Trevor thought this was all going to be his. When he learns it's not, he could do anything."

"He could kill me."

Gage looked into her fearful eyes. Her entire being was steady, though. She wasn't as scared as most people would be. She was strong. "Yes."

Her brown eyes slid closed. She drew a slow breath, her chest rising with the silent move. She slowly let the breath out again and met Gage's gaze.

"Are you sure you want to do this?" Gage asked.

She laughed mirthlessly and shook her head. "No. Not even a little bit. But Mr. Davis was my favorite patient. He was a kind man. He said he appreciated me talking to him, but I appreciated him just as much. He has given me advice and support and kindness for the last year. Three things I never believed I deserved. I've made mistakes, Mr. Stevens, but I'm not the same person I was. Mr. Davis knew that. He knew who I am. Who I've worked hard to become. And if he believed in me, I'm going to do this."

Gage nodded. Every piece of him wanted to pull her into his arms. To keep her safe and protect her. She was fierce. She was strong. After sitting in the same room with her for thirty minutes, Gage knew exactly why Robert Davis chose Dawn Patterson as his beneficiary.

She was magnificent.

Dawn turned back to the paperwork set before her and signed the last sheet. She pushed the entire packet across the desk toward Gage. "I hate to be this person, but the letter mentioned something about a trust for my daughter."

"Yes, that's the next thing I need you to sign."

"Okay. Sorry. That sounds greedy."

Gage shook his head. "Not at all. It sounds like what a good parent would do. Take care of their kid."

Dawn's smile was strained.

Gage went through what the paperwork stated. Since Savannah lived with her dad full time, he had to sign the paperwork, too. Gage offered to set up an appointment with Owen Patterson to have him sign everything, but Dawn insisted she would take it to him.

"He's going to want to review everything. He doesn't always trust me. He'll have his lawyer go over it. If that's okay."

Gage nodded. "Of course. You are welcome to do the same."

Dawn shook her head and signed her name to the next batch of paperwork. "I'm good. I know Mr. Davis would never do anything that would cause me harm." She looked carefully at Gage, narrowing her eyes and letting a smile show through them. "You might be the same, but I'm not committing to that yet."

Gage barked a surprised laugh. Usually reading a will and discussing final arrangements with an heir was painful and challenging, but Dawn Patterson made it all much easier. "Well, I hope I can live up to your expectations."

"Me, too."

Dawn returned to signing her name, reading the pages as she went. The curtain of her hair fell forward, blocking half of her face from view. She tucked it behind her ear and chewed on her lip.

"Can I ask you a question?" Gage asked after a few minutes.

Dawn looked up at him and nodded.

"Why didn't you attend the funeral?"

Dawn inhaled a sharp breath.

"I apologize. That's none of my business."

"No, it's okay. The last time I saw him, we were talking when Trevor walked in. Trevor cleared his throat and startled me. I left because I never want to intrude on the time a resident has with family, but also because Trevor made me uncomfortable. I would usually check on Mr. Davis before I left for the day, but I didn't want to risk running into his son, so I didn't go back there. The way our schedules work, I was off the next three days. I didn't find out Mr. Davis had died until I went back to work, which was the same day as the funeral."

"And you couldn't leave work," Gage said.

Dawn shook her head. "I asked another nurse when I found out. I was going to try, but we were short-handed and there was no way I could leave. It almost killed me to not be there. I went to the cemetery after work. I saw his grave and sat there and talked to him for a while, but I felt like someone was watching me, so I went home."

"Someone was watching you?"

She shivered and shrugged. "I didn't see anyone, but you know how you get that feeling? I was out in public. There was probably someone from the cemetery looking to finish something and go home. I was just being paranoid."

"You never know. And you need to be careful, Ms. Patterson."

"You can call me Dawn."

"Then please call me Gage."

"Gage. I like that name."

Gage smiled at her honest words.

She smiled back.

Time stood still for a minute. Just the two of them, staring at each other. Gage leaned forward, drawn to her without conscious thought. The desk was between them, but his body didn't care.

Until she tore her gaze away and hastily scribbled her signature on the last line. She shoved the paperwork toward him and grabbed her handbag. "I'm guessing that's everything?"

Gage shoved his runaway desire back into the box where it belonged and nodded. He cleared his throat as he stood, buttoning his suit coat and hoping she didn't notice the beginning of his erection.

"Thank you for coming in, Dawn. I will get everything filed and we can work on getting you access to Mr. Davis's house and company."

"His house?" she squeaked. She seemed to do that when she was surprised.

"Yes. He has a large home with staff that is now yours. Along with all of his other properties. Vehicles, investments.

It all belongs to you. Now that you've signed agreeing to this, we can meet again at your convenience to review it all. Unless you have time to do it now."

She shook her head, backing toward the door. "No, I should go talk to Owen. Get this paperwork to him so we can get things set up for Savannah. I'll be in touch, Gage. Thank you."

Her hasty exit made Gage feel like an ass. He made her uncomfortable because he couldn't keep his irrational desire under control. Instead of making her feel comfortable, she was running out the door because he was no better than Trevor Davis.

He followed her to the door and locked it behind her. Then he swore in the empty office and promised himself he wouldn't get drawn in by her next time they spoke.

Dawn clutched the paperwork for Savannah's trust fund to her chest and tried to suck in a breath.

Holy shit. Gage Stevens was hot. And he was far too tempting for Dawn's fragile hold on her independence.

"Do not sleep with the lawyer," she whispered to herself in the dark. The warm spring air was why she felt so hot. Not because the sexy lawyer looked like he wanted to kiss her.

Running was self-preservation. If she'd stuck around, she would have given in, or taken the lead and kissed him. For all she knew, she was completely misreading Gage Stevens. He didn't say anything that made her think he was trying to get her into bed.

"You're an idiot, Dawn," she grumbled to herself.

She knew better than to get involved with a man who

looked like Gage Stevens. A man who was well-dressed and smart. A man who could have any woman he wanted. A man with light brown skin and dark brown eyes and those cheekbones.

"Gah!" she shook her head and shook away the fantasy. Gage Stevens was not looking at her like she could be his dinner. He was being a nice guy, and Dawn needed to remember that.

She pulled her phone from her handbag and tapped on Owen's number. She put the phone to her ear and hoped her ex-husband would answer.

"Yeah?" he said, not sounding happy she was calling.

"I'm sorry to interrupt your night, but I need to see you. I have some news and some paperwork I need you to sign. It's nothing bad, but I'd rather speak in person."

Owen sighed heavily. "Can we meet at my lawyer's tomorrow?"

Dawn inhaled a breath and fought back the pain. She deserved the way he treated her. She hadn't done anything to gain favors. But she'd done the work. She was trying. At some point, she was hoping she'd earn a place in Savannah's life that didn't require lawyers and mediation and approval.

"I work tomorrow. That's why I'm calling now. I can leave the paperwork with you and you can take it to your lawyer. I assumed that's what you would want to do."

Owen was quiet for a minute. Dawn crossed her fingers that he would agree. She didn't expect much from him, but she knew the one thing she could say to help her case.

"I don't have to come in. You can come outside so Savannah doesn't have to see me. All of this is for her, but as the parent with sole custody, you need to sign this."

"What is this? What's going on, Dawn?"

"I... I really think it's best if we talk in person. If tonight doesn't work, I'm off Wednesday, Thursday, and Friday."

"It's fine." He exhaled loudly to let Dawn know she was inconveniencing him. "Are you coming over now?"

"If that works, I can be to you in ten minutes."

"Okay. I'll see you then." He sounded like he was facing a firing squad instead of his ex-wife.

"Thanks, Owen."

"Uh huh."

Dawn hung up and headed that way. She tried to come up with the best way to explain it to Owen, but by the time she arrived at his house, the house they'd bought together when Savannah was two, she was no closer to being able to explain it. Or to contain her excitement.

Owen walked outside as Dawn got out of her car. She was disappointed he wasn't going to let her in the house, but she offered the option, so she couldn't complain.

"Hey, thanks for letting me come here."

"What's going on, Dawn? Are you in some kind of trouble?"

Dawn stuffed down her frustration and shook her head. "No. The opposite. I... I'm a billionaire."

"You're a what now?"

"One of my patients died last week. He left me everything he owns. His company, his house, a bunch of other property. It's amazing." Dawn was having trouble getting the words out. She was smiling so big she thought her face was going to break.

"Amazing? Do you actually think you can handle all of that?"

"Owen."

"What? Dawn, you're an addict. You almost died less

than two years ago. And you now have a shit-ton of money and you think I'm going to be happy for you?"

Dawn let out a shaky breath. "Well, it doesn't really matter what you think because we're divorced. You have no say in anything I do."

"Dawn, this isn't about me wanting a handout—"

"No, it's about you punishing me for the rest of my life. I fucked up, Owen. I know it, you know it, Savannah knows it, and you're going to make sure none of us ever forget it."

"Dawn—"

"Just stop, Owen. I didn't come here to fight with you or to hear how big of a disappointment I am and always will be. Part of the arrangement is a trust fund for Savannah."

"A trust fund?" Owen snapped.

"Yeah, a trust fund. Money for her to use for college or a house or whatever the hell she wants when she's older."

"Do you think this is going to make her forgive you?"

"I didn't do any of this. All of this is part of the arrangements set up in my inheritance. Mr. Davis had this all drawn up before he died, but we needed to sign everything."

"Robert Davis?" Owen asked, sounding less skeptical.

"Yes. He was my patient. We were friends. He was a wonderful man, and I'm..." Dawn sucked in a breath. It still hurt that he was gone. Someone new moved into Mr. Davis's old room, and it was hard for Dawn to go in there and get to know the new man. All Dawn wanted was to give Mr. Davis a big hug and sit down and talk to him for hours. But she wouldn't be able to do that ever again.

"His funeral was all over the news. He was crazy rich."

Dawn straightened her shoulders and met her ex's gaze. "And now I am. Here's the paperwork. I've already signed it. You need to review it all with your lawyer. I hope you're willing to do this for Savannah, but don't you dare put this on me if you don't want to do it."

"Dawn."

"No, Owen. You've been happy to punish me and tell me how I'm not a good mother. I know. I've accepted that. I'm doing what I can to make up for it. This has nothing to do with that, but this will help Savannah and her future. This is a good thing, and I know you don't trust it because it's coming from me, but don't stand in the way of our daughter having an excellent future because you hate me so much."

"I don't hate you, Dawn," Owen whispered. "I loved you. Our marriage was not perfect, but for most of it, I loved you."

"I loved you, too. And I still love Savannah. I always will. Do this for her. You can have all your doubts about me and what I'm capable of, but don't stifle her opportunities because you don't believe in me."

"It's just a lot. Running a company? Managing everything he did? I don't want you to fall back into your old habits. To make all these promises to Savannah and then end up like you did before. Or worse."

"Then sign the paperwork. A trust means no one can touch the money until Savannah is old enough. The lawyer will be the executor, but that can be changed to your lawyer. But don't come at me and tell me I'm going to let Savannah down when you're the one standing in the way right now."

"I'm not—"

"Yes, you are. You're not a lawyer, Owen. Take this to yours and let him help you decide what to do. Don't throw it in my face right now. Put Savannah first. That's what I'm doing."

Owen finally took the envelope Dawn was trying to

hand to him. As soon as it was out of her hands, Dawn turned to walk back to her car.

"Is this so Savannah will agree to dinner with you?"

Dawn stopped and shook her head, anger and pain and regret fighting for first place. She knew Owen was protecting their daughter, but it hurt that he felt the need to protect her from Dawn.

She turned and looked at the man she once thought she'd spend her life with. Before he told her he'd fallen out of love with her. Before he said he thought it was best for them to get divorced. Before she lost everything.

"You are going to think whatever you want, Owen. You're going to tell Savannah whatever you want. But no. I'm not trying to manipulate her or buy her love. I'm not doing this for any reason than it was given to me, and I'm not willing to stop her from having an amazing life." Dawn took a few steps toward her car, then stopped again. "Have your lawyer get in touch with mine. His contact information is in that packet. And keep that paperwork safe."

Owen looked down at it like it was going to burst into flames. "This is real, isn't it?"

Dawn nodded. "Yes. Have a good night, Owen."

He stood on the sidewalk leading to the front door while she got in her car. She watched him in the rearview mirror until she turned the corner, then pulled to the side of the road and let the tears fall.

6

———

GAGE DIDN'T HEAR ANYTHING FROM DAWN FOR THE REST OF the week. He asked her to call him when she was ready to get access, and when he didn't hear anything, he wondered if she changed her mind about what she was getting into.

He made a note on his calendar to call her after lunch on Tuesday, and was surprised when Betsy told him Dawn Patterson was calling early Tuesday morning.

"Good morning. I was going to call you this afternoon," Gage said in greeting.

"I apologize for not reaching out. I was working last week. And trying to wrap my head around all of this. I didn't intend to ignore you."

"You have nothing to apologize for. I received the paperwork for Savannah's trust fund and will finalize that today. I'm assuming that's why you called."

She let out a whoosh of breath that told Gage that was news to her. "Um, no. I... I'm happy to hear that."

"You didn't know?"

"No. I... You don't need to know my family drama. Thank

you for setting that up. I'm very grateful to you for your help. This is all so much more than I ever imagined."

"What is?" Gage leaned back in his chair and tried to be an ear for her. She didn't sound like she had anyone else to talk to.

"I've been doing some research about Davis Developments and Mr. Davis and the magnitude of all of this is just... I don't know if I can do this."

"Dawn, listen to me. Mr. Davis didn't grow this company overnight. Unfortunately, you're inheriting it overnight. You're behind. But that doesn't mean you're not capable. He wouldn't have chosen you if he didn't believe you could handle it."

She inhaled a jagged breath. "I hope you're right. Um, so I'm off for the next few days. I go back on Friday for the weekend, then I'm off next week Monday through Wednesday. You said I need to get things set up. I guess I should do that."

Gage thought through his day and made a quick decision. "Are you available for lunch?"

"Excuse me?"

"It's a lot to go over. I have a few appointments this morning, but I can clear my afternoon if you're available. I will order in lunch and we can go through everything in detail. I can fill you in on a lot more about the company and Mr. Davis."

"You knew him," she breathed. "I guess I should have realized, but... I'd like to know more about him."

"Are you okay with lunch? And all afternoon if you need it. I want you to feel comfortable with everything you're stepping into."

She exhaled slowly. "Yes. That sounds good. Thank you, Gage. Is that still okay?"

"Of course, Dawn. Is noon okay?"

"Yeah. My day is wide open. Can I pick up lunch? Is there something you like?"

"You don't have to do that."

"You said you have appointments. It's the least I can do. What do you like?"

"I'm pretty easy, actually. I'll eat just about anything."

"Okay. There's an Indian place not far from my apartment. Is that okay?"

"Definitely. I love Indian food. Thank you, Dawn."

"Thank you, Gage."

Gage hung up with a smile on his face. He was looking forward to his lunch meeting. Even as he told himself he shouldn't be.

The rest of Gage's morning dragged on. He got a report from Rose Protection Agency that was boring. Boring was really nice. Gage appreciated the update that said there was no update. And he appreciated the company continuing to monitor his office and home.

"Are you sure you don't need me this afternoon?" Betsy asked mid-morning when Gage told her to take a half-day, without needing to take vacation.

"I'm sure. I'll send all calls to voicemail. I'll lock the doors. You'll be bored if you stick around. It'll be a good chance for you to spend some time with Albert. Did you talk about you taking some time off until all of this with Trevor Davis is resolved?"

Betsy nodded. "We did, but we both agreed it doesn't make sense. Albert promised me he'd be careful at home and when he goes out. I'm not ready to sit around the house just yet. Maybe in a year or two, but you're not getting rid of me just yet, Mr. Stevens."

Gage smiled. "I wouldn't get rid of you ever if I had my

way. But I also want you to be happy. You can go out today and not tell Albert you had the afternoon off. Catch a movie. Do some shopping."

Betsy laughed. "I think he has one of those tracker thingies on me. Knows where I am at all times."

"It's in your phone," Gage said.

"What?" Betsy barked. "You mean he really is tracking me?"

Gage chuckled. "Those phones come with an app that lets you track others. And if you're family and have your accounts linked, it's automatically tracking both of you."

"Show me." Betsy handed over her phone, then grabbed it back to unlock it.

Gage flipped to the app he was talking about and showed Betsy. "See, this is him. You're sharing your location with him, so he does know where you are. Or he has the ability to know. He might not use it, but you can track each other right there."

"Well, I'll be. I never knew that."

"It's handy, I imagine. Lots of parents use it to keep an eye on their kids."

"Well, good to know. Now I can see where he is, too."

Gage laughed and shook his head. "Albert's never going to forgive me."

"He'll never know. I'll blame the grandkids."

Gage laughed again. Betsy kept him on his toes. "As long as it helps."

"It helps. Thank you, Mr. Stevens. And thank you for the afternoon off. I think I'll work on those baby clothes for my daughter. The doctor thinks she might go into labor a little early."

"Then you better get moving on that," Gage teased her.

"I will. Today will help. You be careful, Mr. Stevens."

"I will. Let me know when you're ready to head out, and I'll walk with you."

Betsy nodded. They'd been careful, and careful usually led to complacency. Gage didn't want to let down their guard and have Trevor pop up when they weren't paying attention.

Gage finished his last appointment of the morning and checked the time. Dawn would be there in fifteen minutes. Betsy was still there. Good timing.

"Are you trying to get rid of me before your appointment arrives?" Betsy asked.

Gage shook his head. "Not at all. Why?"

"I'm finishing up a few things. It might take me thirty minutes."

"That's fine. Let me know. I don't want you walking out alone."

"It's the middle of the day."

"Please, Betsy. I would feel more comfortable."

She hesitated a moment, then nodded.

The door swung open, and they both looked. Dawn Patterson appeared with a large bag of food that could have easily fed another five people and a big smile on her face.

A smile that punched Gage in the gut again. He really needed to get that reaction under control.

"Hi," Dawn said, lifting her gaze to find Gage's, then trailing to Betsy. "I'm Dawn."

Dawn set the food down and walked straight to Betsy with her hand out.

Betsy shook Dawn's hand. "Nice to meet you, Ms. Patterson. I'm Betsy, Mr. Stevens's assistant."

"She's much more than that. She's the one who keeps this place running."

"It's so nice to meet you. I'm guessing you're the one who answered the phone this morning."

"That I am," Betsy said.

"Your voice is so soothing. I was anxious to call, and when I heard you, I felt better. I'm so happy to put a face to the voice."

Betsy blushed and giggled. Gage had never seen either, but not many of his clients went out of their way to interact with Betsy. Not many were like Dawn Patterson.

"Are you joining us for lunch? I realized when I went to order that I never asked what you like, so I ordered their six most popular dishes."

"Six?" Betsy asked.

Dawn shrugged. "Five is so predictable. And when you ask for six, they have to think about it. I'm guessing we got something good in there that I wouldn't have thought to order."

"I like you."

"I like you, too, Betsy. Will you join us? Oh! Do you like Indian food?"

"Oh, honey, I like all food. You don't get hips like these from being picky."

Dawn put her hands on her hips and laughed. "Same!"

Betsy chuckled. She looked over at Gage and raised her eyebrows.

"I am always happy to have you join me. And there's definitely enough to eat."

Betsy looked back at Dawn and nodded. "Okay. I'll stay. As long as I'm not in the way."

"I can't imagine you would be," Dawn said.

Gage grabbed the food and left the two of them to talk. He couldn't help but smile at the easy way Dawn had with Betsy. He wondered if it was what made her such a good nurse and so well-liked.

Gage set the food out on the table in the break room. He

didn't know what all the options were, but it all smelled amazing. He took plates and glasses from the cabinet above the sink and set them out next to the food, letting the ladies choose first before he filled his plate.

They came in mid-conversation and didn't stop as they loaded plates and took seats at the small table against the wall. Gage fixed his plate and joined them, listening to their conversation.

"My daughter is fourteen. Her birthday was just last month," Dawn said.

"That's a tough age," Betsy told her.

Dawn nodded. "It is. I haven't made it any easier. It's been a rough few years."

"You said you're divorced?"

Dawn nodded again, avoiding Gage's gaze as she focused on Betsy.

"Divorce is tough, but when it's the right move, there's nothing wrong with it."

"It was the right move for us, but Savannah got caught in the middle of a lot."

"Is she excited about your inheritance?"

Dawn shook her head. "I haven't spoken to her. I... When I talked to my ex last week, he wasn't very positive about everything. He doesn't think I can handle all of this."

Gage resisted blasting the guy for putting any doubts in her head. Especially when he turned around and made additional demands for the trust fund for their daughter. Demands that said he wanted exclusive control of it, meaning he could retrieve money whenever he wanted to.

Gage already didn't trust the guy, and to learn he was dumping on Dawn made him even less of a fan.

"What do you think?" Betsy asked.

Dawn set her fork down and leaned back in her seat. "No one's asked me that."

"Then I'm glad I did. It's not an easy task ahead of you. You can walk away. You can sell the company and properties. You can do whatever you want. But I get the feeling you already know what you want and what you can handle."

"I want to do it," Dawn whispered.

Betsy grinned. She reached over and patted Dawn's hand. "Then do it."

Gage had never been happier to know Betsy and to have kept her on when he took over the practice than at that moment. He knew Betsy was special when they met, and when she was given the chance, she proved she was.

Judging by the look on Dawn's face, she had a confidence that was missing before. One only Betsy could have given her.

Fuck you, Trevor Davis. Dawn Patterson's in charge now.

DAWN WANDERED around Gage's office while he walked Betsy to her car. Dawn didn't know if he wanted a moment alone with his assistant or if there was another reason, but she thought it was sweet.

Betsy was sweet, too. The older woman was welcoming and friendly. She made Dawn feel like she was capable of anything and everything. It reminded Dawn of her aunt. Dawn's mom was never around much, but they lived with her mom's younger sister, Judy. Aunt Judy was like a big sister to Dawn. She would offer advice and taught her how to be independent and made Dawn feel like she wasn't a burden.

When Judy died, Dawn left home. Her mom didn't care,

and it was better for both of them without the buffer Judy provided. Every few months, Dawn got a text from her mom, but they would never be accused of being close. Dawn hadn't had anyone she was close to since Aunt Judy.

"Sorry about that," Gage said, striding into the office.

Dawn jumped. She was so lost in thought she hadn't heard him return. "No problem. I apologize if I intruded on something."

Gage shook his head. "Nothing at all." He looked pained and gestured to the chairs around the round table off to the side.

Dawn sat in the one without the paperwork in front of it, leaving the other one for Gage.

He sat and folded his hands on top of the folder. After a moment, he looked up at Dawn. "We had a break-in last week. During Mr. Davis's funeral. Someone broke in here and at my home."

"Seriously? Who would do that?" Dawn didn't know if he was accusing her or sharing information.

"I believe it was Trevor Davis. Somehow, he knows the will was changed, and I think he's trying to figure out who his father left everything to."

"Okay. I thought everything was set or something."

Gage nodded. "It is, and it was before then. But Trevor doesn't seem like someone who cares about laws or wills."

"He really is going to come after me, isn't he?"

Gage exhaled slowly. "I don't know, but you need to be careful, just in case."

"Is it safe for me to be here?" Dawn glanced around. She didn't know Gage Stevens anymore than she knew Trevor Davis. They could be working together. Gage could be the one who gets her somewhere and Trevor swoops in and forces her to sign something that hands him the keys to the kingdom.

"Yes," Gage said forcefully. "I have a top of the line security system. I walked Betsy outside so she's never alone. If I'm not here, she's not here. Same with you. I'm letting you know about this so you know what's going on."

Dawn laughed mirthlessly. "I don't know what's going on. A man I didn't know well decided to give me his fortune instead of his own kid. And now his kid is going to come after me in order to make sure he gets what he wants. How does any of this make sense?"

Gage inhaled slowly and let the breath out. "It doesn't. None of it does. I've had clients change their wills for any number of reasons, but for it to happen so close to Mr. Davis's death and for him to change it to someone outside his family is unusual."

Gage's words put Dawn on the defensive. She recoiled slightly, sitting up straight and facing the man who just told her she was being given something she didn't deserve.

She already knew that. She knew that the moment he told her about the will. But she didn't ask for it. She didn't talk him into it. She had nothing to do with the change.

"I had no idea Mr. Davis had this kind of money, or that he was going to leave it all to me."

Gage looked closely at her, close enough that Dawn fidgeted in her seat. She fought the urge to hide her gaze or squeeze her hands together.

Gage pushed his chair back and turned to face her. He reached out and took one of her hands in his.

Dawn sucked in a breath at the intimate contact. He was holding her hand, but it felt so much bigger. So much more personal. Like a caress from a lover.

Dammit, she needed to stop thinking about him like that.

Then he spoke. "I never suspected you of any wrongdoing, Dawn. It only took a few minutes with you to see what Mr. Davis saw. To know you are the kind of person who is not only capable of running his company, but compassionate enough to do it with the care it requires. It's not going to be an easy task. It's a big company, and there's a lot to it, but you're not going into this alone. I've been his lawyer for years, and I will be here for you every step of the way. I believe in you. So damn much. This was a huge ask, and one I wished Robert had been able to make in person instead of only leaving behind a letter for you. But he made the right choice. You are going to do an amazing job."

Emotion welled up in her throat. No one had ever spoken to her like that. Had ever had pure blind faith in her abilities. It was intoxicating and empowering. She didn't want to let him down. She wanted to kick ass and prove him right.

And she would.

She sat up straighter and tugged gently on his hand. She didn't stop to think about what she was doing, she just leaned in and kissed the man who made her feel like she could do anything.

His lips were warm and soft. His breath whispered over her cheeks. For half a second, Dawn thought she misread everything and almost pulled back, but then he moved his mouth against hers.

Gage's hand squeezed hers. His other one cupped her neck, holding her in place. He kissed her softly, in no hurry to move things along.

Dawn sighed happily and licked his lips. He tasted good, and then he opened for her, and he tasted even better.

And when he let out a soft growl, she knew she was in trouble. She could easily get lost in him, and she wanted to. God, she wanted to. Damn the promise she made to herself. Damn the independence she was striving for. She could do both. Enjoy Gage and stand on her own.

But first she was going to enjoy kissing the sexy lawyer who was giving her billions of dollars. Life was good.

7

———

DAMN THE CONSEQUENCES. DAMN THE LINES. DAMN everything that meant he should stop kissing her. She whimpered against his lips, like she was just as lost as he was to what they were doing.

A kiss. A simple kiss. And it was rendering him senseless. Gone were all the thoughts of her being his client and the whole thing being wrong. All he cared about was making sure she knew he was all in on whatever she wanted this to be.

All. In.

She sighed happily and eased back. She nibbled her lower lip and looked up at him with a tentative smile. "Thank you for believing in me."

Gage raised one brow and smirked. "I will always believe in you. Feel free to show your appreciation of that any time you want."

Dawn exhaled a laugh. "I haven't felt like a sure bet in a long time."

Gage shook his head and finally released her. Even though he knew about her past, she didn't know he knew.

He wasn't going to let on. He wanted her to trust him with the truth. With her past.

"Mr. Davis clearly knew you well enough to believe you were."

Again, she laughed like she was either surprised or didn't believe it. "I'm not sure why."

"One thing I learned about Robert over the years was that he saw things no one else did. He was a very intuitive person. It's one of the reasons he was so successful."

"One of the reasons?"

"He was also smart as hell and surrounded himself with people who were just as smart or smarter."

Dawn grinned. "Does that include you?"

Gage snorted and shook his head. "I'm not sure I could ever count myself as being near as smart as Robert. He was a unique man."

Dawn nodded thoughtfully. She was quiet again, taking her time to process whatever she was going to say next. "Do you really think he made the right decision?"

Gage nodded without hesitation. "Absolutely. I do wish he'd had a chance to speak to you in person, though. Maybe even bring you into the company and show you around himself."

"That would have been nice. Do you even know who I would talk to when I go there? Or where there is?"

Gage chuckled. "Yes, I'll make sure you have all the information you need and ways to contact people. The company has been running without Robert for a while, so they won't expect you to jump in and handle things. You can ease in and be as involved as you'd like to be."

"Is Trevor involved in the business?"

"No. Not at all. Trevor never had an interest in it. And Robert never wanted him involved. I believe that's why he left everything to you. He wanted to make sure Trevor couldn't get access to anything."

"Well, that's something at least. And I'd like to be involved. I don't know anything, but I'd like to learn. Hopefully someone will be willing to show me a few things."

"Tabitha Martin is the COO of Davis Developments. She's the one who's been running everything since Robert stepped aside."

"And she knows about me?"

"She knows someone has been named the beneficiary and will be coming in, but she doesn't know your name. No one does. But it's only a matter of time."

"Until all of this blows up in my face."

Gage shook his head. He understood her apprehension, but he hoped it was temporary. Trevor would get over his anger and move on. "Let's hope that doesn't happen. But if it does, we'll figure it out. I'm not going to leave you blowing in the wind, so to speak."

Dawn smiled at him. Determination once again filled her gaze. She nodded sharply and returned to the paperwork they were reviewing. She was ready to step into her position. And Gage was happy to see her do it.

GAGE AND DAWN walked out of his office together. He wanted to invite her to dinner, but the weary look in her eyes and the stack of paperwork she carried with her said she was overwhelmed and in need of some sleep.

"You will call if you need anything, right?" Gage implored.

Dawn deposited the messenger bag full of files onto her front seat and stood to face him. She closed the door and nodded. "I will. I'm sure I'll be in touch again soon. But I can't thank you enough for all you've done."

"Partly, it's my job. Partly, I know you're going to be good for Davis Developments. And partly, I'm selfish and wanted to spend more time with you."

The blush that stained her cheeks made Gage want to kiss her again, but he resisted.

"I could quickly become addicted to you," Dawn whispered, almost a confession.

"I don't know that I think that's a bad thing."

She smiled mirthlessly. "I'm not sure it's a good thing. For now, I'll just say goodnight and thank you. Again."

"Good night, Dawn."

He waited until she got in her car and pulled away before he went to his SUV. He noticed someone sitting in a vehicle a few spaces away from him. They didn't appear to be paying Gage any attention, but it still caught his attention.

Gage started his SUV and took a minute to watch the other person. He couldn't see clearly through their windshield, not even well enough to tell if it was likely a man or woman in the vehicle. Figuring it was coincidence the person was parked there, Gage pulled away from his office.

He made two turns, and a minute later, he spotted the vehicle three behind him.

He was being followed.

His heart thumped hard. His palms were slick against the steering wheel. Going home wasn't a good idea, even though Trevor had already proven he knew where Gage lived.

What should he do?

Gage tried to remain calm. He didn't speed, and he didn't make quick moves. He took turns leisurely, like he was planning them even though they sent him in circles and had him doubling back over roads he'd already driven.

Despite all that, the vehicle and his shadow remained.

Gage debated calling Marcus, but he didn't like the idea of wasting police resources for something he could handle. He hoped.

Gage pulled into a gas station and parked near the door. He got out of his SUV and headed inside, watching to see if the other vehicle pulled up.

A Black woman got out and looked around. She tugged her jacket down over her hips, outlining the gun tucked underneath.

Shit.

A young woman with two kids was inside. As was the clerk, an older couple, and a man who looked like he was in his late twenties. Lots of people who could be collateral damage if the woman following Gage was trigger-happy.

He should have called Marcus.

Gage headed to the bathroom, hoping the woman saw him head that way and followed instead of hanging out near the innocent customers. He turned the corner and tried not to be obvious he was looking.

She was following him.

Gage paused on the other side of the corner, knowing his only chance to get out of this without anyone getting hurt was to catch her by surprise.

She stepped around the corner, and Gage grabbed her arm. He spun her around and pressed her to the wall, face first.

She let out a soft *oof*.

"Why are you following me?" Gage snarled in her ear. He was bigger than her, but she was strong, and she was fighting back.

"Get off me."

"Not until you tell me why you're following me. Did Trevor send you?"

She shook her head. "If you'll let me reach into my pocket, I can get my badge."

"You're a cop?" Gage didn't believe that for a second. And he didn't let her up.

She shook her head. "No. I'm FBI. I'm one of the agents working the whole case, and I was asked to keep an eye on you. To make sure you were safe."

"Why wasn't I informed?" Gage still didn't believe her.

"Because if you knew, you would potentially draw attention to me and then Trevor Davis would know I was there."

"Because he sent you."

"Call Marcus," the woman said with a sigh. "My ID is in my left inside pocket. Read it to him, and he'll confirm my identity."

"Marcus who?" Gage asked. One more piece of information.

"Captain Marcus Patrick. He's the one who asked me to follow you. Said you're in danger. Already had your office and home broken into and wanted to make sure you're safe."

"And he didn't tell me so I wouldn't give away your presence."

"Just call him," the woman spat.

Gage kept his arm against the back of her neck. He reached into her jacket and retrieved the ID she mentioned. Lorelei Sloane. Why did that name sound vaguely familiar?

He held the ID in the hand holding her to the wall and got his phone out. He tapped Marcus's name and waited for his friend to answer.

"Patrick."

"Do you know a Lorelei Sloane?"

Marcus snorted. "Caught her, huh? I knew she wouldn't take too kindly to the assignment."

"I did fine," Lorelei argued, clearly able to hear the conversation.

"Then why is Gage calling me?" Marcus asked.

Lorelei grumbled. "Can you let me up now?"

Gage took his arm from the back of her neck and held the ID up to the woman who claimed to be her. Gage couldn't find any variance from her picture to the woman in front of him.

"Everything okay?" Marcus asked with far less humor.

"Yeah," Gage answered. "I didn't realize you were going to have me followed."

"I figured you would argue if I asked, so I didn't ask."

"I would have definitely argued. Do you have someone following...?" Gage looked at Lorelei and then past her to the rest of the convenience store. He couldn't see around the corner, or know if anyone was listening to their conversation.

"Yes. Although he hasn't been caught yet," Marcus said, likely for Lorelei's benefit.

Lorelei scowled and snatched her ID back from Gage, tucking it back in the pocket he got it from.

"What else are you keeping from me?" Gage asked. He knew there was a lot going on, and he knew it was an open investigation, but he didn't like being kept in the dark. And he really didn't like being treated like he was vulnerable.

Marcus sighed. "Not over the phone."

"When?"

"Thursday night. We're already planning it," Lorelei said.

"Give him the information," Marcus told her, through Gage.

"Copy."

"And stop tailing me?" Gage asked, although he wasn't entirely sure who he was directing the question to.

"Yeah, yeah. For now. We reserve the right to resume that anytime," Marcus said.

"Fine," Gage agreed, knowing he'd fight it, even if he wasn't sure he'd win.

Gage hung up and faced the woman who looked no happier than he was about their situation. "Do I need to be worried?"

"Haven't you been paying attention to the news the last year? We should all be worried," Lorelei said.

Gage sucked in a breath. He had his suspicions about Trevor, but knowing others agreed with them, and had evidence that linked him to the hell Niagara Falls had been through in the last year, made Gage anxious instead of relieved.

"Be at this address Thursday night at seven. Don't tell anyone else about it. You can confirm the address with Marcus, but don't do it over the phone or in text. We have no idea who is watching and who is being watched."

"We?"

She smiled, her eyes lighting up. Her brown skin was smooth and free of makeup. He put her age somewhere around mid-thirties. She didn't look familiar to Gage, but he knew her name was.

"Yes, we. You'll meet everyone in two days. If you show up."

"And you'll stop following me until then."

She snorted. "You act like I wanted this assignment. It was a favor to Marcus. I owed him. I'd much rather be finding the man who's messed up so many lives than babysitting you, but..." She shrugged as if there was no more explanation.

"Well, thanks. I think."

Lorelei clapped him on the back, then moved to the hallway, peering around the corner before she walked away from him.

Gage watched her go, wondering what in the hell just happened. And who 'we' was. And how he got involved in all of this.

Dawn treated herself to dinner on the way home from Gage's office. She considered ordering a pizza and picking it up, but she wanted to celebrate.

She was rich! Not just a little rich, but a lot rich. No, the money wasn't in her accounts, but she had access to it. Gage helped her sign in to the bank accounts, and he gave her the paperwork she needed to take to the bank so they could change everything to her name. Which she planned to do first thing in the morning.

It was surreal. She wasn't sure she'd ever get used to it, but when she sat down at the table in the fancy restaurant with cloth napkins and tablecloths, she didn't think it would take as long to get used to as she feared.

Her meal was exceptional. Her server was willing to help her figure out what to order. Dawn wanted to experiment. She splurged on caviar to start with, surprised by how much she enjoyed it. For dinner, the server recommended grilled swordfish with goat cheese mashed potatoes and asparagus. A glass of sweet wine was the perfect addition, and another thing Dawn never would have allowed herself to get without so many zeroes in her bank account.

When she finished eating, she left the server a very large

tip in thanks for all her help, and Dawn left feeling warm and cozy and full.

She twirled her keys around her finger on her way to the car. She carried the messenger bag full of paperwork, feeling silly taking it into the restaurant until she made it around to the driver's side of her car.

BITCH was spray-painted across the entire side of the car. The black paint dripped, mocking Dawn and turning her stomach. Whoever did that was just there.

Dawn spun, looking around the darkening parking lot. She didn't see anyone, not who looked like her assailant. No one was running away with cans of spray paint in their hands.

Dawn almost laughed at the thought. If only it were that easy.

"Are you okay?" a woman asked, surprising Dawn.

Dawn spun and shook her head. "No, not really."

"Do you want to call someone?"

Dawn stared at the car. It was paint. It was mean and ugly, but her insurance would charge her more if she filed a claim. And it would cost her more than she was willing to spend out-of-pocket to have the car repainted.

"No. I'm fine."

"Are you sure?" the woman asked.

Dawn took a closer look at her. She was polished and perfect. Her hair was tied up in a complicated twist. She looked at the car in disgust, like she couldn't imagine anyone saying that to her.

"I'm fine. Thank you. Enjoy your night."

The woman pressed her lips into a tight smile and backed away. She went toward the restaurant without glancing backward.

Dawn felt bad for being short with the woman. She was trying to be nice, and Dawn snapped at her.

But Dawn didn't feel like dealing with it. She didn't want to have to think about anything. She wanted to revel in her good feeling, her full belly, and her good news.

Too bad someone didn't want her to do any of those things.

The door handle was coated in paint, but there was no way Dawn could climb across the console separating the driver's side and the passenger seat. She dug through her handbag, hoping she had something she could use to protect her hand.

Tissue? Too thin. Napkin? Ripped. Paper? Still too thin.

Dawn snickered when she saw her sanitary napkin at the bottom. She tossed it in there when she got her period weeks ago and never used it. But if there was anything that would absorb liquid and not bleed through...

She unwrapped it, laughing at the wings flapping in the light breeze. Dawn stuck the pad to her hand, shrugging before she grabbed the door handle and lifted it.

She pulled the car door open, doing her best to avoid brushing against the paint. Dawn fell into the seat, reaching to close the door.

She shook her head and peeled the pad from her hand, wrapping it back in the packaging, then stuffing it in the cupholder. Her hand was free of paint.

It felt like a victory. One point for Dawn, zero for Trevor. Unless you counted the word painted on the side of her car for all to see.

Maybe she could use some of that money she just inherited to buy a new car. One that didn't tell everyone she was a bitch.

Dawn smiled to herself. Good idea.

8

Gage's phone rang Thursday morning just as he took a sip of his coffee. "Good morning, Betsy. Are you here?" He was already up and out of his seat, ready to meet her in the parking lot.

"Mr. Stevens, this is Albert."

Gage's stomach sank. "Albert. Is Betsy okay?"

"No, sir, I'm afraid she's not. There was a man waiting outside our home for her this morning."

"Where are you? Where is she?"

"She's home. She's fine. He scared her more than anything, but she's pretty shaken up. I heard her shout and came out. The man ran off."

"Did you call the police?"

"No. Betsy doesn't want to make a fuss."

Gage almost chuckled at the word. He could hear the frustration in Albert's voice and understood it more than he knew. "Albert, may I come to your home? I know that's an invasion, but I would like to ask the police captain to join me and speak to you and Betsy."

Albert was quiet for a moment, either weighing the

choice or trying to convince Betsy. "I'm not sure how she'll feel about that."

"Albert, we believe we know who is behind all of this. Captain Patrick has been working on a case to bring him in. This will help."

"She didn't see his face."

"That's okay. I'd still like her to report it."

"Okay, Mr. Stevens. I will watch for you. I'd also like to ask if Betsy can take some time off."

"Yes, of course. I told her she could when all of this began. As much as she wants or needs, and I will cover her full salary until she feels safe returning to work."

"Thank you, Mr. Stevens."

"I'm sorry this is happening, Albert. I'll see you soon."

"Yes, sir."

Gage hung up and immediately called Marcus. He relayed all the information he knew, and Marcus agreed to meet him at Betsy and Albert's house in fifteen minutes.

Gage locked up the office and shook his head as he got in his SUV. He shouldn't have been surprised, but it pissed him off Trevor went after Betsy. She was an innocent woman with no stake in anything happening. She didn't do anything wrong. But Trevor didn't see reason.

The city roads turned to more residential before Gage pulled over in front of Betsy and Albert's house. It was a small cottage, one they moved into after their kids had outgrown their previous home and the two of them were left with more space than they wanted to maintain.

The neighborhood was nice and the people were friendly, according to what Betsy said. There was no doubt the person who was waiting for Betsy was Trevor. Not to Gage.

Marcus pulled up behind Gage, and both men got out.

They shook hands before turning to the house without a word. Marcus's face was set in the same grim lines Gage knew were on his own, and they both radiated frustration.

Albert opened the door as they approached. Gage made the introductions and let Marcus walk inside ahead of him.

"I'm so sorry about this," Gage said to Albert. They were in the entryway of the house, without Betsy.

Albert shook his head. "Not your fault. Betsy explained the situation to me. I should have walked her out."

"You shouldn't have had to," Marcus said. "But it's good you were here."

Albert nodded to Marcus. "I don't want to think about what would have happened if I hadn't heard her."

"It's best if we make a plan to avoid this happening again," Marcus said.

"Where's Betsy?" Gage asked.

"In the kitchen. She needed to busy herself. Nervous energy. She's baking," Albert said with a wry grin.

Gage groaned and rubbed his stomach. "If I'd known that, I would have been here sooner."

Marcus raised his brows and fell into line behind the Albert and Gage.

The scent of dough and the sweetness of something else met Gage halfway down the hallway to the kitchen. Betsy was a sensational baker, and Gage had benefited from her talents many times over the years she'd worked for him. But fresh out of the oven was a whole different form of delicious.

"Mr. Stevens and Captain Patrick are here," Albert announced as he made his way into the kitchen first.

Gage made his way straight to the woman he considered family and hugged her. "I'm so sorry," he said.

Betsy hugged him back, her trembling frame telling

Gage she had more than nervous energy inside her. Fear was still there, too. "You didn't have to come."

"Well, Albert didn't mention you were baking. If he had, I would have pushed harder for an invitation," Gage teased.

Betsy laughed and swatted Gage. She turned to Marcus and wiped her hands on her apron. "Captain Patrick. I apologize for the state of my home."

"Nothing to apologize for, ma'am. I wish we were seeing each other under better circumstances."

"Me, too."

"Tell them what happened, Betsy," Albert encouraged.

Betsy looked flustered with all the attention, and the memory of what she'd been through. "I wasn't paying attention. I should have been. I got to my car, and he came up behind me."

"Take your time," Marcus said when Betsy paused.

Betsy drew a shaky breath and nodded. "He had a knife. He pushed me against the car and said if I didn't tell him who was named on Mr. Davis's will, he would kill me."

Gage exchanged a glance with Marcus. It was what Gage thought. Definitely Trevor, or someone Trevor paid to intimidate Betsy.

"What did you tell him?" Marcus asked.

"I didn't tell him anything. I screamed when he grabbed me, and Albert came running out."

"The man was close to her, his body on top of her, pressing her into the side of the car. I shouted at him to get away, and he looked up and saw me, then took off," Albert provided.

Marcus nodded. Gage inhaled sharply. It could have been so much worse.

"Were either of you able to see anything that could tell

us something about the man? Color of his skin, eyes, if he had an accent? Any tattoos or scars on visible skin?"

"His eyes were brown. He was white, but his skin was darker than mine or Albert's. He wore a black mask that was pulled all the way down to his neck, so I couldn't see anything else," Betsy said.

Marcus nodded and looked at Albert. "Did you see the man?"

Albert shook his head. "I was too far away to get a good look at him."

"And you don't have a doorbell camera or anything like that, do you?" Marcus asked.

Albert and Betsy both shook their heads.

"It's a safe neighborhood. We never thought we'd need something like that," Albert said.

"You shouldn't. No one should. We should all be allowed to live a safe life and not worry about someone coming onto our property and threatening us. Unfortunately, Trevor Davis doesn't play by the rules," Marcus said with a regretful shake of his head.

"What should we do?" Betsy whispered.

Marcus looked at all of them in the room, meeting everyone's gaze before he spoke. "If you're able, I'd get out of town for a little while. He's only interested in the woman who was given what he believes is his. He's not interested in you, but he's willing to hurt you to find out."

"That poor woman," Betsy said. "What is he going to do to her when he finds out who she is?"

Gage shook his head. He'd been wondering the same thing.

"There is a team looking into this whole situation. If you're willing, I'd like to provide the two of you with protection, at least until you're out of town," Marcus said.

Albert and Betsy exchanged a look. Albert's was one of worry for the woman he'd loved his entire life. Betsy's was one of fear with a hint of determination.

"That would be nice. Thank you, Captain," Albert said.

"The last thing we want is for Trevor Davis and the other people we believe he's involved with to harm anyone else. Too many lives have been lost because of them," Marcus said.

"Mr. Stevens..." Betsy began.

Gage stepped forward and shook his head. "Do not say anything about work. I told you before that I was willing to pay you to be gone as long as you felt necessary."

Betsy nodded, ducking her head in thanks. "Thank you, Gage."

"You're welcome, Betsy. I want you safe. Both of you."

"Are you going to be okay?" Betsy asked.

"I have the security systems at my house and the office. I'll probably change my routines. But just like you, Trevor only wants to know who his target needs to be. He's not interested in me."

"Dawn is such a nice lady. I hate to think he's going to go after her."

"He will," Marcus said. "If she's standing between him and what he believes belongs to him, he will. But we're working on stopping him for good. Putting an end to what he's done in our city."

"That would be the best thing possible," Albert said.

Marcus nodded. "I agree."

DAWN PARKED in the parking lot outside the headquarters for Davis Developments and looked up at the impressive building. Known for their innovative and environmentally friendly designs, the building in front of her showed that same creativity while also being beautiful.

Dawn did some research into the company over the last week, hoping she would learn more about it before she had to act like she had any idea what was going on, but she was wholly unprepared. She didn't know much of anything about construction and even less about business.

But Mr. Davis believed in her, so she was going to try.

Dawn opened the front door and was greeted by a friendly man with a warm smile. He was young, maybe mid-twenties, and well-dressed. His dark skin was a shade darker than Gage's. His eyes held the same kindness.

"May I help you?" he asked. He was positioned behind a desk with a secured gate next to him and no way inside without going through him.

"Yes, hi. I am supposed to meet with Tabitha today."

The man nodded. "Dawn Patterson? I just need to see some ID."

Dawn retrieved her wallet and handed over her license. She was impressed and a little surprised at the security, but she suspected the projects they worked on had to be kept quiet. Or at least not wide open to whoever wanted to walk in and see what they were doing.

"Thank you, Ms. Patterson. I'll let Tabitha know you're here. You can have a seat for a moment. There's coffee, water, and snacks if you'd like to grab something."

"Thank you." Dawn turned to the reception area the man indicated and helped herself to a small bottle of water. She carried it while she looked at the photographs on display. Buildings around the area that Davis Developments had built. Community centers, large homes, hotels, and campuses used for anything from colleges and universities to large corporations.

"Ms. Patterson," a husky voice said from behind Dawn.

Dawn turned and smiled. "Please, call me Dawn."

"Dawn. Nice to meet you. I'm Tabitha." Tabitha extended her hand and shook Dawn's with a firm grip. Her smile was kind but guarded. She was tall, well over Dawn's five-five, with brown hair pulled back from her face in a low knot. She wore pressed pants and a bright blue button-down shirt that shimmered with her movements.

"Nice to meet you. Thank you for allowing me to come by today."

Tabitha's smile tightened. "I have to say I'm not sure I had an option."

Dawn was a little taken aback by the other woman's words. Her shock must have shown on her face, and Tabitha hurried to continue.

"Forgive me, but as my boss, I don't have the option to tell you no."

Dawn understood the thought, but she wasn't there to exact her superiority. She was there to learn about the company and see if she could help, then decide what path she intended to take. "I hope you'll learn that I'd rather have someone who is willing to tell me no than someone who will say yes because it's what they believe I want to hear."

Tabitha regarded Dawn carefully, then nodded. "I can respect that. Shall we go to my office?"

Dawn nodded and let Tabitha lead the way.

Tabitha didn't speak on the walk past the reception desk and down the hallway to the right. Dawn took the time to look at the additional pictures and to study the woman she was following.

Tabitha appeared to be a little older than Dawn. She was

clearly put together, but her nails were worn like she knew her way around a tool bag. If Dawn had to guess, Tabitha earned her position by working her way up and Mr. Davis trusted her to run the company because of her wealth of knowledge.

Tabitha stopped at a door and retrieved a key from her pocket. She unlocked it, then pushed the door open for Dawn to go in ahead of her.

It was a large corner office with glass on two walls. The view outside the window overlooked the Niagara Gorge and beyond to Canada. It was definitely a position of power.

"Feel free to have a seat, Dawn," Tabitha said, gesturing to the small table near the windows.

Dawn sat, studying Tabitha as she joined Dawn. Dawn wasn't sure what the other woman thought of her being there, or of her taking over. Dawn wanted to learn but not push anyone out.

"I'm sorry for your loss," Tabitha said after a moment. "Mr. Davis was a good man."

Dawn nodded, smiling. "He was. And thank you, although he wasn't my family."

Tabitha's face showcased her surprise. "I assumed you were a relative."

Dawn shook her head. "I worked in the care facility where he lived for the last year. We became friends, I guess you could say. He was very kind to me, and he was my favorite patient."

"Friends?"

Dawn chuckled at the expression on Tabitha's face. "Just friends, I assure you. He never told me about any of this, so I question things."

"What do you mean?"

Dawn shrugged. "I told him a lot about my personal life.

He asked, and I trusted him. I talked to him about my family and my past. But I had no idea he owned this company or his properties or... much of anything about his family. He told me his wife died years ago, and he lost his oldest son, and his younger son wasn't someone he was close to, not that I blame him, but there's just... Sorry. I didn't mean to unload all of this on you."

Tabitha smiled. "It makes me feel better, actually. His son is..."

"A creep?" Dawn provided.

Tabitha chuckled. "That'll work." She sobered. "He's also cruel and possibly dangerous."

Dawn nodded. "I've learned that, too."

"Trevor threatened me when I took over for Robert. When Robert fell and went to Angel's Grove, I was already running most things, but Robert pulled back even more. Trevor showed up at one of our job sites one day and told me if I tried to stand in his way, he'd make sure I was no longer standing."

Dawn gasped. "What did you do?"

Tabitha shrugged. "I told Robert I would leave the company if he didn't keep Trevor away from me and everything this company was involved with."

Dawn's brows shot up. "Did it work?"

Tabitha nodded. "I think so. I never saw Trevor at another job site, and he doesn't ever come here. But without Robert around, I'm not sure what's going to happen."

"If it makes you feel better, I'll be the one he's after." Dawn shivered at the thought. She couldn't avoid it when she got in her car that morning and made sure she parked where the moniker he gave her wouldn't be seen by anyone unless they intentionally went to that side of her car.

"It doesn't make me feel better. Trevor worries me. I'm a

single mom. I have a teenage son and my ex isn't around, so it's just us."

"I have a teenager daughter," Dawn said. "But she lives with her dad because I made some mistakes."

"We've all made mistakes. What matters is how we choose to live after our mistakes."

"Mr. Davis used to tell me something similar."

Tabitha smiled. "Who do you think I got it from? He was a good man. I considered him a friend, too."

"It's good to know he didn't leave me floundering then. I don't know anything about construction or running a business, but I'm hoping I can count on you to help me figure out what I need to know."

"Of course. But I do have one question first."

"Sure?"

"Are you closing the company?"

"What? No. Why would I do that?"

Tabitha looked a little surprised. "Well, someone's been taking money from our accounts. I assumed it was whoever was taking over. Getting money out of the business before selling everything."

Dawn shook her head. "No. I haven't touched a thing. Why would someone do that?"

Tabitha raised her brows. "I think we both know the answer to that question. And to who is doing it. What we don't know is how he's getting access."

"And how we're going to stop him," Dawn added.

"I think it's time for a crash course in business, boss."

Dawn grinned. "I guess so."

9

––––––––

Dawn's stomach growled loudly, again. She clenched her hand over it, embarrassed at the noise her body was making.

Tabitha flashed her a look of apology. "I should have ordered lunch earlier. I apologize for not watching the time."

"We're both adults here. I could have said something at any point, but I was just as lost in all of this as you are. No, that's not true. I'm much more lost."

Tabitha chuckled. "You'll get the hang of it."

A knock on the door caught their attention.

"Come in," Tabitha called.

The man who'd been at the front desk earlier walked in. He carried a paper bag that smelled like heaven. "Lunch is here."

"Thank you, Keith," Tabitha said. "Did you grab your lunch, or do you want to join us?"

Keith shook his head. "I ate earlier. I brought lunch today."

"As long as you took some time for your break."

"I did, Tabitha. Thank you."

"Thanks, Keith."

Keith closed the door behind him as he left, and Tabitha opened the bag of food. She took out each item, setting their subs on the table followed by the chips that came with them. Tabitha went to a mini-fridge along the side wall and asked what Dawn wanted to drink.

"Water for me, please."

Tabitha grabbed two bottles of water and set one in front of Dawn. She settled into her seat and unwrapped her sandwich, taking a minute to say a prayer.

Dawn couldn't remember the last time she prayed for anything. Religion had never been a big part of her life. She was raised going to a Lutheran church, but her parents were the people who went on Christmas, Easter, and a few other days throughout the year. Dawn didn't hang on to the tradition, and Owen wasn't religious, so her faith slipped away without any thought.

"My parents were devout Catholics," Tabitha said when she picked up her sandwich. "My mom said she would have been a nun if she hadn't met my father when she did. She was in the process of deciding when he came into her life, and she believed it was God's way of telling her she was meant to share her faith in other ways."

"Wow. It's obviously important to you, too."

Tabitha nodded. "It is. I stopped going to church for a while when I was married. My ex wasn't big on it, and it was hard when my son was little. I always felt like something was missing, though. I started going back once my son was a little older and put him in Faith Formation, which is basically Sunday school. It helped me to realize I wasn't meant to stay married."

"That's not an easy decision," Dawn said, thinking of her

own choice to get divorced. Not that it was her idea, but she eventually agreed to it.

"It wasn't. We tried, though. We went to counseling, and we talked to each other a lot. It just wasn't right. When our divorce was final, he decided to leave the area. Said it never felt like the right place for him, but he stayed because I wanted to be here."

Dawn's brows jumped up. "He left his son?"

Tabitha nodded. "That was a hard one to take. Nick struggled a lot. Robert actually helped me with him. He gave me as much time off as I needed to be there for Nick, and he came by and spent time with us. He was like a surrogate grandfather to Nick at a time when he needed a man around."

"That sounds like something I would think he'd do. Although, like I said, I don't feel like I knew him, so maybe I shouldn't think that."

Tabitha examined Dawn closely, scanning her features and making Dawn shift in her seat. "I don't think Robert had a lot of people in his life who were only there for him. Who didn't care about his money or what he could do for them."

"That's not who I am," Dawn argued.

Tabitha nodded. "Which is exactly why he didn't tell you. You were there. I understand it was your job, but you were there. You spent time with him. It might have been your job to take care of him, but it sounds like you went above and beyond for him."

Dawn's cheeks warmed at the praise in Tabitha's voice. "I tried not to play favorites, but all the other nurses knew if Mr. Davis needed something, I would make sure it was done. We just connected, at a time when I had no one else."

"There's nothing wrong with that. And him not telling you about his fortune was probably because he knew he didn't need to. You treated him like a person, not like a rich guy who could help you."

"Do you think he worried I'd change if he told me?"

Tabitha breathed a laugh. "No. I think he either figured you knew or he planned to tell you but ran out of time."

Dawn nodded thoughtfully. She hoped that was the case. The letter Mr. Davis left her meant a lot, but hearing those words from him would have meant even more. She understood no one got to choose when their time was up, whether they had money or not. And Mr. Davis was no exception to that.

"Just spending today with you, a few hours, has shown me that you are going to be very good for this company."

Dawn smiled, but it fell as soon as her thoughts went back to what they'd been doing before lunch arrived. "If we can figure out how the money is leaving. He must have some kind of access we don't know about."

Tabitha nodded. "I was thinking that, too. Now that we've changed the passwords, hopefully it stops."

"Do you think that'll make a difference?"

Tabitha shook her head. "Unfortunately, no. I asked IT to look into it at the end of last week and they couldn't find where anyone was logging in to the system, so it's likely they have a way around it. We just have to figure it out."

"Which is obviously not easy."

"Nope."

Tabitha and Dawn ate their lunch in thought, both trying to figure out how Trevor could be accessing the systems without accessing the systems. He had to have a way to login, but it wasn't showing up.

"Should we get back to things?" Tabitha asked as she balled up her trash.

Dawn nodded and threw hers away, too. They cleared

the table again, bringing out the laptop Tabitha was using to show Dawn all the projects they were working on.

The rest of the day went by quickly. Before Dawn knew it, Tabitha was packing up her things and apologizing for having to leave to get her son.

"Since I'm the only one, I have to get him," Tabitha said.

"You don't have to explain yourself to me. I'm not coming in here with the intention of changing anything about the way you run the company. I want to learn and help, if I can, and support Davis Developments. It'll take me a while to get up to speed on everything, but I am not going to say you're doing anything wrong."

"Thank you. And thank you for coming today. It was a great day. Tomorrow?"

Dawn was about to agree when she realized she had to work. Her other work. "Actually, I can't. I have a shift at Angel's Grove."

Tabitha drew back sharply. "You still work there? I assumed you terminated your employment when you found out about all of this."

"Until I feel like I'm making a difference, I don't feel right taking money from Davis Developments, and that could be a while."

"But you have all of Mr. Davis's money. His house, his bank accounts. I would imagine it's enough for you to live off of for a long time."

Dawn nodded. "It is, but it's still his. I... Every time I think about spending it, I feel guilty. I didn't do anything to get that money. It should help others, not just line my pockets."

"There's nothing wrong with treating yourself. Or living on that money. But you have to do what feels right to you."

"Thank you," Dawn said. She didn't know many people who would understand.

Tabitha led the way outside, waving to Keith and reminding him to go home at a reasonable time. He assured her he would and said good night to Dawn.

Dawn walked with Tabitha at the fast pace the other woman set. She was heading straight for Dawn's car, which surprised Dawn that Tabitha was walking her there.

"You don't have to walk me to my car," Dawn said, knowing there was no way to avoid Tabitha seeing the paint on the side if she got close.

"What?" Tabitha asked. She pointed to the car parked next to Dawn. The only one Dawn worried about when she chose to spot at the back of the lot. "That's my SUV."

Dawn shook her head. What luck. "Oh."

"Are you parked next to me?" Tabitha asked.

Dawn nodded and knew Tabitha would definitely see the paint job. "Yes, and—"

"Oh my God, someone painted your car! We have to call the police. We have cameras. Hopefully, it caught them." Tabitha already had her phone out.

"It happened a couple nights ago," Dawn admitted.

"What?" Tabitha lowered her phone and looked at the paint. "Did you call the police?"

Dawn shook her head. "I treated myself to dinner, and this happened. If there was ever a sign that I shouldn't be spending Mr. Davis's money, I figure this is it."

"You should buy a new car."

"That was my first thought, but the more I considered it, the more I felt guilty. And figured someone will just paint a new car."

Tabitha nodded, alternating between staring at the car and Dawn. "Do you think this was Trevor?"

Dawn shrugged. "It's possible. I don't know who else it would be, but it's not public knowledge that I'm the one who inherited everything."

"It will be after today. There's no way he's not going to find out."

"I thought you said he isn't involved with the company."

"He's not, but everyone here has been curious who's taking over and what's going to happen to them. Your presence, once people start talking, will likely tell Trevor what he obviously already assumes."

Dawn stared at the word and nodded. "I guess I need to be ready then. Because he's coming."

"Stay safe," Tabitha said. "And come back whenever you have another day off. And seriously, think about using some of that money you have to make things easier. You deserve it."

"Thanks, Tabitha."

Dawn waited for Tabitha to get in her SUV and drive away. Then Dawn got in her BITCH car and thought about her day and her life. She wanted to be ready to spend the money, but every time she thought about it, something held her back. Who would she be with unlimited funds? Would she fall back into old habits? Or were those habits influenced by the people she was spending her time with?

Dawn hadn't felt the desire for drugs in over a year. Rehab was a good thing for her. But temptation changed when opportunities arrived.

GAGE PARKED on the street in front of a house in a nice section of the city. Kids played outside and people walked their dogs. The house he was going to was well-maintained and nice. It wasn't fancy, neither was the neighborhood, but it was nice. The kind of place where bad things didn't happen and people were there for each other.

It wasn't too different from his neighborhood, although Gage was sure a lot of people would disagree. Outside looking in was always different than reality. Gage was happy with his reality.

He was also confused about why he was there. He confirmed the address with Marcus when they were leaving Betsy's that morning, but it wasn't a place Gage knew. Then again, he would have been more surprised if he recognized the place where this supposed group was meeting.

Gage pressed the doorbell and waited for someone to answer. A white man with dark hair and a slightly receding hairline opened the door.

"Um, hello," Gage said at the man's raised eyebrows. "I'm Gage Stevens. I was told to come to this address."

"Nice to meet you," the man said, stepping back for Gage to enter. "Marcus and Lorelei told us to expect you. I'm Wray Allen. Everyone's in the living room."

Gage shook hands with Wray and followed the direction of his nod. Gage turned the corner into the living room and found it full of people.

"Gage. Glad you made it," Marcus said, approaching Gage.

Gage nodded to his friend and took stock of the others in the room. A few of them were vaguely familiar, but most were strangers. He recognized Jessica German from when Marcus asked Gage to defend her against a murder charge for... Karli Sloane. Whose cousin was Lorelei Sloane. Gage felt like an idiot for not making that connection sooner.

Marcus hung back with Gage and pointed out all the people in the room. Besides Jessica, Karli, and Lorelei,

Marcus identified Stacey Allen, Mackenzie Chambers, Edie Warren, and Raina London. Marcus's wife, Francesca, came over and hugged Gage. He didn't know Frannie well, but the times they'd met, Gage liked her.

Then there were the men. Most of them were paired up with one of the woman Gage had seen on the news in the last year, according to Marcus. Stacey's husband, Wray, was a firefighter, and the group was gathered in their home. Braden Wright worked with Wray and was dating Jessica. Cade Murray was a PI and with Karli. Holden Cross was a paramedic and involved with Mackenzie. Adam Johnson was Lorelei's partner in the FBI and engaged to Raina. And Gage already Drake Foster and Pryce Murphy and knew Pryce was involved with Edie.

"This is quite a group you have here," Gage said.

Marcus nodded. "It all sort of came together when we realized everyone was fighting the same man. We've been putting the pieces together since we learned Damon Street was pulling the strings."

"He's dead, though. It didn't stop."

"Which was why we started looking into Trevor, but we didn't know his last name until you told me."

Gage sucked in a breath and looked at the woman he knew was held captive by a man named Trevor. Edie Warren was a victim of violence, abuse, and rape. But she was standing across the room looking like she didn't have any shadows in her past.

Gage couldn't imagine feeling safe. Not after a situation like she'd been through. Gage lost his mother to a random act of violence, according to police at the time, and had his home and office broken into. He hadn't felt safe since he lost his mother, and the break-ins only served to amplify that feeling.

"So, you guys meet and try to bring down this organization?" Gage asked.

Marcus nodded. "If anyone found out I was bringing civilians into this, I'd be out of a job. It's an active investigation, one that's not led by my department but we're involved with it. Every person here has a vested interest in stopping all of this. My job is worth the risk if it means putting an end to what's been happening."

"Why bring me in?" Gage asked.

"You found the missing piece," Lorelei Sloane said, joining them at the edge of the room. Her dark gaze assessed Gage in an instant, then scanned the room.

Gage got the feeling she saw things no one else did. As an agent, she was smart and capable and tasked with taking down some of the worst criminals in the country. Gage didn't envy her job, but he did respect the hell out of it. "What do you mean?"

"We knew someone was footing the bill. We knew there was a money trail, but we had no idea where to look for it. You found it for us. Which means you get to join in the fun," Lorelei said, as though that was all the explanation Gage needed.

"I'm limited on what I can share," Gage said, knowing that wasn't an answer law enforcement liked to hear.

"And we respect that," Marcus was quick to say. "We would never ask you to violate privilege and risk your license. However, it's my understanding Trevor Davis is not your client."

Gage nodded slowly. "That's true."

"Which means any information you know or discover about him is not bound by privilege."

"Also true."

"And we know you are just as interested in putting an end to all of this as the rest of us are."

Gage nodded. "I am."

"Then I think it's time we fill you in on the whole story. From the beginning. When my wife was a witness to a murder I investigated, and we had our first run-ins with Damon Street and Clyde Davis."

Gage's brows shot up. "Robert's older son?"

Marcus nodded. "Little brother is only following in the footsteps laid out for him. But we need to stop him before he puts an end to our city."

Gage drew a breath. "Tell me everything."

10

Gage's head spun as they told him all the things Trevor Davis had been involved with. Or if not Trevor, people he was a known associate of. Damon Street, Clyde Davis, Oscar Hyatt, Silver James, and others.

Gage had his suspicions, but it was all so much more than Gage ever assumed. If he'd known, and if he'd realized Trevor was the missing piece, he would have risked his license to go to Marcus.

But it was too late for that. Marcus knew what Gage suspected. Marcus and his team had figured out far more than the public knew, but Trevor was still in the wind.

"Do you think Trevor is the one in charge?" Gage asked when they'd all shared the details.

Food had been delivered, and people had traded places in the living room, eating and talking and standing around in turn so everyone had a chance to tell their story to Gage. Stacey and Wray had each taken a break to spend time with their sons, eating in the kitchen with them and taking them upstairs to settle them into bed.

Marcus shook his head as the others looked around the

room at Gage's question. "I don't know. I've been about six steps behind this whole time. I had cops working under me and handing over information to these people for years. Cops who were breaking the law and helping keep all this activity quiet. If it wasn't for Stacey and her dedication to tracking down Holly's killer, I don't know if we'd have ever figured all of this out."

Gage nodded, understanding that the connections were flimsy. Almost everything they had was circumstantial. In a court, it would be hard to prove any of what they were saying. But they didn't need to prove all of it in court. Damon Street was dead. So were Silver James, Oscar Hyatt, and Clyde Davis. Two of the cops who assisted in the criminal activity were also dead with the third in jail. The criminals were cleaning up after themselves, but it didn't help the victims. The people like Edie Warren and her cousin Tonya, and all the people still missing. The ones who were being victimized every day they weren't found.

Gage looked at Edie. "He has more women?"

Edie nodded. "There were four or five others with me at all times. I was in a few different places, but I don't remember any of them. I know there are more. And probably far more than I ever saw."

Gage tried to process everything he learned, knowing a lifetime wouldn't be long enough to understand why someone would do the things Trevor did. But all of the information did confirm what Gage originally thought. Trevor needs the money from his father's estate and company. The walls were closing in, and it would be that much more important for him to find a way to get that money.

"The woman who inherited everything," Lorelei began,

"is being followed. She spent the day today at Davis Developments. Her vehicle was spray-painted two nights ago."

"Seriously?" Gage barked. "So you're following her but allowing things to happen to her?"

Lorelei traded a look with her partner, Adam. Adam raised his brows and looked at Marcus.

Marcus stepped forward and put his hand on Gage's arm. Gage fought the urge to shake his friend off.

"Gage, they are watching her but not interfering. And they were watching her, not her car," Marcus said in a soothing tone that grated on Gage's nerves.

"She doesn't deserve this," Gage growled.

"I agree. We all do. But until we can bring Trevor Davis in, it's going to keep happening. We have to catch him doing something. Right now, we have no proof he's involved with anything."

"Edie's seen him. Why can't she identify him?" Gage asked, wondering why he was the first to think of that.

"Well, until you told me his last name, we didn't know who we were looking for. Since then, we've tried to find a picture of him, but none exist. Plus, Edie's testimony wouldn't hold up in court." Marcus gave Edie a sympathetic smile.

Gage started to question why when he realized what Marcus meant. Drugs were forced on Edie for months. Any attorney would tear her apart on the stand and convince the jury she was an unreliable witness and couldn't be counted on for her testimony.

Shit.

"So we're back to square one," Gage said, feeling as defeated as when he walked in there.

"Not entirely," Marcus said. "We know he's after Ms.

Patterson. We know he's going to try to get the money. We will catch him."

"You're using her as bait?" Gage was incredulous.

Lorelei shook her head. "Not bait. But we don't want to scare her more than necessary, so we're watching her and waiting."

"For him to kill her. Great fucking plan," Gage spat. He thought the police were the good guys. They would protect people. Instead, the police and FBI were waiting for an innocent woman to be hurt before they would do anything.

"Gage," Marcus said.

Gage glared at his friend, then let his gaze drift to the others. "Listen, I want to agree with this, but I've met Dawn. She's a kind person. I understand why Robert gave everything to her. She's someone you can trust. Someone who will do what's right. Even knowing her past, she's making up for it. I think Robert saw that. I can't just sit here and let you leave her unprotected."

"She's not," Lorelei insisted.

"Are you sure about that? Because I promise you, someone breaking into your home and your office, violating your personal space, threatening you and hurting you, and the police swooping in later to say sorry but we needed proof is not fucking good enough," Gage snapped.

"You're in love with her," Lorelei announced.

Gage shook his head. "I don't know the woman. And no. But I feel a responsibility toward her. I'm the one who brought her into the middle of this. Without Robert changing his will two days before he died, without me being the one who told her, she would still be living a life without a thought to this evil waiting for her."

"Is that all it is?" Lorelei asked.

Gage glared at the woman. "Yes."

Lorelei held his glare and studied him without looking around the room.

Everyone else was silent as the two of them squared off.

Gage didn't like being questioned. Yes, he was attracted to Dawn, and yes, that kiss they shared had been replaying in his mind for days, but he would feel the same protective instincts about anyone in this position. The desire for her to be safe had nothing to do with his desire for her to be his.

"Okay," Lorelei said, deflating the tension in the room with one word.

Gage tried not to sag with relief.

"What's the next step?" Mackenzie asked.

"Same as the current step. Find Trevor Davis and bring him in," Marcus said.

TREVOR SAT in the back of the SUV and stared at Angel's Grove. Darkness had fallen, blanketing the area with a thick layer of fog. The spring night was cool. A good night for Trevor. Time to move his body.

The door at the front of the building opened, the automatic sliding doors parting for the woman who walked through them. The woman Trevor had been waiting for.

He knew he could be patient, but he wasn't known for his patience. And neither was his boss. She was putting the pressure on him to get the money he promised he'd deliver. Money that his worthless fucking father waved under his nose his entire damn life, then swept away at the last fucking minute.

If he could kill his father again, Trevor would. It was a joy to watch the old man's life end. To see the look on his face after he was gone. To know Trevor got the last fucking word. Forever.

"Fuck you, old man," Trevor muttered.

"What was that, sir?" Trevor's driver asked.

"Nothing, Jeeves. Pull up next to her."

Jeeves, whose real name was something Trevor never bothered to learn because he was the fucking help and didn't fucking matter, eased the SUV around the parking lot to where the good doctor was walking. There were cameras everywhere, but Trevor and Jeeves had done enough recon to know where the cameras were and how to avoid them.

Lucky for Trevor, there were no cameras in the employee lot. He snickered. Privacy and all that shit. It was his favorite rallying cry. Made his life so much easier.

Jeeves stopped the SUV a few feet away from the woman, close enough that she had no choice but to pay attention to them, but far enough away for Trevor to be able to get out and grab her if she didn't willingly get into the SUV.

"Good evening, Dr. Walden," Jeeves said. "Would you come with me, please?"

Dr. Walden looked at the SUV and back at Jeeves. She was careful, studying him. She was smart, probably why she was a doctor. She thought she could recall some feature and be able to tell the police later. She gripped her keys tighter, sliding one between her index and middle fingers like she was going to use it as a weapon.

Trevor grinned in the backseat, behind tinted windows Dr. Walden couldn't possibly see through.

"How do you know my name?" Dr. Walden asked.

"We have some questions for you," Jeeves said, not answering her question.

"Who is we?"

"My employer."

"Who is your employer?"

"Come with me, ma'am," Jeeves said, his voice edging toward harder. Jeeves might be the help, but he wasn't all useless. Trevor knew the man could snap a bone or take down someone without a second thought. He wasn't helpless, and he wasn't useless.

"No," Dr. Walden said. She moved to go between two vehicles, but she wasn't fast enough.

Trevor anticipated her retreat and her argument and was halfway out of the SUV when she refused. Since she was running away, it was easy for him to grab her bag and tug her back toward him.

She shouted, but a hand over her mouth was an easy solution to that. Along with a hissed promise that she would die more slowly if she fought him.

The whimper she let out was enough for Trevor. He was going to enjoy her. She wasn't his type, and she didn't do anything for him, but he was going to have fun torturing her.

Jeeves was out right behind Trevor, knocking the doctor out with a quick strike on the back of her head, then helping Trevor put her in the backseat.

Trevor climbed in after her, slapping the seat for Jeeves to take off.

Jeeves drove away slowly like he wasn't in a hurry. Anything else would have caused suspicion, and they didn't want that.

The doctor stirred a few times on the drive, but she didn't wake up until Jeeves pulled into the warehouse and Trevor opened his door. She sat up and looked around, then reached for the door handle, like getting out of the SUV was going to be helpful.

She stopped short when she got out, seeing the cavernous space with nowhere to go and nowhere to hide. She ran anyway, heading straight for the door.

Trevor laughed, the sound echoing off the metal walls. He watched as she flinched, then laughed harder when she tripped over a seam in the floor.

She finally made it to the door and pushed, but nothing happened. The door was sealed off a long time ago. For that reason. The only door that opened was the one they drove through. The one that could only be opened by a remote in the SUV.

"You're not getting out of here, Dr. Walden. You might as well come have a conversation with me," Trevor shouted.

"About what?"

"About my father," Trevor said, knowing his voice would carry.

Silence met him for a few seconds. He could feel her relaxing. A conversation was easy. "Who's your father?"

"Robert Davis."

"I assure you, there was no negligence on the part of the staff. Your father received excellent care. His death was sad, but unfortunately, that's how so many of our guests leave Angel's Grove," Dr. Walden said, infusing the right amount of sympathy into her voice. She drew closer as she spoke, as though figuring out Trevor just wanted answers. He was a heartbroken son. That was why he wanted to speak to her.

She finally stepped back into the light. Her clothes were wrinkled but definitely expensive. She looked less worried than she'd been a minute ago.

"Will you tell me about his last few days?" Trevor asked, knowing she wouldn't pick up on the reference.

She moved closer, putting her hand on the back of the metal chair Trevor motioned to. She stepped around the seat and pulled it away just slightly. She folded her hands on her lap and nodded. "Sure, I can tell you about his last few days. Is there anything specific you want to know?"

Trevor shrugged. "Whatever you want to share."

"Okay, well, I only saw him a few times. He was having trouble breathing toward the end. He was slowing down quite a bit. He was always in good spirits, though. He would smile whenever I would come in, and we would talk about anything from family to hobbies."

"I'm surprised he didn't talk about work. It was his favorite topic."

Dr. Walden looked a little unsure. She shifted in her seat, something she wore scratching across the metal. "Well, he did some, but not all the time. He told me he was proud of you." Her smile was as fake as her words.

Trevor barked a laugh. "He did, huh?"

Dr. Walden nodded, shifting again. "Yes, of course."

"Of course." Trevor stood and walked behind Dr. Walden. "Of course. Was that before or after you declared him mentally fit to make the changes to his will that cut me out?"

Dr. Walden squeaked in response to Trevor's arm locking around her throat. She grabbed at his arm, trying to pull him free. She gasped, wheezing for breath.

Trevor released her, delighting in the way she sucked in a breath and coughed. He moved around to the front of her, crouching in front of the woman.

Dr. Walden looked up at him. The fear in her eyes made Trevor grin. "I didn't know what he was doing."

Trevor raised one brow. "Really? You had no idea he was writing me out of his will? Giving everything he owned, all his money and his company and his property, to someone who wasn't related to him."

"He didn't tell me all that."

"But he did tell you who it was going to, didn't he?"

The truth flashed in her eyes. She knew. There was no question.

Trevor stood and stepped over to the table he asked to be left in the space. The table that had all kinds of tools he could use to encourage the doctor to tell him what he wanted to know.

Tools he could also use to dismantle her body once he had the truth, but he was still deciding about that.

Trevor picked up a set of brass knuckles. He slid the device onto his hand and faced the doctor.

Her eyes widened. She gripped the edge of the seat. "What... What are you doing with that?"

Trevor flexed his fingers. "Well, that depends on you."

"On me?" she squeaked.

Trevor nodded and moved closer. "Yes, on you, Dr. Walden. Because if you tell me what I want to know, this will be a much easier process."

"All you want to know is who your father left everything to?"

Trevor nodded and met the doctor's gaze. "He didn't get around to sharing that piece of information when he told me he cut me out of the will."

She inhaled sharply.

"My boss keeps telling me I'm too short-tempered. That if I was a little more patient with people, I would be able to get what I want so much easier. But that isn't always my experience."

Dr. Walden eyed Trevor's fist.

"I keep thinking if I'd done what she said, I might have been able to get the truth out of my father. But I have a hard time with that. You know how it goes. Someone gives you bad news, and you react. You pick up the pillow on the floor and you hold it over their face until they stop fighting you and give in to death."

"You killed your father?" she breathed.

Trevor shrugged. "He made me mad. He said he didn't want me to have his money. That I didn't earn it. But he was wrong. I did earn it. I deserve it. And you're going to tell me who has it so I can get it all back."

"That's all you want?" Dr. Walden's throat bobbed as she swallowed.

"To know who my father left everything to?"

She nodded.

Trevor nodded. "Yeah, that's it."

"And you're not going to hurt me?"

Trevor chuckled. "Now, Dr. Walden, I never promised that. I just said this will be much easier if you tell me what I want to know. You're still going to die."

"What?"

Trevor snorted. "Did you really think there was a chance you were getting out of here alive?" He shook his head and tsked. "And I thought you were so smart. Guess I was wrong."

"Please don't kill me," she begged.

"It's not time for you to beg yet. There's still a lot of time for that."

"I'll tell you who it is. Just don't kill me."

"You'll tell me who it is?"

She nodded. "If you promise not to kill me."

Trevor examined his knuckles like he was actually considering her offer. She was dead no matter what, and he was going to get confirmation of what he already knew, but if she made it easier on him, he would make it fast.

"Fine."

"That's it?" she breathed, exhaling like she couldn't believe that worked.

He shrugged. "Sure. Who did my father leave everything to?"

"Dawn Patterson. She's a nurse at Angel's Grove. She's—"

Blood poured from the slice Trevor made across Dr. Walden's neck. Her words stopped. Fear lit her gaze for a second before her eyes went dark.

"Clean this up," Trevor said to Jeeves. He walked out of the room with his phone already dialing. "I have confirmation."

11

———————

"Has anyone seen Dr. Walden?" Dawn asked the other nurses at the desk. She logged into the computer and looked up to meet the confused gazes of her coworkers.

"I thought I saw her car outside," Sue said.

"She was here yesterday," Terry added.

"But no one's seen her today?" Dawn asked.

The other two exchanged a look and shook their heads.

"Not that I can remember," Sue said. "I'll ask around."

Dawn nodded, wondering where Dr. Walden could be. It wasn't like her to not show up, or to not stop by the desk a few times at the beginning of the shift to make sure everyone knew what was going on that day.

Dawn checked on another patient and went about her day, pushing Dr. Walden from her mind. She went into the break room for lunch and smiled at Mandy.

"You're still here?" Mandy asked.

Dawn put her frozen meal in the microwave and hit the button to start it before she turned to Mandy. "There's still hours left on our shift. Where else would I be?"

Mandy shook her head, surprise in her eyes. "I figured

you'd quit once you inherited all that money from Mr. Davis."

"How do you know about that?" Dawn hissed, taking a seat with Mandy. She thought it was still a secret. One she wasn't in too much of a hurry to expose.

Mandy narrowed her eyes at Dawn. "Dr. Walden and I were the ones who signed the paperwork. That cute lawyer needed someone to declare Mr. Davis of sound mind. We were the witnesses to his signature."

"You and Dr. Walden?" Dawn asked. Her breath hitched.

Mandy nodded. "Yeah. I figured you knew that. Or did something change?"

"Have you seen Dr. Walden today?"

Mandy sneered at Dawn. "No. Why?"

"She's missing. Sue said she saw Dr. Walden's car, but no one's seen her."

"That doesn't mean she's missing. You're being pretty dramatic."

Dawn shook her head and pulled her phone out of her pocket. "I don't know that I am." Dawn walked out of the room and called the only person she knew would take her seriously.

"Stevens," he answered, sounding like he didn't know who was calling.

"Gage?"

"Dawn?"

"Hi."

"Hi."

Dawn's cheeks burned. She felt like a teenager with a crush. But that wasn't why she called. "Hey, sorry. Hi. Um, one of the doctors from here might be missing."

"Missing? What do you mean, missing?" Gage was all business with that bit of information.

"Well, I might be overreacting, but I haven't seen one of our doctors here all day. Another nurse swore she saw her car."

"What doctor?" Gage asked. His tone said he knew the answer already.

"Dr. Walden. The one you had sign the will."

Gage swore under his breath. "Let me make a call. Are you at work?"

"Yeah. I'm just getting lunch."

"At work, or are you leaving the facility?"

"No, I'm... I'm at work. I'm not leaving."

"Don't leave, Dawn. Stay inside, make sure someone knows where you are at all times. Don't go in any stairways or elevators alone. Stay in public places as much as possible."

"You're scaring me, Gage."

"I know, and I'm sorry, but until we know if Dr. Walden is missing or just involved in something and no one's seen her, I don't want you alone."

"Okay," Dawn breathed. Fear trickled down her spine and settled in her gut like the lunch she'd planned to eat.

"Is this your phone number, or are you calling me from Angel's Grove?"

"It's my number."

"Okay. Keep your phone with you. Don't go anywhere without it. I'll call you back as soon as I know something."

"Okay."

"Dawn?"

"Yeah?"

"I'm glad you called me. You can always call me, okay?"

"Thanks."

"We'll talk soon."

"Okay."

Gage hung up, leaving Dawn staring at her phone and wondering how in the hell something that should have been good news had messed up so many things in her life. She was a billionaire, and instead of being able to enjoy it, she was trapped at work and worried one of her coworkers was in danger because of her.

Dawn walked back to the break room and opened the microwave. She carried the tray to a table and sat down, barely processing what she was doing.

"What's going on?" Mandy asked.

Dawn shook her head. "I don't know."

"Did something happen to Dr. Walden?"

"I don't know."

"Is someone going to come after me?" Mandy half-screeched.

Dawn looked up at her. She wasn't close to Mandy. Mandy always seemed a bit selfish and too good for everyone else, including the patients. She was good at her job, but the job was a stepping stone for Mandy. "I don't know anything, Mandy. All I know right now is you are one of only a few people who knew Mr. Davis named me as the one to inherit his fortune, a fortune I never knew about until after I was told it was mine. A fortune his son is very upset didn't go to him. I don't know what happened to Dr. Walden, and I don't know if there's a reason to worry. What I do know is I'm not going anywhere alone today. I'm going to be aware of my surroundings, and I'm going to do my best to stay alive through today, and tomorrow, and all the days after that."

"Stay alive?" she screamed. "You think someone's trying to kill you? They could come for me? Why the hell did you drag me into this?"

"I didn't do anything! I didn't ask for this. I didn't plan it.

And I sure as hell don't want anyone to be hurt because of it."

Mandy shook her head with disgust. "This is all your fault."

Dawn's stomach tightened, rejecting the food she hoped to eat. She pushed the tray away and shook her head, fighting the tears welled up. "I didn't do anything."

"If you hadn't gotten so friendly with Mr. Davis, he wouldn't have named you. If you'd treated him like all the other patients and just did your job and moved on, none of this would be going on. I'm supposed to be getting engaged soon. I'm going to get married. My life is just starting. I'm not going to get killed because of you!"

"What is going on in here?" Sue hissed from the door.

Mandy swung her frantic gaze to Sue. Her chest heaved with each breath. Her hands tightened into fists. She looked wild and savage.

"I'm sorry," Dawn said.

"She's going to get all of us killed," Mandy snarled, her voice breaking on a sob. "It's her fault Dr. Walden is missing."

"What are you talking about?" Sue caught Mandy as she collapsed and turned her attention to Dawn. "What is she talking about?"

"Mr. Davis left me his estate, his company, and all his money. His son is angry and wants it back. The lawyer said the son doesn't know I'm the one who inherited everything, but Dr. Walden and Mandy were the ones who signed the will, so Mandy thinks..."

"Oh, no," Sue breathed. "We have to do something. Call the police. Someone."

"I already did," Dawn said.

"What did they say?" Sue asked.

"It's being looked into. I would guess someone will be here soon. I hope."

"Here? Someone is coming here?" Mandy cried.

"The police, honey," Sue said, leading Mandy to a chair. "We're safe in here. No one gets in without ID and a reason."

"I'm too pretty to die," Mandy crowed.

"I know, honey, I know," Sue said, as if being pretty was a reason to live.

Dawn threw her lunch away and left the two of them alone. She was only adding to the stress of the situation. Plus, she wanted more answers.

Dawn called Gage again.

"Are you okay?"

"Yeah. I just... one of my coworkers blames me for this. I needed to hear a friendly voice."

"You are not to blame, Dawn. Not even a little bit. Robert should have told his son, and you, about the change. And regardless of that, Trevor is responsible for his actions."

"Do you think he hurt Dr. Walden?"

Gage's silence was enough of an answer, but he spoke anyway. "It's possible. The police are on their way to Angel's Grove since someone said they saw her car. Another team is going to her house."

"What if they don't find her?"

"They'll find her, Dawn. I know they will."

"Okay."

"Dawn?"

"Yeah?"

"Can I take you to dinner tonight?"

She sucked in a breath, surprised at the request. Her heart thumped hard at the possibility of dinner with Gage, but her brain knew it was a bad idea. "I work a twelve-hour shift today and tomorrow. I'm usually pretty exhausted when I get home."

"When's your next day off?"

"Monday."

"How about Monday then?"

She smiled despite the situation. She could still hear Mandy crying in the break room. Her stomach rumbled at the missed lunch and twisted with her fear. She had patients to see and a busy day left, plus an impending visit from the police.

But none of that mattered. None of it meant she couldn't live her life and enjoy time with a kind man who was proving to be there for her more than anyone else in her life. "Yes."

"Good. Marcus just texted me they're at Angel's Grove. I'm going to tell him to ask for you. Captain Marcus Patrick is the one looking into all of this. Check his ID."

"Okay. Thanks, Gage."

"See you Monday, Dawn."

Dawn hung up with a smile, immediately feeling guilty for the excitement coursing through her.

She checked in at the nurse's desk and told Terry she was going up front to meet someone. It would be all over the floor by the time she got back that she'd inherited billions of dollars and put them all at risk.

Maybe it was time to start thinking about a job change.

The thought sent a pang through her heart. Dawn loved what she did. But she hated the idea of anyone being in danger because of her.

She'd have to think about that.

A tall man was at the desk when Dawn turned the corner to walk down the hallway. He flashed a police badge at the man behind the bulletproof glass, keeping visitors out unless they were allowed. Harold was a large man who used to be in the military and had a soft spot for elderly patients. He spoke softly and kindly to all the guests, making each of them feel safe and cared for. He'd give his life to protect Angel's Grove.

Dawn's phone buzzed with a text. She pulled it from her pocket and saw the request from the desk to meet a visitor.

She texted back that she was almost there, and Harold turned to see her with a wide smile.

"This is Captain Marcus Patrick," Harold said. "He said he needs to speak to you."

"Did you check his ID?" Dawn asked.

Harold blanched slightly but nodded. "I did."

"And he is who he says he is?"

Harold nodded. "Unless he has a good fake, yes."

Dawn looked up at the captain. The man didn't blink, and didn't argue at her appraisal. She scanned him carefully, not that she would have known if something was off, but it made her feel better. "Who called you?"

His lips quirked up. "Gage Stevens."

"And why are you here?"

"Dr. Walden is missing."

"Dr. Walden is missing?" Harold snapped. "What? Since when?"

"Did she arrive at work this morning?" Captain Patrick asked Harold.

Harold shook his head. "Not since I've been here, but that's not unusual. She works odd hours at times."

"Do you have security footage of the parking lot?"

"You think something happened to her?" Harold asked.

"We're looking into every possibility."

Harold nodded and buzzed the door for Captain Patrick to enter the building. With both men in the small office space, Dawn felt crowded. She started to back up, but Captain Patrick grabbed her arm.

"I'd like to keep you close, Dawn. Please."

Dawn hesitated, but she nodded when she saw the kindness in his gaze. If Gage trusted him, Dawn would, too.

Harold cued up the video from the night before. He zipped past shift change, slowing down to confirm none of the people walking out were Dr. Walden. Two hours after the others left and the new shift arrived, Harold stopped.

"There she is," Harold said, pointing to Dr. Walden.

The doctor waved to the man behind the desk and walked out the front door. The door camera followed her for a minute, then she went out of frame as she stepped off the curb toward the employee section of the lot.

"Do you have more cameras?" Captain Patrick asked.

Harold shook his head. "Only the one pointing at the road. We can see if she drove out."

The view on the screen changed to the road coming into Angel's Grove. Harold went to the exact time Dr. Walden walked out the door and let it play. Six minutes after she walked out the door, an SUV pulled out. More time passed and Harold sped the video ahead, but Dr. Walden's vehicle never left.

The tension in the small space built higher and higher until Dawn asked, "Did she leave in that SUV?"

"I'd say it's likely," Captain Patrick said. "Do we have a shot of the SUV arriving?"

Harold clicked a few more buttons and retreated to before shift change. Forty minutes before employees started arriving, the same SUV pulled into the lot. It parked out of view of the cameras, and the windshield was too dark to see who was in it, but Dawn already knew the answer to that question.

It had to have been Trevor. And he took Dr. Walden.

Captain Patrick flashed her a look that said he'd come to the same conclusion. "Is there somewhere we can speak?"

Dawn nodded and turned to walk out.

Captain Patrick thanked Harold and handed him a card. He asked Harold to send copies of the videos they just watched to the email address on the card, then followed Dawn to the small room off the front hall where they typically told family their loved one had died.

Dawn sank onto one of the chairs, folding her hands in front of herself. "She's dead, isn't she?"

Captain Patrick nodded. "I would guess she is, but until we have confirmation, we can't go there."

Dawn looked up at him, shocked he would admit that.

"I know I shouldn't have said that, but I also believe you are in danger, and this is proof."

"What about Dr. Walden?" Dawn snapped.

"We will do whatever we can to find her. I know this is not an easy situation. Did you recognize the vehicle? Do you have any idea who could have been behind Dr. Walden's presumed disappearance?"

Dawn shook her head. "I don't recognize the vehicle, but we both know who was in it."

Captain Patrick raised an eyebrow at her.

"I'm not stupid, Captain. I know it was Trevor Davis. I know he killed Dr. Walden to confirm I'm the one his father left everything to. I'm assuming you know that as well. Otherwise, it's unlikely the police captain would have shown up for a woman who's only been missing a few hours."

Captain Patrick rubbed the back of his neck. "There are a lot of moving pieces in this, Ms. Patterson."

Dawn laughed mirthlessly. "Meaning I'm not really important. I'm just a pawn in this thing."

Captain Patrick's face pinched with his agreement. "I wouldn't put it that way."

"How would you put it, Captain?"

"We've been chasing this organization for a long time. You're the most recent target, and we will do everything we can to protect you."

"But you don't think you actually can. Is that how it is?"

"I didn't say that."

Dawn shook her head and stood. "You didn't have to."

"Ms. Patterson—"

"Captain Patrick, at least have the courtesy to tell me the truth. Are you doing anything to make sure Trevor Davis ends up behind bars? Anything that will put an end to whatever it is he's doing?"

"This is an active investigation. One that I'm not at liberty to discuss."

"Which means no. Great to know, Captain. Thanks. Now, if you'll excuse me, I have to get back to work."

"Ms. Patterson?"

Dawn stopped just outside the door and looked back at the captain.

"Please be careful."

Dawn nodded. She had no intention of dying.

The rest of her shift was less eventful. Dawn sent Gage a quick text letting him know Captain Patrick showed up and did nothing. Then she turned her phone off and tried to shake off her frustration.

By the time Dawn got home, she was exhausted and starving. She turned on the TV for background noise and stuck her leftovers in the microwave. She grabbed her food and sank onto her couch. She took a bite and got lost in the cooking show she was watching, marveling at the talent of the chefs she watched.

Two hours later, Dawn woke with a start. The TV still played softly. Her neck ached from sleeping slumped over on the couch. She stood and stretched, then she heard a noise.

A soft rattle. Then the slide of metal on metal.

She looked at her door. The knob moved slightly.

Someone was trying to get into her apartment.

12

———

Dawn scrambled for her phone and dialed nine-one-one. She stared at the doorknob, trying to figure out what she should do. Block the door? Grab a knife? Scream?

"Nine-one-one. What is your emergency?" the voice on the other end of the line said.

"Someone's trying to break into my apartment," Dawn whispered.

"What is your address?"

"Three-oh-nine West One Hundredth Street. Apartment four-eighty-nine."

Clicking echoed through the phone. "Is there somewhere you can hide?"

"Hide?" Dawn hissed. "It's a studio!"

"Do you have a bathtub?"

"He knows I'm here. He's after me."

"Do you have something you can use to defend yourself?" the woman asked. "The police are on the way."

Dawn looked around the apartment. Her only option was a knife. Or a frying pan. "Nothing that'll do much harm.

Not without getting close. I don't know if I can do it. I'm a nurse. Hurting someone goes against everything in me."

"I understand. Hopefully the person will leave when they hear the sirens."

Dawn strained to hear. The rattling hadn't stopped, and she didn't hear any sirens. "How long until they're here?"

"Less than two minutes," the woman said. "Are you Dawn?"

"How... How do you know that?"

"Your name comes up with your address."

"Oh, okay."

"I'm Mackenzie. With your permission, I'd like to call Captain Patrick. He's the police captain."

"I met him earlier today. Why are you calling him?" Dawn kept her voice low as she stared at the door and waited for someone to throw it open and come at her. The knife in her hand was heavy. The metal warming in her palm despite the chill coursing through her.

"I want him aware of this. I want him to know someone is trying to get into your apartment. Is that okay?"

Dawn scoffed. "Sure. Maybe he'll be able to find out who killed me."

"No one's going to kill you, Dawn. The police are on their way up the stairs to your unit. You should hear sirens. There are two cars there."

Dawn held her breath and listened. Mackenzie was right. Sirens whooped through the night, breaking through what would have been a quiet night if she hadn't brought the police to her apartment.

Voices outside her apartment drew closer before they stopped at her door.

"There's an officer outside your door, Dawn. Are you okay?"

"Yeah. Yeah. Thank you, Mackenzie."

"You're welcome, Dawn. I'm happy I was able to help."

"Me, too." Dawn hung up, feeling like she was going to be sick. A knock on the door almost had her dropping the knife, even though she expected the knock.

"Police. Can you open your door, Ms. Patterson?"

Dawn set the knife on the counter and walked to the door. She opened it, hating that she lived in a place that didn't have peepholes so she could make sure they were who they said they were before she opened the door.

Two officers stood outside her door, one blocking her from exiting. "Ms. Patterson, are you okay?"

Dawn nodded and wrapped her arms around herself. "I think so."

"I'm Officer Pryce Murphy, and this is Detective Drake Foster. May we come inside?"

Dawn shrugged and stepped back. Two more officers were right behind the two who came into her apartment, but the others stayed outside.

Dawn thought she saw someone on the ground, but the officers blocked her view.

"You said you heard someone trying to break in?" Detective Foster asked.

Dawn nodded. "I was sleeping on the couch. Something woke me up. After a minute, I heard it again and saw the doorknob moving. Like someone was checking to see if it was unlocked. Then I heard metal, like when you slide your key into a lock."

"And that's when you called nine-one-one?" Officer Murphy asked.

Dawn nodded again. "I didn't know what else to do."

The cops shared a look, and one of them noticed the knife on the counter. "Arming yourself is a good idea."

"I can't take credit for that one. The woman on the phone suggested it. I'm not sure I would have been strong enough to use it."

"We understand," the detective said. "Did you see anyone or anything outside your apartment?"

Dawn shook her head. "I didn't look. I figured it's the same man who kidnapped my boss."

Foster and Murphy exchanged another look. "Who's your boss?"

"Dr. Walden. Hannah Walden. She went missing last night. Because of me."

"Because of you? What did you have to do with her disappearance?" Detective Foster asked.

"Nothing, but the man who took her wanted information about me." Dawn shook her head and dropped to the couch. "I figured he was here to kill me. So he could get his money."

The cops were quiet for a long minute. Dawn didn't want to look up at them and see the looks they were likely giving her. The ones that would vacillate between crazy and full of herself. No one who walked into her apartment would think Dawn had anything of value, or enough money for anyone to care about.

"Dr. Walden's body is outside your apartment, Ms. Patterson," the officer said.

"What?" Dawn breathed, pushing to stand. She had to see for herself. It took her a second to realize he said *body* and not Dr. Walden. "No. She's dead?"

Detective Foster nodded. "It seems whoever killed her wanted to send you a message."

Dawn raced to the bathroom, not bothering to close the door before she emptied her stomach. She dry-heaved when nothing else came up, her fear and anxiety and sadness all warring inside her.

And then the anger showed up. Dr. Walden was innocent. She had nothing to do with Mr. Davis's choice to give Dawn all his money. Dr. Walden didn't deserve to die for doing her job.

"Trevor Davis did this," Dawn snarled, her head still in the toilet. "He's the one who's after me. He killed Dr. Walden."

"We will do a full investigation, Ms. Patterson," one of the cops said.

Dawn didn't want to hear placating words or empty promises. She pushed to her feet and washed her mouth out with a handful of water from the sink. She turned on the cops and glared at them. "His father left me his fortune. His father was Robert Davis. Trevor is a nasty man who feels like he can take whatever he wants. I didn't ask for this, and neither did Dr. Walden. You have to stop this. Stop him."

"We're working on it," Officer Murphy said.

"Work faster," Dawn snapped.

Another knock on the door sent all Dawn's bravado running for the hills. Her stomach flipped, and every pore in her body felt like it wet its pants.

"It's Patrick," a voice said from the other side of the door.

Officer Murphy went to the door and opened it. The captain stepped into Dawn's apartment, making her feel claustrophobic for the second time in less than a day.

His gaze slid around the room before landing on Dawn. "Ms. Patterson."

Dawn nodded, unable to squeeze words out.

The three officers looked at each other. The detective and officer both stayed silent with their captain in the room.

"Do you have somewhere else you can stay for a few days, Ms. Patterson?"

Dawn scoffed. "You mean like Mr. Davis's mansion? That I've never been to and don't believe is better?"

Captain Patrick didn't call out her nastiness or her attitude. "My wife and I own a shelter. There's a room available for you if you have nowhere else to go."

"But I can't stay here." She wasn't asking since neither was he.

"I can't force you, Ms. Patterson. But seeing as how a body was left outside your door, I would recommend going somewhere else."

Dawn shook her head. "It's definitely Dr. Walden?"

Captain Patrick nodded. "I'm sorry. We were all hoping we would find her alive."

"What happened to her?"

"Her throat was cut."

Dawn closed her eyes and tried not to collapse. "Definitely not an accident then."

Captain Patrick shook his head. "Definitely not."

"And I'm assuming you have no new leads on Trevor Davis."

Captain Patrick sighed. "No, we don't."

"Is this guy a ghost? I've met him. I know he exists. Why can't you find him?"

"When did you meet him?"

"The day his father died. Trevor was there visiting Mr. Davis."

Captain Patrick nodded like he already knew that. Which was hard to believe since she'd only met Captain Patrick that morning. Except.

"Gage told you that, didn't he?"

Captain Patrick appeared caught off-guard that she

would call him out. He took a second, then nodded. "He did."

"And it's significant, isn't it?"

"We're not sure. It could be."

"Where is this man? Besides outside my door while I'm sleeping so he can drop off my boss's dead body."

"We don't know," Captain Patrick admitted.

"Then where can I go that would make me safe? Where is safe?"

Captain Patrick shook his head. He offered his home, but Dawn wasn't sure she'd feel better there. In a shelter? Which meant there would be others who were in danger. She couldn't risk bringing more danger to them. Risking more innocent lives.

There was only one person who was already in this as deep as she was. One person who knew what she was going through.

Dawn looked around, searching for her phone. She spotted it on the kitchen counter next to the knife. She snatched it up and tapped on Gage's name.

"Hello? Dawn? Are you okay?"

"I need a place to stay. Someone tried to get into my apartment and left Dr. Walden's body outside as a gift."

"Are you okay? Did he get inside?"

"No. But Captain Patrick suggested I find another place to stay for a day or longer."

"I have a guest room. You're welcome to it as long as you need a place to stay."

"Thanks. Can you text me your address?"

"Yeah. Um, is Marcus still there?"

"He's right here."

"Do you mind if I speak to him?"

Dawn handed the phone to Captain Patrick without answering Gage's question.

He lifted the phone to his ear and said, "Patrick."

Dawn ignored his side of the conversation and went to her closet. She grabbed her suitcase and tossed it on the bed. She opened her drawers and shamelessly grabbed clothes and tossed them in. She went into the bathroom and grabbed everything she would need for a few days. When she was sure she had everything, she zipped up the suitcase and set it on its wheels on the floor.

Captain Patrick offered her phone back to Dawn. She slid it in her pocket, then unplugged the charger from the wall and tossed that in her purse.

"I guess I have a place to go."

"Gage asked me to follow you, or drive you, but I'm assuming you'll want you own vehicle."

"If it doesn't blow up when I start it," Dawn said with a mirthless laugh.

"We will check it out," Captain Patrick said.

At the same time, Officer Murphy said, "Explosives aren't his style."

Dawn snorted. "Lucky me. Just dead bodies and thinly veiled threats."

"We will find him, Ms. Patterson," Detective Foster said.

Dawn nodded. "Sure."

GAGE PACED in his living room, watching the street out front for Dawn's car to pull up. When his phone rang, adrenaline rushed his system, but when he heard her voice, it was worse.

Someone tried to get into her apartment. Gage wasn't

foolish enough to think it was actually Trevor. He was too smart to risk getting caught. He had people to do things like deliver a body and scare the hell out of someone.

But that didn't mean Trevor wasn't behind the whole thing. There was no doubt he was.

Headlights flashed across the front windows as someone pulled into the small driveway that separated Gage's house from his neighbor's. Another car pulled in right behind it, half in the street.

Dawn got out of the first car with Marcus in the car behind her. As they walked to the door, Gage turned off the alarm and opened the front door. He stepped out onto the porch.

He wanted to ask Dawn if she was okay, but the look in her eyes answered the question for him.

"Thanks for following her, Marcus," Gage said. He reached for the suitcase Dawn dragged up the porch steps.

"Sorry it was necessary. Are you good here, Ms. Patterson?" Marcus asked.

Gage was annoyed his friend asked, but he tried not to let it get to him.

Dawn nodded. "I'm fine." Her voice was soft, weak, terrified.

Marcus looked at Gage and tried to convey a message Gage wasn't sure he received. All he knew was he was going to keep her safe and put an end to all the shit happening because of Trevor Davis.

"It's time, Marcus."

Marcus nodded, not arguing and not pretending he didn't understand what Gage was saying. Dawn needed to know everything. She needed to be brought up to speed on the whole situation.

"We'll talk tomorrow," Marcus said, waving and walking back to his car.

Gage followed Dawn into the house and locked the door. He set the alarm and asked if she wanted something to drink.

Dawn snorted a laugh. "Do you have anything that'll make me forget that a madman wants to kill me and will do anything to make that happen?"

Gage shook his head slowly. "I don't think I have anything like that. But I am sorry, Dawn. Are you okay?"

She swallowed, her throat working to complete the action. She wrapped her arms around her waist and shook her head. She rolled her lips in, chewing on them as her face slowly crumpled.

A sob tore from her throat, then another. By the time Gage took the two steps to reach her, she was sinking to the floor. He caught her and helped her to the couch, pulling her onto his lap and holding her close while the adrenaline and fear crashed over her and poured out.

"I didn't ask for this," she whimpered. "I didn't want this. It wasn't my fault. Why is this happening?"

"It's not fair. I know," Gage whispered.

Dawn nodded against his chest, letting the tears and pain out. She trembled in his arms, her entire body shaking with the force of her pain.

Gage held her and let her cry. He feared this would be the result when Robert changed his will. Gage knew Trevor would be angry. Trevor was proving to be exactly who Robert thought his son was. Gage knew there was a reason Robert wanted to lock Trevor out of the will, but the truth of who Trevor was was so much worse than Gage ever feared.

Dawn slowly calmed down. Her tremors eased. The sobs faded to whimpers and quieted.

Gage wondered if she was asleep. He wasn't ready to move. To wake her up and put her to bed. He wanted to sit there for a little longer and hold her. To know she was safe.

"Thank you for letting me stay here," she whispered.

"You're welcome," Gage said.

"Is he ever going to stop?"

Gage shook his head. "I don't know."

"If he kills me, he doesn't get anything. What's his end game?"

"I'm not sure he cares."

"What do you mean?"

"I mean Trevor Davis is a dangerous man, and I don't think he's rational."

"So this is sport for him?"

"That's what I'm afraid of."

"So no matter what I do, I'm going to end up dead."

"No," Gage said. "I'm not going to let that happen."

"How are you going to stop him? He killed Dr. Walden."

"I don't know, but I'm not going to let anything happen to you."

Dawn stiffened and scrambled to get up, as if she just realized she was sitting on his lap. She moved to the seat next to Gage. "I'm sorry. I didn't mean to..."

"I didn't mean to make you uncomfortable."

She breathed a laugh. "That's the opposite of my problem right now."

"What do you mean?"

She looked up at him. The expression on her face was unreadable, but the look in her eyes was one of desire. "I don't trust myself with men. I have made mistakes. And leaning on you is probably the last thing I should be doing."

"I'm the reason you're in this mess, Dawn. If you can't lean on me, who can you turn to?"

She chuckled. "That's what I was thinking when I called you. But it's not fair to put you in the middle of all of this, either. And it's not fair of me to... to want you when I'm a walking corpse."

"You're not a walking corpse. And the other part..."

Dawn grunted, a sound of curiosity.

"You're not alone in that, but you've had a hell of a night. I'd never forgive myself for taking advantage of you when you're upset."

"Then I guess I'll have to take advantage of you."

Gage laughed softly and shook his head. "Let's get some sleep. You can take advantage of me tomorrow. Because I can promise you, I'm not letting you back to your apartment until Trevor Davis is behind bars or in the ground."

"You sure know how to romance a woman," Dawn said wryly.

Gage chuckled. "Yeah, it's shocking I'm single, isn't it?"

Dawn looked at him and nodded. "It is, actually. You're a pretty amazing man, Gage Stevens. Thank you for taking me in."

"Thank you for calling me."

13

GAGE FIXED THE SHEETS ON THE BED IN THE ROOM THAT wasn't his and listened to the woman who wasn't his use his bathroom. He hadn't lived with a woman since he was a teenager. He'd forgotten what it was like, the things a woman did before she went to bed.

The water turned off and a few seconds later, the door opened. He'd left his bedroom door open in case she needed anything else, but the sight of Dawn walking out of the bathroom, her face scrubbed clean and her breasts swinging free under the tee she wore as a nightshirt paired with shorts that exposed her thick legs to his view, made Gage regret that choice.

He swallowed his groan and willed his dick to calm down long enough for her to go to her temporary room and close the door.

But of course that couldn't happen so easily. Not when Gage was still in the room she was supposed to use. She looked toward his room, then turned toward hers and approached.

"Did you give me your bedroom?" she asked.

He nodded, not standing holding a pillow in front of himself to hide the effect she had on him. "It's at the back of the house and quieter. But the stairs lead that way if you'd rather sleep in here."

She smiled at him. "I'd rather sleep in here because I feel bad evicting you from your own bedroom."

Gage shook his head. "It's more comfortable. And there's no porch on the back, so there's no way someone could get into the room from the outside."

She shivered at his words, her smile slipping off her face.

He wanted to kick himself for reminding her of the danger she was in. He could have just pretended everything was fine, but he had to throw it in her face. "I apologize. I shouldn't have said that."

She shrugged. "It's why I'm here. God, all of this is so messed up."

"The police will find Trevor, and you'll be safe."

"Will they? It sounded like they've been looking for him for a while."

"They have been, but they didn't know as much as they do now."

"What does that mean?" Dawn asked.

Gage sat on the edge of the bed, giving her space to join him on the mattress. He wasn't sure how she felt about the invitation, but she didn't hesitate to sit next to him. Her thigh was a few inches from his, but he could feel her heat and smell the lotion she used before leaving the bathroom.

"Do you remember the news stories about Damon Street?" Gage asked.

Dawn nodded. "He was a psycho. I'm glad he's dead."

"Unfortunately, he wasn't operating alone. The police believe Trevor Davis might be the one who took over the company Damon had."

Dawn's eyes widened. Fear drained the blood from her face. "No."

Gage nodded. "When Marcus was going after Damon, they rescued a woman named Edie Warren."

"I read about that."

"Edie was being held by a man named Trevor."

Dawn sucked in a breath.

"Edie didn't know Trevor's last name, or if Trevor was his real first name. A few months ago, they started trying to follow the money, to see how this company was being funded. Without knowing all the players, they didn't have a lot of leads. Damon had a company that he was running things through, but without him in the picture, Marcus and his team knew someone else was funneling money from somewhere."

"Through Davis Developments," Dawn breathed.

Gage shook his head. "Robert wouldn't have done that if he was going to cut Trevor off, but I'm guessing Trevor was counting on his dad's money to fund the operation."

Dawn shook her head. "No, that's not true. Trevor has access. He's been pulling money out since his dad died. Either he was getting money another way before, or he was hiding it better, but I was there yesterday. I spent the day with Tabitha trying to learn what I could and find where the money is going. Tabitha said it's been happening since Mr. Davis died. She assumed it was me, or whoever was taking over, but it wasn't."

"Shit," Gage breathed. "That means Trevor has a way of getting money from Davis Developments without the inheritance."

"And he's using it. Tabitha and I worked to find out how he could be getting into the accounts, but we aren't financial investigators. We changed some passwords and had IT look into any outside access, but I wasn't in touch with her today. I don't know if it worked."

"If it did, he's going to be more angry and more likely to come after you."

"He left a dead body on my doorstep. I think it's safe to say he's coming after me."

"Unfortunately, if he wanted you dead, he'd have already killed you. He knows where you live."

"And what I drive."

"What do you mean?"

"You obviously didn't see the message on my car. Someone painted *BITCH* on the side."

"Why didn't you tell me?"

Dawn shook her head and shrugged. "All of this is way over my head, Gage. I feel like I'm drowning in it. And we barely know each other. It's bad enough I called you tonight."

Gage leaned over, cupping her jaw and turning her head until she met his gaze. The despair and loneliness in her eyes yanked on his heart. He felt it deep inside. He had since his mother died.

But with Dawn in his house, opening up to him, there for him in ways she didn't even realize, he felt that knot inside him loosening for the first time in longer than he could remember.

"I want to kiss you so badly right now."

"Then why aren't you?"

Gage inhaled, drawing her closer. "It would be taking advantage of you. It wouldn't be right."

"You keep talking about right and wrong like it would be bad if something happened between us."

"I feel responsible for everything going on around you.

And if we explored whatever this is, I'd worry I'd lose focus or something would happen to you."

She snorted. "Sorry, but too late for that. He knows who I am. He's coming for me. It might just be intimidation, but I got on this train the day we met. The day you told me Mr. Davis left me everything. I chose this. It's more than I expected, and a hell of a lot scarier, but I chose this. I am not backing down. I'm not going to give him the satisfaction of knowing he can get to me. Of knowing I won't follow through on what Mr. Davis asked me to do."

Gage watched the conviction cross her face. The determined set of her shoulders and the subtle shake of her head that he wasn't even sure she realized she was doing. She was amazing. Strong and confident and beautiful.

And he couldn't resist any longer.

He surged forward, catching her by surprise when his lips landed on hers. She gasped, but it only took a second for her to turn the full force of her strength to him.

Her arms wound around his neck, and she leaned into him. Gage teased her lips with his tongue, groaning when she allowed him access.

He cupped her jaw and tilted her head to the side, diving into her mouth like it held all the treasures of the world. She climbed on top of him, her knees hitting the mattress on either side of his hips, and he pulled back.

"Dawn?"

"Please don't stop," she whispered. She lowered herself onto his lap. There was no possible way she missed the reaction he was having to her. She ground down on his erection, and he knew she not only felt it but wanted it.

"Fuck," he hissed. His hands slid to her ass, molding her cheeks and encouraging her to use him to feel good.

She threw her head back, raw pleasure clear in the way

her lips parted and her eyes closed. She moaned softly, rocking against his cock.

Without her lips accessible, Gage ran his tongue over her collarbone. She jerked at the touch, then settled into it, wrapping her fingers around his head and caressing his short hair to hold him in place.

"More," she whispered, so softly he wasn't sure she knew she said the word out loud.

Gage met her thrusts, listening as she panted her way closer to a release. He wanted to feel her let go, but they were both fully clothed, humping like teenagers who didn't know what they were doing.

Except Gage knew exactly what he was doing. He knew how good she would feel wrapped around him. He knew how good she'd smell when she came. He knew how quickly he'd lose his fucking mind with her.

"Gage," she breathed as her body shook. She twitched and thrust against him, her movements erratic and erotic as she finally let go and came on his lap.

He kept a hold of her, unsure how she was going to feel but unwilling to release her or let her run back to his bed and hide from him.

"That was not what I intended," she said, dropping her head to rest her forehead against his.

"What did you intend?"

She shook her head. "I don't know, but leaving you without a release was not my plan."

"You don't owe me anything."

She snorted. "Owe you? I owe myself. Missing out on watching you lose your mind is a travesty. One I deserve the chance to rectify."

Gage chuckled. "You are not like other women."

"I'm going to choose to take that as a compliment."

"I meant it as one."

She pulled back and met his gaze. Hers was glassy and fully pleasured, but clear enough that she was definitely in control. "I don't feel like you're taking advantage of me, Gage. Or that you're responsible for any of this. I just want that out there before I ask you to come to your own bed and fuck me until neither of us has a choice but to fall asleep."

Gage's dick twitched between her thighs, and she grinned.

"I'm glad a part of you is on board. How about the rest of you?"

Gage shook his head. "You are very good for my ego."

She smiled at him, her cheeks turning pink. "I can't imagine how that's possible. You're gorgeous and could have any woman in the city. I'm just lucky a psycho is after me and I needed a place to crash."

Gage's good humor slipped with her words. He pulled her in so he could feel all of her against him. "I think the same about you having any man you want. And I don't think I'd say you're lucky, but I am grateful you called me. That you felt you could trust me."

"I know I can."

"Good."

"So?"

"So?"

"Your bed or this one?" Dawn asked. She wiggled her hips, rubbing against his barely holding on dick.

He groaned. "Mine. I want to see you in my bed."

She jumped off his lap and started for the door.

He grabbed her hand and spun her back to him, standing as she turned. He pulled her in tight, kissing her hard as he let his hands explore her curves.

He released her just as quickly, loving the dazed look in her eyes. "I'll be right there."

She nodded and walked ahead of him. He turned off the light in the spare room, then rushed through his bedtime routine before joining her in his bed.

She was curled up on her side, the lamp on his nightstand illuminating the room and casting shadows across her face.

Gage saw the anxiety in the eyes she averted from him and the lip she nibbled. He sat on the edge of the bed instead of sliding under the covers with her. "I can go back to the other room."

"No! I don't want that. I feel safer with you in the same room. It all just hit me. Dr. Walden is dead."

"I'm so sorry about that."

Dawn shook her head. "You had nothing to do with that. You didn't hurt her."

"I should have realized he'd go after whoever signed it to find out who was named in the will."

"No. Trevor is psychotic. He doesn't get off the hook for that."

"Definitely not."

"I just wish things were different."

"Aside from the obvious and not wanting a psycho after you, what do you wish was different?"

She shrugged. "For one, I wish you were lying next to me right now."

He chuckled and laid down, easing himself under the blanket.

She moved closer to him, and he lifted his arm. She rested her head on his shoulder and slid a hand across his stomach.

It was intimate, personal, and nice. Gage let out a breath,

wanting to remember the moment when Dawn went back to her apartment and her life and no longer needed him to protect her.

"I wish Mr. Davis told me he was going to leave everything to me. I wish we met under different circumstances. I wish my relationship with my daughter was better. I wish I knew what I was doing with my life."

She fell silent, giving Gage a chance to think about what she admitted. He'd dated women for months at a time without having such an honest conversation with them. Maybe it was the circumstances, or maybe it was just Dawn, but he liked hearing about her thoughts.

"If you could do anything right now, what would it be?"

"Kiss you again."

Gage exhaled a surprised laugh.

"You asked."

"Dawn?"

"Yeah?" She looked up at him, her eyes going wide when she saw the look in his eyes.

He didn't want to hold back from her. Not now. Maybe it was a bad idea. Maybe she'd regret it later. Maybe things wouldn't work out. But at that moment, all Gage wanted was Dawn.

She propped herself up on her elbow and leaned toward him as he surged toward her. They met in the middle, a scramble of hands searching for skin, lips crashing, tongues tangling.

They both ended up kneeling in the center of the bed, bodies pressed tight together. Gage groaned when her cold hand slid between them and wrapped around his erection.

Not willing to miss his chance, he lifted her shirt and cupped a full breast, his palm rubbing over a very perky nipple.

She stroked him, and he plucked her nipple. He added his other hand, breaking their kiss to bring her oversized breasts to his mouth. The shift had her hand falling from around his dick, but he didn't care when he tasted the sweetness of her nipples.

"Oh, God," she murmured.

Gage licked both nipples together, the plump globes large enough for him to tease them at the same time. He nibbled and sucked and worshipped her breasts, intensely aware of the effect his actions were having on her.

"Gage," she whispered.

He let her breasts fall and yanked his shirt off, reaching for hers next. Chest to chest, he devoured her mouth again, pressing his tongue between her greedy lips and loving the way she tangled with him, not giving in and not backing down.

Hands grabbed waistbands and shorts were shoved to their knees. She wrapped her hand around him once more, but Gage won the battle when he pressed two fingers into her dripping core.

She cried out immediately, her body still sensitive and ready for more.

"Tell me to stop, Dawn."

"Don't stop," she begged. "Please don't stop."

Gage withdrew his fingers, adding a third to stretch her channel. He rubbed his thumb over her clit, and she hung off him. Her teeth sank into his shoulder, the bite grounding him right before she came with a cry.

Her hips rocked against his hand, her clit brushing the heel of his palm with each gentle stroke. When the tremors slowed, she collapsed onto her back, kicking at the shorts that kept her from spreading her knees wider.

"More," she said.

Gage climbed off the bed and let his shorts and boxer briefs slide to the floor. He dug a condom out of the box in his nightstand and rolled it on before positioning himself between her thighs.

She licked her lips and watched him. Her eyes tracked his movements until he lined himself up with her entrance.

"Slow or fast?" Gage asked.

"Yes," Dawn said with a chuckle.

Gage pressed into her slowly, hoping she was ready. Her body stretched easily for him, and he surged in the rest of the way, sinking all the way inside her until his balls slapped her skin.

"Holy fucking shit," she moaned. "Oh, God."

"Is that a good thing?"

"Fuck me, Gage," was her only answer.

He didn't need to be told twice. He withdrew enough to get space between them, then slammed back into her hard. Their bodies slapped together, the sounds of their fucking echoing in the otherwise silent house.

She panted, he grunted. She dragged her nails down his chest, he pressed a thumb to her clit. She screamed, and he followed her right over the edge and came harder than he'd ever come in his life.

Holy fucking shit was right.

14

———

Dawn had never propositioned a man in her life. She'd never asked one to fuck her. She liked it. A lot.

Being terrified and stalked and wondering if she was going to live to see tomorrow gave her a new sense of power. Not that she was hoping to die, but she knew if she did, she didn't want to die feeling like she'd never lived.

And before Gage, she'd definitely never experienced anything like *that*. "We need to do that again," she breathed when she could force words out.

Gage chuckled softly. "I won't tell you no."

"That's good because I'm not very good at hearing no from you."

"Just from me?" he asked.

She shrugged when he pushed up to look at her. She was pretty content with his weight on top of her. "I'm not usually like that."

"I'm not sure I want to ask what you're usually like when you have sex with other men."

She snorted. "You make it sound like I do that so often."

He shrugged and rolled off her. He walked out of the

room to the bathroom, leaving the door open and the light off while he took care of the condom and washed his hands. He was back in a minute, pulling her close under the covers. "We don't know each other very well. And that's okay. I'm not trying to get you to tell me everything. Just saying I don't know how often you're having sex. You don't have to tell me."

She snuggled in closer, her head on his chest rising with each breath he took. "It's been a while. Eighteen months. I... I'm an addict."

He stiffened under her head, then slowly relaxed in a way that told her he wasn't really relaxed.

"I wasn't trading sex for drugs or anything like that. My ex-husband and I got married when I got pregnant with our daughter. I tried to convince myself we could make it work, but we fought more than we got along. Nothing bad, just bickering. We weren't right together, but we wanted to give her a good life."

"You can still do that."

Dawn nodded. "We're trying. Well, he's trying. She's... When things went sideways with Owen, I moved out. Got an apartment and told myself I didn't need him. Met a neighbor who was funny and looked at me like I was worthy. That makes me sound so bad, but—"

"It makes you sound human," Gage said.

Dawn was quiet for a minute, absorbing his words and letting them dissolve the lump they created in her throat. "Thank you." She cleared her throat and continued. "We started hanging out, and eventually we started sleeping together. As things with Owen deteriorated, it was nice to know someone wanted me. Then the drugs showed up. Nothing major at first, but it escalated quickly. Eighteen months ago, I overdosed and my daughter had to call nine-one-one and do CPR on me until the paramedics showed up."

"Shit," he breathed.

"Yeah. So, I don't blame Savannah for hating me or not wanting to be around me. She's with her dad full time. He's a great father. And I can't compare."

"You shouldn't have to compare. You're not the same person."

"No, but we're both her parents, and he's the only one who hasn't caused her major trauma."

"You can't give up. A kid needs to know they matter. Especially to their parents."

She tilted her head to look up at him. "You sound like you're speaking from experience."

Gage nodded slowly. "I never knew my dad. Ran off before I was born. My mom was amazing. She worked hard to provide for me. Always made sure I knew she loved me."

"She sounds pretty great."

"She was. She died when I was in high school. Wrong place, wrong time."

"Gage, I'm so sorry."

He nodded, but the pain of losing his mother was still etched on his face. Time didn't heal all wounds. "Thanks. I ended up in a good foster home. I know how lucky I was. I did what she always told me to do and made something of myself."

"Good for you. That couldn't have been easy."

Gage laughed mirthlessly. "Not even a little. But I wanted to find the person who killed her."

"The police never did?"

"No. It's still unsolved. But I told you about my mom because I understand what Savannah went through. To a point. I lived through the fear and pain of losing my mom.

She needs to know you're doing everything you can to make sure she's safe and okay."

"I know. I am. The trust will help ensure that, and I'm not giving up on trying to build a relationship with her."

"Good. Because she should know how strong and amazing her mom is."

"Oh, yeah? You think I'm amazing?"

Gage flipped them over and settled between her legs. He hardened when she spread her thighs wide to give him space. "I think you're sexy and smart and strong and amazing and beautiful and so fucking good."

"Speaking of fucking good," Dawn whispered.

She pulled Gage down for a kiss and rubbed herself against him. He let her do it for a minute before breaking the kiss with a curse as he reached for a condom from his nightstand.

"I told myself I'd go slow this time," he said as he lined up at her entrance again.

"Slow is overrated."

He slammed into her, creating spots in her vision as her body went from sensitive to ready to jump in a flash.

"Oh, fuck, Gage."

He pulled out and did it again. Her toes curled, her body thumped with need. Her core scorched.

He pounded into her, relentless as he fucked her into another orgasm. The buttoned up lawyer had a secret in his pants.

He chuckled.

"Did I say that out loud?"

He leaned down to whisper in her ear. "Yes, you did. But that's not the only secret I have." He licked her ear and dipped his tongue inside.

Dawn never knew ears could be so sexy, but the warm

feel of his tongue distracted her enough for her orgasm to sneak up on her and shove her over the edge.

"Oh, fuck, yes," she moaned, unable to hold back her words.

"Fuck, you feel good when you come on my dick," he grunted.

"Tell me."

"You're so damn wet. I wish I could sink into you without anything between us. Feel your come soaking me. The way you tighten around me when you come is so good. Ugh, yeah. Do that again."

She squeezed her inner muscles, and his stroke faltered, then sped up.

"I love seeing your skin flush red. The way your body reacts when I fuck you."

"Oh, fuck," she said as she tipped over again.

He pumped hard and fast, following her over the edge and grunting his release. He collapsed onto her again, his twisty chest hair scratching against her sensitive nipples.

Dawn wrapped her arms around him. She pressed her nose to his neck and inhaled deep. She licked a bead of sweat the trickled down his throat.

He groaned. "It's been a while for me, too."

"What?"

Gage rolled off her, lying on his back and throwing an arm over his head. "Since I've been with anyone."

She slapped his chest. "You're seriously telling me about sex with other women while you were still inside me?"

Gage climbed out of bed and went to the bathroom.

Dawn watched his ass flex and relax as she walked away. She chuckled, knowing she did almost the same thing. But still.

He came back, and she scowled at him. "I wasn't trying to upset you."

She smirked at him and pulled the blanket back for him to crawl into bed again. "I'm just teasing you. But you could have waited a few minutes."

Gage snickered. "True."

"Do you want to tell me about her?"

Gage drew a deep breath and let it out slowly. "She was someone I met through mutual friends. It started out slow, but we ended up spending more and more time together. It became something without either of us really trying to make it something."

"So it was convenient?"

"I guess. That makes it sound like I didn't care about her. I did, but I was never in love with her."

"Were you in love with someone else?"

He shook his head. "I don't think so. I wanted to be a few times. Women I thought my mother would have liked. Women I was willing to build a life with. But no one that I felt like I could be myself around."

"Are you yourself with me?"

He nodded. "I am."

"Good."

They were both quiet for a few minutes. Dawn started to fade, the day finally catching up to her. She yawned widely, and Gage kissed the top of her head.

"You should get some sleep," he whispered.

She nodded against his shoulder, knowing she wouldn't be able to resist the pull of sleep. She drifted off, knowing she was safe with Gage.

Sunlight strained to breakthrough the room darkening curtains Gage hung in his room. He was usually up far before the sun, but with his room facing east, the first thing he did when he bought the house was hang the curtains just in case he found himself in bed after daybreak.

As he held Dawn, who slept peacefully in his arms all night, except for when she woke him and rode him silently to an orgasm that had both of them panting and reaching for each other as they drifted back to sleep. She was beautiful with her dark lashes fanning her cheeks and her blonde hair wild and wispy around her face.

Gage knew he should get a start on his day, but he couldn't bring himself to leave her in bed alone. Not when she was at peace for a few minutes.

Dawn stirred, her naked ass rubbing against Gage's morning wood, and she stilled for half a second before melting against him. "Again?" she asked, her voice thick with sleep and teasing.

"You're still here," he said as an answer because it was the only one he could offer. With her in his bed, he was hard. There was no other option.

She shifted her hips, teasing him until he hooked her thigh and lifted her leg on top of his. He teased her clit with a glancing brush before dipping into her core.

"It seems I'm not the only one ready this morning."

She moaned and jerked against his hand.

He bit her earlobe. "Do you like it when I slide my fingers deep into you?"

"Uh huh," she moaned.

"What about when I rub your clit?"

"Please," she begged.

"Spread wider for me," he demanded.

She stretched her leg wider, tipping slightly onto her back so she could spread her thighs.

"Are you going to soak my sheets?"

"Maybe. You feel so good."

"So do you." He pushed deeper into her, gritting his teeth to keep himself from losing control while he pleasured her.

"Oh, yes," Dawn moaned, the words dragged out as her entire body trembled. "Shit."

"I know that's not all you have for me. Unless you're sore."

"I can be sore later."

He stopped. The last thing he wanted was to hurt her. "Dawn."

"Please, Gage." The whimper was enough to do him in.

"Too bad I don't have a shower that we can both fit in."

"Too bad," she said with a thrust of her hips against his hand.

He ground the heel of his palm into her clit with each thrust inside her. She met his movements, grunting in frustration when she didn't come fast enough.

Gage dragged his fingers out of her and drew the soaked digits to her clit. The slippery come let his fingers slide quickly over her clit, setting her hips into motion as her orgasm raced toward her.

"Come for me, Dawn. Come hard, then I'm going to fuck you hard."

She moaned and mewed and came with a long, low sound that tightened like a fist around his balls. The sound was everything an orgasm should sound like. Pleasure and release and joy all rolled into one sound.

Gage grabbed a condom he was grateful he had the foresight to leave on the nightstand and ripped it open. He tried to roll it on with one hand so he didn't have to let go of Dawn, but it wasn't working. He shoved the condom down his length, reciting law texts to keep from blowing before he sank into her.

She rolled onto her back and spread her thighs, thoroughly spent and flushed and looking like his every fantasy come to life. Gage paused for a second to memorize the way she looked. Nipples red from his repeated sucking. Thick nest of hair between her thighs. Dimpled skin with stretch marks and rolls. Blonde hair spread out on his pillow. She was fucking stunning.

And for the moment, she was all his.

"Gage?" she whispered.

He smiled. "Just thinking how gorgeous you are."

Her skin flushed even darker, his words embarrassing her and delighting him. He learned through their night that she enjoyed dirty talk, but she didn't handle compliments well. He vowed to shower her with so many she couldn't help but see herself the way he saw her.

"Come here."

"Are you ready for me?"

"You made sure I am," she teased, "but you're welcome to verify."

He kneeled between her legs and let his gaze travel down her body. Her pink skin was plump and wet and tempting. If it wasn't their first night together, he'd bury his face between her legs and lick her clean. Instead, he lowered his hand.

She jumped when he touched her. He spread her folds, feasting his eyes on her glistening skin. He pressed one finger inside her, and she clenched around it like she was as close to the edge as he was.

"You're pretty wet," he said.

She nodded, nibbling her lower lip.

"Do you want to come again?"

She nodded. "You inside me."

"You want me to fuck it out of you?"

Her eyes widened with his words. She nodded sharply.

Gage thrust into her with his finger, building her closer before he withdrew. She whimpered when he pulled his finger out. He lifted on his knees and lined himself up with her, thrusting deep in one stroke.

She cried out, but he didn't let up. He pounded into her, letting his orgasm race through him and take control.

"Gage," she moaned. "More. Yes. Oh, yes."

He kept going, needing her. Needing to feel her ripple around him. Needing to let go.

"Oh, oh, oh. Yes. Oh, shit. Yes. Gage, yes!" she pulsed, gripping him and pulling him deeper with each thrust.

Her orgasm raced through him, the grip on his dick triggering his orgasm and sending him soaring with her. "Dawn. Oh... fuck!"

He collapsed, unable to support his body long enough to finish his orgasm. She let out an *oof* when he fell on her, and he rolled them so she ended up on top of him.

His heart pounded hard. Sweat beaded on every inch of his body. He was hooked on Dawn. One night and he wanted more.

"Where have you been all my life?" she whispered.

He chuckled. "I know what you mean."

She exhaled a laugh. "Wow."

"Same."

They laid there a few more minutes before she climbed off him and went to the bathroom. He took his turn after her, then they got dressed and decided food was a good idea before they passed out from sex exhaustion.

Dawn made coffee while Gage pulled out eggs and bacon and bagels to make breakfast. She sat at his table and sipped from her mug, watching him.

"What?"

She smiled and shook her head. "This is nice. A day ago, I never would have expected to wake up in your house."

"A day ago—"

"Shit! I forgot I'm supposed to work today."

"Can you call in?"

Dawn nodded. "I can. And I should. But I also need to decide if I'm going to keep working there. I'm not sure I can do both that and Davis Developments."

"You don't sound too happy about that."

She shrugged. She sipped her coffee.

Gage got the feeling there was something she wasn't saying, so he waited for her to find the words.

"I went there as a personal penance for my overdose. I wanted to make up for what I'd done, for what I'd put Savannah through. It seemed like a good place to stay away from drugs. And the people needed someone to be there for them."

"It sounds like it made a difference for you."

"I never intended for Mr. Davis—"

"That wasn't what I meant. I meant it sounds like you turned things around. That it was good being there."

Dawn nodded. "It was. It is. But Mr. Davis was my favorite patient. It's hard for me to walk into his old room and take care of the man who's there now. And with Dr. Walden... I should have left before. She might be alive if I had."

Gage abandoned the stove and walked over to her. He rested his chin on her head. "Like you told me yesterday, you're not responsible for Trevor's actions."

"I know, but—"

"No. You can't take that on yourself. I hate she was killed, but it's on him, not you."

Dawn was silent and still for a minute. When she moved, it was to reach up and hug him around the neck. "Thank you."

"You're welcome." Gage returned to the stove and finished cooking their breakfast. He let her take a bite before he dropped his news on her. "Aside from deciding what to do about work, we need to talk."

She set her fork down slowly and looked up at him. "Okay. About what?"

"There's a group looking into Trevor. Police, FBI, and some locals. They were following you."

"What?"

"I just found out about it. I wanted you to know."

"Why the hell didn't they stop someone from leaving a dead body outside my door?"

"That's the first question I think we need to ask them."

15

Dawn was furious. Shaking with rage. Someone was following her, and instead of protecting her and scaring away the person who carried a dead body to her door, they did nothing.

She ate breakfast in silence, then called into work. She was grateful for the call-in service they used so she didn't have to tell anyone what happened, but Dawn knew the news of Dr. Walden's death would be all over Angel's Grove. So would the news of where the doctor's body was found.

Dawn went to Gage's room and recovered the clothes she left all over his room the night before. She stuffed everything in her bag and carried the whole thing to the bathroom to shower.

As she scrubbed his scent from her body, Dawn knew she wasn't being fair to Gage. He had nothing to do with the people who were not protecting her. He was just the messenger. But she was still angry.

When she finished her shower, Gage took a turn while Dawn debated what she should do. It made sense to go back to her apartment if she had protection, but the protection clearly wasn't very good. At the same time, moving in with a man she barely knew and spent all night in bed with might not be the best thing either.

Especially given her track record.

She hadn't come to a decision by the time Gage walked back into his room wearing boxer briefs and nothing else.

Dawn shook her head, smiling at the temptation in front of her.

"What?" Gage asked, definitely clueless why she was smiling.

"I was just trying to decide if I should go back to my apartment or stay here a little longer, and you walk in looking like the world's biggest temptation."

He chuckled. "Thank you for that compliment. And I don't want you to go back there. But I do want you here."

She sighed. "I told you about my ex-husband and my ex-boyfriend. I... I don't tend to make smart decisions when it comes to men. I jump in with both feet and end up getting in over my head."

"And you think that's going to happen with me?" Gage sat on the bed next to Dawn, not close enough to touch.

"I think it's my truth. I made mistakes in my marriage. I didn't love Owen the way he deserved to be loved. Same for him. It wasn't right, but we never tried to make it right. We went from dating to married with a kid and never slowed down to make sure it was what we wanted. By the time we had our heads above water, Savannah was almost eight, and we coexisted but never connected. We'd gotten so wrapped up in being good parents that we never took the time to be good spouses."

"That's common with kids, though. Not that I know, but it sounds like a lot of people go through the same."

Dawn nodded. "Yes, but because we didn't get married

for love, it made it harder to stay married when the immediate need for a family was gone."

"There are a lot of different kinds of family."

"Absolutely, but at the time, we both wanted the family for her that neither of us had growing up. We didn't think about what we wanted, we only thought about what was best for her."

"I get that. I think a lot of people do the same."

Dawn nodded. "I don't want to keep making the same mistakes. To lose myself because of a man."

"I'd never—"

"That's not a comment about you, or even the other men I've been with. It's about me. I have to own that truth. To accept that my personality makes me want to leap first and look later."

"So, this time, leap with your eyes open. If you find yourself looking around and not liking what you see, take a step back."

She let her gaze run down his bare chest, over the abs her mouth watered to lick. The bulge in his boxer briefs twitched, and he groaned.

"All right now."

She laughed. "I definitely like what I see." She groaned. "But that's what I'm talking about."

"You're attracted to me, so we can't be together?"

"You make it sound so dumb."

"That's not my intention. I'm just trying to understand."

"Can you explain it to me if you ever do?"

He laughed and slid his arm around her waist, pulling her against his side.

She wrapped an arm around his back. His skin was warm and soft. He smelled like the soap in his shower. The desire to drag him back to bed and forget about the day was strong. Stronger than she thought was safe.

"Dawn?" he groaned.

She looked down. Her fingers were stroking the hair just below his bellybutton. His dick grew beneath his boxer briefs. She yelped and pulled back.

"Not the reaction I was expecting," Gage said somberly.

Dawn jumped up and paced in front of him. "This is what I'm talking about. Instead of stomping my way into the FBI office and demanding someone tell me what the fuck is going on, I'm thinking about how good you smell and how good you feel."

"We need balance. Good and bad. Simple and not. Sexy and chaste."

"You're telling me this is perfectly normal?"

He shook his head. "Nothing is normal. Nothing about any of this is normal. If things were normal, you wouldn't be here because someone left a body outside your door. If a billionaire hadn't left you his entire estate to keep his son from getting his money, we might not have met. None of this is normal."

"All the more reason for me to go back to my apartment. Give you space and let you go on with your life."

"I don't want that, Dawn. Just because how we met isn't normal doesn't mean I want it to end. I had a lot of fun last night. And I wouldn't sleep if I was worrying about you."

"Ah, so, this is purely selfish. You want me to stay here so you can sleep."

He laughed and nodded. "Absolutely. Will you take pity on me and stay here until we know Trevor is in custody?"

She fought her grin and failed. "I guess. I wouldn't want you too tired to help others."

He smiled wryly. "You're so generous."

She smiled. "Speaking of generous, can you help me set up a way to donate money to charities?"

Gage nodded. "Of course. Or you can set up your own charity."

"I can do that?"

Gage shrugged. "Sure. If there's something you think needs to be done. You have the means to do it."

"Wow. I'm still getting used to all this. I... I have to think about that."

"Until then, let's go find out why you were so vulnerable last night."

Dawn nodded, then sighed when Gage pulled on a button-down shirt. He chuckled and finished dressing before leading her outside to his fancy SUV. Maybe she should think about one of those.

WHEN GAGE REACHED out to Marcus, Marcus gave Gage an address and said to meet him there at ten. Gage wasn't sure what to expect, but a strip mall in the middle of the city on a Saturday morning was not it. And the door? There was a rose on it.

"Where are we?" Dawn asked, holding Gage's arm with a grip that said she was just as confused and scared.

"I'm not entirely sure." Gage looked back and forth down the walkway, wondering if they were in the wrong place. He reached for his phone when the door with the rose opened in front of them.

"Mr. Stevens," a man said.

"Zeke. Is this you guys?"

Zeke nodded. "Yes, sir. Rose Protection Agency. My boss thinks he's funny not having a sign out front, but clearly it's just confusing."

Gage let his hand rest on Dawn's lower back as she went ahead of him toward the muscled man who could snap Gage in half if he wanted to.

Dawn's gaze slid down the large man before she nodded and walked inside.

Zeke let the door close behind them and locked it. "I'm Zeke Donovan, Ms. Patterson. I'm sorry to meet you under these circumstances."

"You, too," Dawn said.

"Do I want to know how you know who she is?" Gage asked. Zeke seemed like a good guy when he installed the security system at Gage's office and home, but Dawn wasn't there.

"Marcus let us know about the situation last night. Montgomery, my boss, insisted on a meeting today." Zeke nodded toward a door to the right of a large desk that was unoccupied. "Our assistant isn't here right now, but everyone else is in the back."

Gage let Dawn go ahead of him, led by Zeke. Voices rose as soon as they were through the first door. The space was bigger than Gage expected. They were in a hallway with conference rooms on either side. Both rooms were empty, with glass walls separating them from the hallway. Beyond those rooms was another door that was propped open.

On the other side of that door was a large open space full of people. Some Gage recognized and some he'd never seen before. All of them were talking. The walls were lined with whiteboards, some full and others empty.

Beyond the open space was a row of offices that all sat

empty, once again with glass walls separating them from the bullpen.

Zeke whistled loudly, getting the attention of everyone in the room. They all looked up and fell silent, their gazes locked on Dawn.

Gage looked at her, seeing the blush climb her cheeks. She shuffled her feet and avoided the curious gazes of everyone in the room.

"Everyone, this is Dawn Patterson and Gage Stevens. No pretending you don't know who they are, but fuck, don't treat her like a zoo animal." Zeke glared at the others in the room, earning all of Gage's respect.

One man stepped forward. Another large man, covered in tattoos like Zeke was. He moved through the desks and chairs with ease, as though none of them were even there. When he made it to them, he extended his hand to Dawn first. "Montgomery Rose. Thank you for meeting with us today, Ms. Patterson."

"Call me Dawn," she said. "Do you... Are you...?"

"This is my company, Dawn. We run private security and offer protection when needed."

"Were you the one who was supposed to be watching me last night?" Dawn asked, letting her displeasure show.

Montgomery shook his head. "No. We refuse to follow people without telling them. Unless it's a special situation. Our protection is a little more in your face."

Dawn chuckled. "Then I wish I'd met you before now."

"Unfortunately, I'm to blame for what you went through last night," Lorelei Sloane said, stepping next to Mont-gomery. "Lorelei Sloane, FBI. My team was supposed to be watching you, but signals were crossed last night."

Dawn sneered at Lorelei. "A dead woman was left on my doorstep. A woman I knew well."

Lorelei nodded in acknowledgement of the epic fuck-up. "I apologize for that. It never should have happened. That's why we're all here."

Dawn looked at the others in the room. Gage stood to the side, knowing he was only there as an accessory. He didn't mind at all. He wasn't nearly as important as Dawn, and he was happy to let her be the one they were all worried about. She needed to be.

"Okay, let's circle up," Marcus said, grabbing the attention of everyone. "Dawn, there are a lot of people in the room. Instead of going around the room and expecting you to have any idea of who's who, I'm going to say there's local police." Marcus paused for his officers, Detective Foster and Officer Murphy, to raise their hands. "FBI." He stopped for Lorelei Sloane and her partner to wave. "Rose Protection Agency, who's kind enough to let us all convene here." Montgomery, Zeke, and a dozen other men raised their hands. "F-BOMB, who usually works on border issues, but has been involved with this from the beginning." Another group of men raised their hands. "And the group who calls themselves Curvy Vigilantes." Marcus turned to the women Gage met the other night.

Dawn looked around the room, her eyes getting bigger with each group that was introduced. One woman stepped forward. Gage thought she was the nine-one-one operator, but he wasn't positive.

"I'm Mackenzie. We haven't met, but we spoke last night."

"You're the nine-one-one operator," Dawn gasped.

Mackenzie nodded. "I am. And I believe we have another connection. Through Savannah."

Dawn's eyes went wide again before her cheeks reddened. "That was you?"

Mackenzie smiled at Dawn. "Your daughter is very strong. I don't usually hear how things go after a call, but it's so nice to meet you."

"I'm not sure things are going so well. That night was the lowest point of my life."

Mackenzie wrapped her arm around Dawn's shoulders and hugged her. "Let's keep it that way. Rock bottom hurts, but the farther you climb, the easier it is to keep from falling back there."

"Thank you," Dawn whispered.

Mackenzie led Dawn into the middle of the room and sat with her. Gage watched the whole thing unfold, impressed and amazed by the group assembled and the work they'd done so far. They did a recap of things for Dawn's benefit, then jumped into the current situation.

"We don't have proof Trevor was the one who killed Dr. Walden, but we have no reason to believe it was anyone else. Out of an abundance of caution, we've picked up Mandy, the nurse who signed the will with Dr. Walden. We don't believe Trevor is going to go after her since he has the information he needs, but we don't want to risk anything happening to her," Montgomery said.

"I've turned protection for you, Dawn, over to Rose. Because we believe you're a target, there's only so much we can do. You're not a witness, and putting you in official protection isn't something I've managed to get authorized yet," Lorelei explained.

"Is that why she was left exposed?" Gage asked.

Lorelei nodded. "The team was pulled off for another job, and no one was reassigned. I am so sorry that happened, but with Rose, it won't. You'll be under surveillance twenty-four-seven."

"Someone's going to be with me around the clock?" Dawn asked.

Everyone in the room looked at someone else. Dawn's tone said that wasn't what she wanted, and they all knew it.

Montgomery stepped forward. "We can talk through the logistics, but that's our plan right now."

"Don't I get a say in this? In my own life?" Dawn asked.

Montgomery slid a look to Marcus, who drew Dawn's attention. "We know this is an inconvenience, but—"

"Inconvenience? That's when the pizza guy forgets your appetizer and you have to go back to the store. This is an intrusion in my life. A big one. Does this mean I can't go to work? I can't see my kid? I can't go to dinner or the grocery store?"

"We can't force this on you, Dawn. This is for your protection," Marcus said.

"What about just catching Trevor Davis? Putting him in jail and throwing away the key. I mean, he killed Dr. Walden. Gage said he kidnapped other women. He's been siphoning money from his dad's company. For all I know, he killed his father, too."

The room erupted with Dawn's accusation against Trevor. Not that any of them were going to argue with her, but the news was a shock.

Gage watched the people in the room. A lot of groups. A lot of people who could be jockeying for power. Instead, none of them were stepping up in his opinion. It looked like they were all waiting for someone else to take control.

"Who's in charge?" Gage asked over all the noise.

They quieted down and looked around, just like he assumed they would.

"Who's calling the shots? Because until someone is willing to say I am, this chaos is a waste of time. For all of us.

A woman is dead. Others have been hurt and killed by Trevor. All I'm hearing is no one's willing to take control over this situation. Dawn's already been left vulnerable. Too many things have been kept from her. Why in the hell should she trust any of you?"

"I'm in charge," Lorelei said, stepping forward. "You're right. We're all waiting for someone else, but at the end of the day, this is an FBI case. If it's not now, it will be once we have solid evidence."

"A dead body isn't enough evidence?" Dawn asked.

Lorelei shook her head. "No. But we know that's the least of what Trevor Davis has done. We've been chasing this for months. Years, in some cases. This organization has riddled this city with pain and devastation for too long. We can't let it continue."

"Then don't. Find him," Dawn said.

Lorelei shook her head. "We're looking. Trust me. He has to have places to go that we don't know about."

Gage crossed the room to Lorelei and held out a folder. One he'd been unsure about handing over until now. "This is proof that I'm violating my attorney client privilege. This is proof that I'm helping you with an investigation. Every single person in this room is a witness to what I'm doing. I could lose my license for giving you this, but I'd rather lose my license than let him get away with anything else."

Lorelei held the folder but didn't take it. "What is it?"

"It's a list of properties Mr. Robert Davis owned before his death. Not all of them were in his name. Some were in his company's name. Some were in his son's names," Gage admitted.

"Your client is dead. It's not a violation," Lorelei said.

"That's a very fine line. One I'm not sure would hold up if someone pressed me," Gage said.

"Do all of these now belong to Dawn?" Marcus asked.

Gage nodded. "Which is why I'm handing this over. I'm hoping Dawn will give you permission to search her properties. And maybe not press charges."

"Yes," Dawn breathed. "Yes. Go get him."

16

———

After the meeting with Rose Protection Agency, a meeting that left Dawn more unsettled and less willing to count on the law enforcement agencies she believed would help, she refused any authorized protection. Trevor was after her, but he also needed her.

At least, that was the resounding thought. She was an asset. One he would exploit every chance he got.

Dawn returned to work at Angel's Grove the day after the meeting and was met with stares and glares. News of Dr. Walden's death had made the rounds, as did news of where her body was found and the reason why. Mandy mouthed off any chance she got, refusing protection and telling everyone it was Dawn's fault that Dr. Walden was dead and that Mandy was sure she was next.

Dawn kept her commentary to herself, but she had a feeling if Mandy showed up dead, there would be more than one suspect.

On her three days off, Dawn considered her options. She'd already thought about leaving Angel's Grove, but after Dr. Walden's death and Mandy's insistence that they were all in danger, Dawn didn't feel she could be effective in the job any longer.

She didn't want to leave them shorthanded, so she waited until the end of her next scheduled shift. A full week had passed since Dr. Walden's body was found, and Dawn was sick of the looks and fear from her coworkers. When she approached management about leaving Angel's Grove, they didn't argue and accepted her resignation effective immediately.

It hurt to feel like she was so easily replaceable. To have them treat her like she wasn't all that valuable to Angel's Grove. Dawn enjoyed working there, and she gave everything she had to the place. And they were quick to toss her aside.

It didn't matter that there were extenuating circumstances. It still bugged her. And hurt, if she was honest.

Gage didn't give her a minute alone to dwell on it, which was nice in some ways, but it also meant processing that truth was a challenge. He was worried about her, and he was distracting her with his body.

That was a damn good trade that Dawn could not complain about. At. All.

"Are you ready?" Gage asked the Monday after Dawn quit her job. He'd refused to let her be alone since their meeting at Rose Protection Agency and drove Dawn to and from work every day.

Dawn nodded and grabbed her new leather messenger bag. She wasn't ready to upgrade everything about her life, but she wanted to start investing in herself and her future. Assuming she had a future.

Gage reached for her hand in his SUV. He held it tight in his as he drove to Davis Developments. "I know you don't like this."

She looked at him. "Being stalked by a psycho?"

Gage breathed a laugh. "That, and me not letting you go anywhere alone."

She shrugged. "I worked really hard to be independent. To count on myself and trust myself."

"I'm not trying to take that away from you," Gage said quickly.

"I know." Dawn was quiet another minute, trying to collect her thoughts in a way that made sense. "I know you want me to be safe. I don't want anything to happen to me either, but it's not easy to turn my entire life over to someone else. No matter how much I like you."

She smiled his direction, and he returned her grin. "If I make you really crazy, let me know, and we can talk about it."

She raised an eyebrow. "Well, there was this one thing you did last night..."

He squeezed her hand tight, telling her he remembered, too. "I'm going to turn this vehicle around if you keep teasing me."

Dawn laughed and shook her head. "We have tonight."

Gage nodded, his smile fading.

"What are you thinking?"

He glanced at her. "It's strange to me how well you can read me already."

"We are basically living together. Talk about jumping in with both feet."

He exhaled at her teasing tone. "That's pretty much what I was thinking about. We're in this bubble. This altered reality where we're living together and you're in danger and things have completely changed for you recently. At some point, you'll go back to your life. Or back to a life. I was just thinking how quickly I've gotten used to you being at my house, even though it's only been a little more than a week."

"I've gotten used to it, too," Dawn admitted softly. "We said we were going to go slow, and we blew right past slow."

"The situation changed."

Dawn nodded. "It sure did."

Gage pulled into the Davis Developments lot. He drove around to one side and parked instead of pulling up to the front to drop her off. He turned in his seat to face her, and she did the same.

Gage tucked her hair behind her ear. "Are you regretting the decision to stay with me? I'm sure we can call Rose Protection Agency and ask someone to—"

"No," Dawn interrupted. "That's not what I want." She shrugged. "I don't want any of this. I want us to be able to get to know each other like a normal couple. I want to learn over time how you like your coffee and what your favorite treat at the end of the day is. I want time to figure out if you wear slippers inside or go barefoot. I want a chance to learn about your family and your past and why you became a lawyer."

"I'll tell you anything you want to know," he said.

She nodded. "I know you will. And I'm grateful for it. But it's still strange. I sleep in your bed every night, and I use your shower every morning. I know the code for your alarm system. I know where your breaker box is. But I don't know your middle name or your mom's name."

"Anthony. And Sharon."

Dawn chuckled and shook her head.

"I know. I'll pull back. If you want to go home, I won't stand in your way. I'll let you drive yourself to work if you want. I just want to know you're safe."

"I know you do. And thank you. We'll talk tonight about everything."

Gage nodded and backed out of the spot. He pulled up to the crosswalk and stopped. "Have a good day."

She leaned across the console and kissed him. "You, too." She grabbed her bag and walked into the building like she owned the place. Because she did.

Keith was at the desk again, like he'd been every other time Dawn had walked in to Davis Developments. "Good morning, Ms. Patterson."

"Good morning, Keith. How are you today?"

"Well, thank you. Is there anything I can get for you today?"

"I'll need lunch again. If you don't mind ordering."

"Of course not. Do you have a place in mind?"

"I'm open to your suggestions. Everything you've gotten has been amazing. And please make sure you get yourself something. And Tabitha, since I'll be working with her all day again today. Do you still have my card saved?"

"I do, Ms. Patterson. And thank you."

"Thank you, Keith. I appreciate your help. I know all of this going on isn't easy on anyone here, and you're the first line of defense. That can't be easy."

Keith smiled. "I have a secret button under my desk. If I see Trevor coming, I can lock the doors. And if someone gets in, Tabitha has already told me to sound an alarm and hide."

"Good advice. I don't want anyone getting hurt."

"If you don't mind me saying..."

"Yes?" Dawn braced herself for whatever Keith was going to say.

"Mr. Davis made the right decision when he gave you everything. People have been worried about Trevor taking over, but since you showed up, it's been a whole different place."

"Thank you, Keith. That means a lot."

"Thank you for keeping this place running, Ms. Patterson."

Dawn nodded, thinking about his words. If everyone thought Trevor was going to shut the place down, why did he need access? The general thought process from the police was he was planning to use it to run money through. So why was he stealing? Why was he pulling money out of the company?

Unless he was also putting money in. Running it through the company investments.

Dawn walked down the hall toward Tabitha's office with the thought in her head. They'd spent a lot of time looking at the money leaving, but they hadn't looked at anything that could have been going in. Was it possible?

Dawn knocked on Tabitha's door and hurried in before the other woman had a chance to say anything. "I think he's funneling money through the company. Could he be doing that? Pushing money in and pulling it out again, but we're only seeing it come out?"

Tabitha's eyes went wide, and she nodded slowly. "Yep. That's definitely possible. I hate when the criminals are smart."

Dawn chuckled and sat in what had become her chair while Tabitha started digging.

GAGE UNLOCKED his office door and locked it right behind him. He stepped over to the beeping alarm panel and put in his code before it alerted Rose Protection Agency that he wasn't fast enough.

It had been less than two weeks since Betsy took her leave, and Gage was already tired of the silence. In the three weeks since the break-in, he'd been working with clients by phone only, telling them he wasn't available for in-person meetings for the time being. A few of them questioned him about it, but most went with it.

But Gage hated it. He liked being around people, more than he realized before his self-imposed isolation.

He powered up his computer and started his work. He didn't bother with coffee anymore since Betsy wasn't there to help him drink a pot every day. She was doing well and was safe, but he hated that she had a scare at all.

And he hated that no one had caught Trevor Davis yet. When Gage supplied the list of properties to Marcus, Gage assumed it would end the whole nightmare. Instead, it only added to Gage's anxiety. If the police searched the places they thought Trevor could be and didn't find him, it was likely he knew they'd been there. And that they were looking for him.

Which only made Trevor more dangerous. As if that was possible.

Gage pushed away thoughts of Trevor and focused. He had calls with two new clients that afternoon and a call in the morning with one existing client who wanted to make a change to his will.

After his morning call, Gage decided to get some fresh air. He unlocked the office and walked outside, taking the long way around the block before returning to his office. He locked himself inside and knew if he was feeling the way he was, Dawn had to be losing her mind.

"No more," Gage said to himself. He couldn't do it. They

had to be free to live their lives. When they got home, he was going to tell Dawn she could drive herself to work. That he was backing off. He wasn't ready for her to go back to her place and be alone while she slept, but Gage admitted hovering over her wasn't sustainable for either of them.

He felt better after making the decision. He didn't unlock the door or turn off the alarm, but he was ready to start meeting with clients again and scheduled one to come in a few days later.

When Gage was done with his day, he drove to Davis Developments. Dawn walked out with a smile on her face. She and Tabitha had hit it off and bonded over being single moms. Dawn had shared her history with Tabitha and was surprised when the other woman was so positive about who Dawn was. All of it told Gage that Robert Davis knew exactly what he was doing the whole time.

If only the man had found a way to stop his son and the terror of his ways before he died.

"How was your day?" Gage asked when Dawn got in the SUV.

"It was good. We figured out that Trevor is putting money into the business and taking other money out. More these days than he's putting in, but it's new information."

"He's using it as a front? How?"

Dawn shook her head, frustration showing on her face as Gage pulled away. "We're not sure yet. He's smart. A lot smarter than we expected. I'm sort of guessing he's been doing this for a while and no one noticed, or Mr. Davis didn't want anyone to know."

"You think Robert was helping him?" Gage asked. He couldn't bridge the gap between the man he knew and his son.

"I don't know. Whenever he would talk about his sons,

he always told me he made a lot of mistakes. That he wanted to make things right with his younger son before it was too late. I got the feeling he would do anything for Trevor, even if it wasn't legal."

"Why give you everything if he was willing to look the other way for Trevor?"

"I wish I could answer that question. That's what I've been asking myself all day."

Gage was quiet for the rest of the drive home. He tried to make sense of the idea that Robert could have been okay with Trevor's business dealings, or the kind of business he appeared to be in. Robert was a good man.

But there was a small safe in his belongings. One Gage had delivered to Robert's house when he moved his personal belongings out of Angel's Grove. Gage never thought to check if the safe had anything in it. It wasn't his, but what if Robert was giving Trevor cash? What if that was why Trevor visited his father the day he died?

"I think Trevor killed Robert," Gage said.

"Yeah, but we don't have proof."

"There was a safe. In Robert's things. If he told Trevor he couldn't have more money, maybe Trevor got angry and killed his father."

"It's possible. But I don't think you're ever going to prove something like that."

Gage shook his head. "It's sad. To hate someone so much that you'd rather kill them than love them."

"Trevor Davis is not a normal person."

"That's for sure." Gage parked behind Dawn's car and put his SUV in park but didn't turn it off. "What do you think about buying a new car?"

"I need to."

"How about now?"

"Now?" she gasped.

Gage shrugged. "You have the money. And you need to get rid of that thing. If you have a car, you can drive to work, and you don't have to have me treating you like a prisoner."

"I—" Dawn's phone rang, interrupting the rest of her sentence.

She pulled her phone out. Her shoulders slumped. It kept ringing.

"It's Owen," she said before swiping the screen to answer. "Hey."

Gage sat quietly while Dawn's ex-husband spoke. He watched her body language closely, resisting the urge to grab the phone and tell Owen off when Dawn tensed.

"It's fine. I can take care of it."

She smiled. That was curious.

"All good. Yep. Four o'clock. I won't forget, Owen. I promise. And thanks for calling me."

Dawn hung up and stared at her phone for a long few minutes. Gage wanted to shake her and find out what Owen said, but he didn't interrupt whatever was going on with Dawn.

"I guess we should go get me a new car," Dawn said eventually.

"Yeah? Why is that?"

"Owen has a meeting at work tomorrow that he can't get out of, and Savannah needs a ride home. She's staying after to make up a test and asked if I could pick her up."

"She asked for you?" Gage asked. That was a really good sign from the little he knew about their relationship.

Dawn nodded, her smile nearly splitting her face in half. "She did. She told Owen she wants me to pick her up since he can't."

"That's a great sign, Dawn."

She nodded, but her smile faded a little. "I hope so. I know Owen told her about the money and about her trust. I want her to want to be around me because I'm her mother and not because I'm rich, but—"

"Nope, don't think that. Be positive. This is a good thing. Maybe we should get dinner out after we buy you a new car. What do you think?"

"Sounds good. My treat."

Gage laughed. "I can agree to that. What do you want to do with your car?"

"Know any local scrap yards?"

17

———

DAWN FELT LIKE NOTHING COULD STOP HER IN HER NEW vehicle. She told the guy at the dealership she'd never bought anything brand new, after she haggled with him on the price and got a few extras thrown in. He was impressed with her negotiating skills, and he upgraded her floor mats for the heck of it.

Dawn was not going to say no to that.

She smiled the entire drive back to Gage's house, insisting on dropping off his fancy SUV so they could drive hers to dinner. When he climbed up in the passenger seat, he whistled.

"You picked a good vehicle," he said.

She inhaled deep and smooth her hand over the soft-as-butter leather seat. "It's so pretty. I've never owned anything this nice in my life."

"You own a lot of nice things. You just haven't moved into your house or driven your cars."

Dawn wrinkled her nose. "None of those feel like mine."

"You're okay stepping in to help with Davis Developments. What's the difference?"

Dawn made a right turn and tried to think of a way that made sense. "I can walk in to Davis Developments and do something. Not that I'm very helpful right now, but I can try. I can learn and do something to make the company better. With his house and cars and whatever else he owned, it feels like it's more than I deserve."

Gage was quiet while Dawn drove, making her wonder if she upset him somehow. When she parked in front of the restaurant, she looked over at him and found him watching her with a strange expression on his face.

"I know it doesn't make sense, but it's—"

"No, it makes sense. I get it. I've seen a lot of people go through the same. Sometimes it's because it's a house they never wanted or because they're having a hard time accepting the person they loved is gone. I haven't really stopped to think about how all of this feels for you. All of the other stuff."

Dawn nodded, grateful he understood. "Maybe I am struggling to accept he's dead, but it's more than that. It's all the secrets, all the things I never knew. And then the magnitude of it. I've don't know how to be rich. I don't want to end up throwing away his money or wasting it. I want him to be proud and to believe he made the right decision."

"He's not going to come back and tell you *whoops, I made a mistake.*"

Dawn chuckled. "I know, but I believe in an afterlife. I believe he's watching or has the option to. He trusted me with something huge, and I know his properties are being maintained by his staff for now. Eventually, I'll have to decide what makes sense, but for right now, I'm just trying to stay alive."

Gage sucked in a sharp breath, like he'd forgotten that reality. He nodded slowly, then leaned across the console.

He caught her gaze and held it as he moved closer, pausing for Dawn to meet him, letting her choose if she wanted to.

Dawn surged toward him, their lips smashing together. She was doing what she always did and falling fast and hard, but for the first time, she didn't feel like it was a huge mistake. Which was terrifying.

And exciting.

Gage pulled back before Dawn, putting much needed head-clearing space between them. He smiled at her, his lips wet from hers and his breath just as ragged as hers.

"Thank you for everything you've done for me," she said. "I didn't know how much I needed someone I could count on until you came along."

"Right place, right time," he said.

She shook her head. "It's more than that to me. You didn't have to offer to help me or let me stay with you. You didn't have to take me to work every day or take me to buy this new beautiful machine. You have gone above and beyond. I can see why you're so well-respected as a lawyer." She smirked.

Gage laughed, as she hoped he would. "Most of my clients don't get quite such personalized experience."

"I should hope not," she teased him.

Gage shook his head at her and laughed. "Let's get dinner before I give in to a very different kind of hunger."

"Such a tease."

Gage chuckled as he got out of the vehicle and met her on the sidewalk. He reached for her hand as they walked in, then rested his hand on her back as she went ahead of him to the table.

Dawn liked the casual way he touched her. The level of comfort she felt with him. It was never the same with Owen, or anyone else. Owen was always more concerned about

Savannah, both when Dawn was pregnant and once their daughter was born. He doted on Savannah, but never did the same for Dawn. There were times she was almost jealous of her daughter and the way Owen treated her.

But time and distance, and Gage, if she was being honest, showed her that she was never meant to be with Owen forever. He was an amazing father, a kind husband, but he was never the right one for Dawn. She wasn't right for him, either.

She wasn't sure she was right for Gage, but everything was easier with him, in spite of all the hell surrounding Dawn.

"What looks good?" Gage asked, picking up his menu to make a choice.

Dawn followed suit. "I've never been here before, so I'm not sure."

"You're never been here?"

Dawn shook her head. "I've always wanted to, but the prices were outside what I could justify."

"And now they're not."

She shrugged. "They're not outside what I can afford, but justifying them is a bit of a stretch. I mean, I can get a steak at a dozen other places."

"Yeah, but none are as good as here. It'll melt in your mouth. Everything is good. If you don't want steak, you can get seafood, pasta, chicken. And you could have told me if you didn't want to come here."

She shook her head. "It's a good night. A little celebration is good."

Gage held her gaze for another minute. It was something she realized he did a lot. Sit and watch her, like he was making sure she was real.

She felt the same about him. He was kind and funny and

gorgeous. She considered herself lucky that he was willing to spend time with her.

"You're pretty amazing, you know that?" Gage said.

Dawn shook her head. "I don't. I think you should tell me exactly how amazing I am."

Gage laughed with her and shook his head. Then whispered all the things he found so amazing about her.

DAWN SHIFTED in her seat the entire drive home. Gage talked her into a glass of wine before either of them remembered she was driving. She didn't hesitate to let him drive, saying she wanted to see what the passenger seat was like.

"Are you uncomfortable?" he asked.

"Incredibly," she replied.

"What's wrong?"

She chuckled. "I'm extremely turned on right now."

"You what?" Gage nearly drove off the road at her admission.

She laughed again. "Are you really surprised by that?"

"Yeah, I am. I haven't touched you in hours."

"You whispered in my ear, and you drove home, and you let me buy this car without trying to butt in and tell me how to do it. You're showing me what a man I need looks like. The kind of man I should have in my life."

"What are you trying to say, Dawn?" Gage parked in his driveway and turned off the car, letting the interior lights turn off while they sat there.

"I'm saying I like you a lot, Gage. And I'm trying really hard to go slow, but it doesn't feel very slow to me right now."

Gage studied her closely in the dim light from the streetlights. He had already memorized her face, her smell, the feel of her body against his. He'd already admitted to himself that he was going to have a hard time letting her go. "Then let's stop pretending this is something different than what we both know it is."

"What is it?"

"It's two people figuring out if we're more. Two people who might be falling in love. Who aren't going to hold back anymore."

Dawn's eyes slid closed. Her lips lifted. She nodded, just slightly. "Okay."

"Let's go inside and take care of your other issue," he said, letting his voice drop.

She shivered and opened the door.

Gage was about to break through his zipper by the time they got inside and reset the alarm. They kissed on their way inside, pulling at clothes while they climbed the stairs, and fell naked onto the bed two minutes after they got out of the vehicle.

"Gage," she whispered.

He kissed her neck and down to her chest. She bowed up, pressing her body to his lips. Her hands went through his short hair. She tried to pull him back to her, but Gage was on a mission.

He nudged her thighs apart and settled himself between them. He kneeled on the floor and looked up at her, catching the look of lust in her eyes above the swell of her stomach. He lowered his head, inhaling the scent of her before he licked her from bottom to top.

"Oh, fuck," she whispered, shoving a pillow under her head.

Gage groaned, loving her reaction almost as much as he loved her flavor. She rocked her hips gently, not holding back anything as he learned the way she liked to be tasted.

"So good," she moaned when he licked her clit. Her body shook, the tremble telling him she was already on the edge, her earlier words absolute truth.

Gage pushed two fingers into her channel and focused his efforts on her clit. It wasn't long before she was moving counter to his strokes and grunting her way through an orgasm that had Gage surging to his feet and needing to be inside her.

He grabbed a condom while Dawn came down from her high. He watched the flush work its way across her naked body while he rolled the condom on his engorged dick. He lined up between her legs and waited for her to meet his gaze.

"Are you ready, Dawn?"

She nodded, biting her lip when he brushed against her. She propped her feet on the edge of the bed and spread her thighs wide. She took all of him in one fast stroke. Her back bowed, her eyes fluttered closed, and her core tightened around him.

"Fuck," Gage hissed.

"Yes. More," she said with a whimper.

"You amaze me every day," he said, starting the speech he gave her at dinner. "You are beautiful and kind. You are smart and generous. You love with your entire heart. You are so beyond worthy of all the good things coming to you. You impress me with the way you've jumped in and fought for something that's only been yours a few weeks. You're amazing, Dawn. Amazing. Amazing. Amazing." The word became a mantra that guided his thrusts.

She met his movements, her skin flushing and her breasts bouncing with each slap of their bodies together. He reached one hand between them and pressed on her clit while the other hand grabbed her breast and rolled her nipple between his fingers.

She let go, coming with a grunt and a scream and a string of praises for his talents.

"So good. Fuck. Gage. Yes. Oh, shit. Yes."

Gage was so focused on her pleasure he forgot about his own. The orgasm that tore through him nearly sent him to his knees. He caught himself on the edge of the bed, his hands landing next to her hips just in time to keep him from falling.

"Fuck. Dawn," he hissed. He groaned and shook as he came inside her.

She reached for him, trying to pull him down on top of her. It was awkward with their legs hanging off the bed, but Gage needed the reprieve and was happy to feel her sweaty body against his.

"Did that help?" he asked after a minute.

She giggled. "No. I think we need to do that again and again and again."

"You're a tough client. I think I'm going to have to dedicate more of my time to making sure you're very, very happy."

"Yes, please," she said.

Gage laughed and kissed her. He'd never laughed or joked with a woman during sex. It was just one more thing that was different with Dawn.

And one more thing he liked.

Dawn let herself into Gage's house the following afternoon with the key he gave her that morning. It was strange being there without him, but also freeing. She hadn't been alone in more than a week, and with the knowledge that someone was watching the house, she felt like she was safe.

She spent the day with Tabitha again, working on finding the leaks that Trevor was using to steal from Davis Developments. It was a full day, but a good one. They found some new information. Information Dawn was quick to turn over to the police and the FBI.

Dawn set the alarm and carried her things upstairs. She wanted to take a quick shower before Gage got home. Tabitha showed her one of the job sites that afternoon, and Dawn felt grimy and gross from walking around in a dusty environment.

She turned on the water and went to the bedroom. She set her handbag on the dresser, then undressed, making sure she didn't get dust all over the bedroom and bagging her clothes so they wouldn't touch everything else. She rushed to the bathroom and stepped into the shower.

"Ahhh," she moaned. The heat from the water felt good. Shampoo, conditioner, and body wash cleaned the day away. She indulged in an extra twenty minutes of hot water, knowing the tank would run out eventually but not willing to get out until she felt the first sign of cooling.

Dawn grabbed her towel and took time drying her skin. She wrapped her hair up in the towel and returned to the bedroom. She was still living out of her suitcase, still temporary, but she knew it had to be that way. They weren't living together. Not for real. It was temporary. And when it became permanent, if it became permanent, it would be for the right reasons.

Dawn sat on the edge of the bed and pulled panties up her thighs. She dug out a soft tee and pulled it over her head. Her hand hit something solid.

"Lotion," she said. She forgot she put the bottle in when she packed in a frantic haze the night she left her apartment.

She squirted a sizable dollop into her palm, then spread the lotion between her hands. She smeared it over her legs, rubbing it in.

"Little things."

She added more and rubbed it into her arms and hands, then smoothed the last of it onto her feet. She felt good. Sexy and confident. It was amazing what something so small could do.

A door opened downstairs, and Dawn froze. She strained to listen, the faint beeping sound rising above the blood rushing through her ears. Someone was turning off the alarm.

Dawn stood quietly and reached for her handbag. She grabbed her phone from inside as footsteps, not quiet ones, started up the stairs.

"Dawn? It's me," Gage said, his voice getting closer.

Dawn exhaled her relief, her shoulders sagging. She stood to put her phone back in her bag.

Gage came around the corner and smiled, his gaze heating when he saw what she was wearing. "That's one hell of a welcome home."

Dawn chuckled. "Tabitha took me to one of the job sites today. We got a little dusty. I couldn't resist the urge to jump in the shower as soon as I got here."

Gage looked at his watch. "You must have been really fast."

Dawn shrugged. "Not really. What do you mean?"

Gage loosened his tie and pulled it over his head. "I mean a part of me thought you'd still be with Savannah right now. How was she? Did you have a good visit?"

"Savannah?" Dawn squeaked. She sank to the bed.

Gage dropped to his knees in front of her. "What's wrong? What happened? Is she okay?"

Dawn shook her head slowly. "I never picked her up. I completely forgot."

18

———

DAWN GRABBED HER PHONE FROM HER HANDBAG. "FUCK. Twelve missed calls from Savannah." She tapped Savannah's name, grabbing her stuff and getting ready to go get her daughter.

A beep interrupted the call, and Dawn pulled the phone away from her ear.

"It's Owen," she said, mostly to herself, as she swapped calls. "Hey. I'm sorry. I'm on my way."

"I already got her," Owen said. "She asked me to call you when she saw you were calling her back."

"Is she okay?" Dawn asked.

Owen laughed mirthlessly. "What do you think, Dawn? Her mother forgot about her."

"I know. I'm sorry. I was at work, and my mind was on something, and the time went by, and I just completely forgot."

"Is that what you want me to tell her?"

"No, Owen. I want to tell her. To apologize. It was a mistake. It won't happen again."

He sighed heavily. A door closed on his end. "I'm trying, Dawn. I am constantly telling her to give you a chance. To let you back in. I know your life is a lot right now, but we were counting on you today. Savannah was counting on you. I was hesitant to ask you for help, but she said she wanted to call you."

"I know. I messed up."

"It's more than that, Dawn. It's everything. It's not being there for her. It's not showing her that you want her in your life."

"I do!"

"I know. At least I believe you. But actions are different than words. She hasn't been able to rely on you for a long time."

"Here we go," Dawn snarled.

"Don't get defensive with me," Owen said. The calm in his voice was enough to piss Dawn off.

"Don't get all high and mighty with me. I fucked up, Owen. I got involved with someone who was horrible for me. I lost myself. I couldn't handle things as well as you did when we split up, and I lost sight of everything. I'm not going to do that again."

"But you are," he said softly.

Dawn's heart jumped. How did he know about Gage? No. It was different. Gage was different. "This is different."

"Yeah, it's money. It's not even a man this time. You're in over your head with this company and the money and everything else. I know you're trying to see it as a good thing, but money amplifies who we are, Dawn. It doesn't really change people, it just makes us more. And what I'm afraid of is you're going to be more unreliable and more self-centered instead of a better parent."

"That's not fair," Dawn whispered. Tears rolled down her cheeks. Shame burned her face. She wanted to be better. To be there for Savannah. And to prove to Owen that she wasn't self-centered.

"I'm not going for fair here. I'm going for truth. I'm the one dealing with a hurt and heartbroken kid who thought her mom would be there for her."

"I'm sure you're pushing her hard to give me chances."

"You have no idea how hard I push her, Dawn. No idea. But when things like this happen, when you don't even call when you're supposed to show up, and then you tell me you were working, what am I supposed to tell her?"

"That I messed up. That it won't happen again."

"Except I can't promise her that. It's happened too many times for me to think you've changed."

"Give me another chance, Owen. Please."

"It's not up to me. It's Savannah's choice."

Dawn sighed. Her throat tightened. She was losing her daughter. She'd made too many decisions that didn't put Savannah first. And it was going to cost Dawn any chance she had at a relationship with her kid. "Okay."

"I'll try, Dawn. I can't make any promises, though."

"Thank you."

"And Dawn?"

"Yeah?"

"I'm not going to keep trying forever. I've never tried to keep her from you, and I never will, but I can't be the only one fighting for the two of you to have a relationship. You need to fight for it, too. You need to show up. Come to a soccer game, or a lacrosse game. Text her. Ask how things are going. She needs to know you're there, even when you're not physically here."

Dawn nodded. "I will. Thank you, Owen."

"No promises, but I'll let you know what she says."

"Okay."

"Have a good night, Dawn."

"You, too." Dawn hung up the phone and stared at the screen until it went dark. She messed up when she overdosed and almost killed herself with Savannah home, but this felt worse. She could accept that her drug use was part of her addiction, and that she could keep that under control as long as she stayed away, but this was completely on her. This was not paying attention to her kid. It was neglect, plain and simple.

"Are you okay?" Gage asked softly.

Dawn startled. She'd forgotten he was there. Listening to her life falling apart. "No."

"What did he say?"

"He said he's going to talk to her, but that I have to show up if I want a relationship with her."

"You didn't do it on purpose," Gage defended.

Dawn shook her head. "It doesn't matter to a teenager. I still did it. She thought she could count on me, and I let her down."

"Don't be so hard on yourself."

"I have to!" She jumped up from the bed and paced the room, feeling caged in and trapped. An hour ago she felt safe there, with the security system and the cozy house she'd allowed herself to believe was a place she could belong.

But now, she knew it wasn't any of that. It was just a place. A home that wasn't hers. A place where she was still the same messed up person who let everyone down.

"What can I do to help you?" Gage asked.

Dawn shook her head. "I... I don't know. This isn't your problem."

"No, but I care about you, Dawn. If it wasn't for all of this with Robert, you would have had a normal day and a normal life and you wouldn't be dealing with everything you're dealing with."

She laughed mirthlessly and shook her head. "None of that matters. I'm still the same messed up person I've always been. I'm not reliable, I'm not there for the people I love. I've chosen to do this. To run Davis Developments. But this is what I was worried about. Like Owen said, money makes us more of what we already are, and I'm not a good person."

"Dawn—"

"You don't know me! It's been a month since we met. Even less than that since we started sleeping together. You don't know what I'm like on a day-to-day basis. What life is like with me. You have no idea if I can ever be counted on. Newsflash! I can't be. I'm a disaster. What kind of person forgets about their kid? Leaves their teenager stranded at school. How can I stand here and think I'm even a little bit decent? I'm not. And all I manage to do is prove that over and over again. And I keep hurting my kid in the process."

Gage was silent through her rant. He stared at her, but he couldn't refute her words. Because she was right. She wasn't reliable. She wasn't a good person. And he had no proof otherwise.

"I'm going to sleep in the other room tonight," Dawn said. She snatched her things from where she'd tossed them over the last week, shoving everything into the suitcase she carried it all there in. She wanted to leave, to go for a drive or just get away, but she didn't feel safe, and she knew Gage wasn't likely to let her go alone when she was so upset.

She was stuck. Because she made choices that put her first. That did exactly what Owen accused her of. She was self-centered. She was just like every other rich person.

And she hated herself for it.

GAGE WATCHED Dawn walk down the hallway to the other bedroom. She closed the door softly, keeping her anger and pain locked inside.

He wanted to call her ex and rip the guy a new one, but it wouldn't have fixed anything. The reality was Gage didn't know Dawn. He saw what he wanted to see, what he thought Robert saw, and he decided that was who she was. But there's more to a person than what they showed others.

Gage changed his clothes and went downstairs to fix dinner. He hoped Dawn would join him, but she never did. He knocked on her door and said there was food downstairs. All she said was, "Okay." She never came out.

He left his door open when he went to bed, wanting to be there for her if she needed him, but she never left her room. She punished herself all night, thinking that was better.

Gage knew all about that. He'd done it enough when his mom died. He'd done it for years. At times, it was still something he indulged in. That soul-deep agony that never went away when you believed with your whole heart that you were the cause of someone else's pain.

It was bullshit. And Gage wasn't going to let Dawn wallow in it.

He got up early and showered with the door cracked so he would hear if she tried to sneak out while he was in the shower. He dressed and went to the kitchen to make breakfast, knowing the scent of coffee would draw her in.

When her door opened, Gage didn't make a sound. He

knew she believed he'd left for work, but he was determined to wait her out.

Dawn took a quick shower, then returned to her room before walking downstairs. She went for the front door, but he called out to her.

"I made breakfast."

"Ahh! I thought you were gone."

Gage waited until she walked into the kitchen to speak. "We need to talk."

She tensed immediately. "Can we come up with a new phrase for when someone wants to deliver bad news? *We need to talk* are the four most ominous words in the English language when they're strung together."

Gage smirked, hiding the look behind his coffee mug. He leaned against the counter, a few feet away from the mountain of food he made for breakfast. Definitely a bribe.

"You're going to ply me with food, then tell me what? To get out? That things are over? That I'm too much trouble? Got it. Can we move on to the part where we pretend things are fine? I'll be gone by the time you get home today."

"Why do you think that's what I want to tell you?"

She breathed a laugh. "Well, last night was so much fun, and the only thing that comes from *we need to talk* is bad news, so it's all about logic."

Gage shook his head. "That's not what I was going to say. At all. I wanted to see how you're doing today and ask if I can do anything and tell you I missed you last night."

She opened and closed her mouth, looking like a fish. It would have been comical if it wasn't accompanied by tears welling in her eyes.

"Dawn," he whispered, taking a step toward her.

She put her hand up and shook her head. "I... I need to

figure out what I have to do to get Savannah back. She has to be my priority."

Gage ground his teeth together. "I'm not trying to steal your focus. I want to support you. To be there for you."

She swallowed roughly, her throat moving with the effort it took. "I need to figure out if I can handle that."

"What does that mean?"

"It means I scorch everything I touch, Gage! It means my marriage imploded because I wasn't a good wife and mother. It means my daughter hates me because I didn't get better after my marriage ended. It means I nearly died because of a choice I made to get involved with the wrong man. It means Dr. Walden is dead and Mr. Davis is dead and everyone around me gets hurt. And it's because of me."

"That's not true. Dr. Walden is dead because of Trevor. And Mr. Davis—"

"Is probably dead because he told his son he was giving everything to me. You know it, and I know it. And he's smart. Too smart. Everyone at that company is in danger because I'm going there every day. I put people at risk. How can you want to step into that?"

"Because I know the good sides of it. I know how much this is killing you. I know you would erase all of it if you could. I know you're not choosing any of this. And I know you're good and kind and unbelievable. And I know you're worth the risk."

She shook her head the entire time he spoke, tears streaming down her cheeks. "Gage."

"Don't box me out. Not yet. Maybe things won't work out for us, but don't let it be because of things that aren't true. Don't let Trevor take something else away."

Her breath hitched with her inhale, and she nodded. "I'll try."

"That's all I can ask of you."

He took a step toward her, relieved when she didn't put her hand up to stop him. He advanced slowly, giving her the chance to stop him before he made it to her.

He wrapped her in his arms and held her tight. She hiccuped and shook and held on to him like he was the only thing keeping her upright.

He didn't let go until her breathing leveled out. She drew a breath and released him.

"Thank you," she whispered.

"I don't know how hard all of this is on you, but I want to be here for you. Please don't shut me out again, okay?"

She hesitated, then nodded. "I'll try. It's my first instinct."

"I get that. It's mine, too. We retreat because we've never had someone else we can count on. Maybe we can be that person for each other."

She smiled, looking like the woman he was falling for.

Dawn had to get to work, so she drank a cup of coffee quickly and hurried through a few slices of bacon and grabbed a pancake to eat in the car.

Gage shook his head at her and teased her about her rushed breakfast.

"We're so close to stopping Trevor. I want to get there and see what IT found."

"Go. Save the company. Dinner tonight?"

Dawn nodded. "Sounds good. Thank you."

She raised onto his toes to give him a soft kiss. It was over far too quickly for Gage, but she was coming back that night. If he had his way, she'd come back every night.

He followed her out the door and secured the house. He was blocking her in, so he backed out of the driveway first, then waited for her to leave before turning the other direction to go to his office.

They got through their first fight. That was better than some of his relationships.

DAWN CHECKED her phone a dozen times since she got up. She sent Savannah a text after she spoke to Owen, apologizing and asking for another chance. She still hadn't heard back from her daughter.

Dawn parked next to Tabitha's SUV and grabbed her messenger bag. She looked at the other vehicles in the lot as she walked toward the front door. She was almost there when a vehicle pulled out of a parking space and came straight toward her.

Dawn glanced at the car, sure they would stop or turn or something. Seconds ticked by like hours, fear paralyzing her. She had no control over her body. No ability to move.

A sound reached her ears, but Dawn couldn't make out what it was. She just stared at the car as it raced toward her. Ten cars away. Seven. Three.

Something slammed into Dawn, knocking her off her feet. The pavement scraped down her side, popping the strap on her messenger bag and cutting through her clothes.

Tires screeched. Or maybe that was her.

Dawn looked up as the car that sped toward her raced down the road to exit the parking lot.

"Dawn! Ms. Patterson! Are you okay?"

Dawn turned and saw one of the men she met when she and Gage went to Rose Protection Agency. "I know you."

"Yes, ma'am. I'm Walker St. Brown from Rose Protection Agency. Are you okay? Are you hurt?"

"Were you following me?"

The man nodded, his hands patting her body clinically.

She hissed when he touched her hip.

"You are hurt. Let's get you inside and get you patched up."

"Someone just tried to kill me."

"It appears that way, yes, ma'am."

"And you saved me."

"Right place, right time."

Dawn nodded, then everything went black.

19

———

Dawn heard voices all around her. Fading in and out, like she was swimming. She tried to move, but it hurt. And something was keeping her still.

Or someone.

She screamed, thrashing against whoever was there.

"Calm down, Dawn. It's just me. It's Walker St. Brown. Please—oof!"

The name and voice melted into her brain. Dawn managed to pry her eyes open. The bright light assaulted her, and the memory of what happened came back. "Walker. The car. Oh, God."

"It's okay, Ms. Patterson." His voice sounded pained. "Are you ready to sit up?"

She nodded, letting him help her into a seated position. She glanced over at the man who saved her life.

"Thank you."

"For?"

"Saving me. I'm sorry I freaked out."

"I'll be okay."

"Did you get hit? What happened?"

"Your elbows are more dangerous than that car," he said with a grimace. He shifted in his seat and adjusted his junk.

"I elbowed you... I hit you... Shit, I'm sorry."

Walker shook his head. "I'll survive. Not the first time I've had my nuts handed to me."

Dawn snorted a laugh. He was adorable. In a giant of a man kind of way. The look in his brown eyes was one of kindness and concern, not frustration. He was attractive, too. Short, dark hair and corded muscles that came in handy when he carried her inside.

"Wait, did you carry me in here?" She realized she was in the lobby of Davis Development instead of the parking lot.

He nodded. "You sort of passed out when that car went flying by. Your side is pretty messed up. I'd like to get you to a doctor."

Dawn shook her head and realized how many people were watching the two of them. "Shit."

"They're worried about you," Walker whispered. "Half of them saw what happened and the other half heard about it and rushed here to check on you. I kept them all away, but they will want to hear from you."

"There's twenty people there. How did you keep them away?"

He glared at her, and she immediately backed up in her seat. His face morphed into a smirk. "It's not that hard."

She chuckled. "You're a good man to have around."

"Not everyone would agree with that, but for today, I'm glad I was here."

"Did you see who was driving that car?"

He shook his head. "I heard the engine and saw you and focused on getting you out of the way. I called my team, but there aren't many cameras around here, so it's unlikely we'll get anything. Plus, we already know who it was."

"Trevor Davis," Dawn said.

Walker nodded. "That would be my guess."

"I guess your team was wrong about him not wanting me dead."

Walker shook his head slowly. "I'm not so sure about that. My guess is if he wanted you dead, you'd be dead. That was meant to scare you."

"Great. Such a comfort," Dawn dead-panned.

Walker barked a laugh. "Well, at least you have a good attitude about it. Let's get you to your crowd and we can find out if they have a medical team here. Otherwise, I'm taking you to a doctor."

"I'd rather go somewhere else if you think I really do need—" Dawn hissed, halting her words when she tried to stand and the pain sliced through her side.

"I think you answered your own question," Walker said.

Dawn glared at him, but he wasn't put off by her weak attempt. It wasn't nearly as terrifying as his glare.

"Let's go tell them all you're okay."

Dawn nodded. She let Walker make sure she was steady before she nodded to him.

The crowd of people pressed toward her as she walked their direction. "I'm okay," she said.

"Are you sure?" Keith asked. "I saw the whole thing. Do you want me to call the police?"

"Already handled," Walker said.

Keith glared at the other man, and Walker tried not to laugh.

Dawn stepped between them. "Because of everything going on, I've had a protection detail on and off." She looked at Walker, and he nodded. "This is Walker St. Brown. He's working with the police and will handle reporting all of this to them. His team is already looking into it. If we have any security footage, it would be great if we could share it with them."

Tabitha stepped forward. "We will send it over." She looked at Walker, who handed her a card. "Thank you. And thank you for watching out for her."

Walker nodded. "Glad I was here today."

"We all are." Tabitha turned to the crowd. "Let's all give Ms. Patterson some space. We are all aware of the situation, and the risks. This is a reminder to be diligent. To be aware and safe. Don't go anywhere alone. Stay with someone else anytime you leave this building. If you feel you need protection, the company will be happy to provide it for you. We want all of you safe."

Dawn nodded in agreement. She would spend all the money she had to ensure no one else got hurt. The idea of Trevor going after anyone else sent a shiver through her.

The group that had come to check on Dawn offered well wishes and thanks that she was okay, one-by-one speaking to her for a second before returning to their jobs.

When they were all gone, except Tabitha, Dawn looked at the woman who'd become a friend.

"Was it him?" Tabitha asked.

Dawn shrugged. "I don't know of any other enemies I've made lately, so I assume so."

Tabitha shook her head. "I'm so sorry, Dawn."

"Thanks. Um, Walker's insisting I get checked out. I really wanted to finish what we started yesterday."

"I'll do what I can, and we'll keep working until we're done. We're close. It'll happen."

Dawn nodded, grateful for Tabitha's friendship and support. "Thanks. If I can, I'll be back. If not—"

"Get some rest. Make sure she gets the good drugs," Tabitha joked.

Dawn almost said something, but she kept her mouth shut.

Walker nodded. "I'll take care of her. Thank you for sending over the footage."

Tabitha nodded, then turned to go back to her office.

Walker led Dawn outside, his pace faster than she could keep up with without racing. She made it out the front door before the pain nearly sent her to her knees.

"Shit," Walker hissed. "I didn't realize how much pain you were in."

"I'll be fine," Dawn whispered.

"We need to get you to a hospital. You're going pale."

Dawn nodded, feeling weaker and weaker. She knew it wasn't blood loss, the scrapes weren't that bad. It had to be anxiety and surviving a near-death experience.

She leaned her head against the headrest while Walker took turns through the city at speeds that couldn't possibly have been legal. When he pulled up in front of St. Nicholas Memorial Hospital, there was already someone waiting for them.

"That's Zeke Donovan. Do you remember him?" Walked asked.

Dawn looked at the man and nodded. "From your team."

"Yes, he's going to watch you while I park the car, but I'll be inside soon."

Zeke opened the door and helped Dawn into a wheelchair. She was already feeling better and thought it was overkill, but she didn't have it in her to argue.

"Sounds like you had a close call," Zeke said on their way inside.

"I'm lucky Walker was there," Dawn told him.

"Walker?"

Dawn turned to look at Zeke. "Isn't that his name? That's what he told me. Who was that?"

"It is. Sorry. I didn't mean to scare you. He isn't the most friendly of guys. Usually pretty quiet. He must like you."

"I'm not exactly single," Dawn said, feeling awkward all of a sudden.

Zeke chuckled. "No, not like that. I'm sticking my foot in it today. He doesn't date, ever, so I didn't mean likes you in that way. Just he isn't the normal grizzly bear around you. Most people have a hard time with him."

"Well, he saved my life, so he can act however he wants to around me."

Zeke laughed and parked Dawn's wheelchair in a room. He came around the front and offered his hands to help her up. "Lorelei Sloane insisted we have someone follow you as much as possible. Like we said when we met, we don't usually follow people without their awareness, but I'm glad we broke that rule this time."

"Me, too." Dawn stood, grateful for Zeke's help when she twisted to go around the wheelchair and her side sent white hot pain through her. "Dammit."

"Go slow," Zeke said. "Get to the bed and someone will be here in a minute. Is there anyone you want us to call? Mr. Stevens?"

"No," Dawn blurted.

Zeke's eyebrow went up, but he didn't comment.

"Sorry."

"You don't have to explain yourself to me. I'm certainly not an example of how to operate in a relationship."

"You're in a relationship. Why don't you tell me about her? Maybe it'll help with the pain."

Zeke chuckled. "I'm not in a relationship. That's why I

have no advice." The wistful sound of his voice said there was a lot more to it.

"But there is someone."

Zeke looked at her, his surprise sparking his eyes. "There was, but..."

"I'm sorry," Dawn said. "I didn't mean to pry. And I'm sorry for your loss."

Zeke swallowed thickly, nodding and avoiding her gaze. "Thanks."

A knock on the door interrupted the awkward moment and brought a doctor into the room. "Ms. Patterson, I'm Dr. Howard. It sounds like you need a few stitches."

"She passed out, too," Walker said from behind the doctor. "A full workup might be the best bet."

Dr. Howard looked between Walker and Zeke, then met Dawn's gaze with a careful one of her own. "Are you comfortable with these two being in here during your exam?"

"Um, what will the exam entail?" Dawn asked.

"First, I'd like to get you into a gown. If you need help, they can help you or I can ask a nurse to come in. I'm going to start with the part of you that's bleeding before we look at head trauma, since you're upright and clearly communicating with me."

"A nurse would be good," Dawn said, her cheeks burning. She didn't know either of the men well enough to want to get naked in front of them. Nor did she feel comfortable asking them to help her change.

"We'll wait outside," Zeke said.

"Right outside," Walker added.

They pulled the door closed behind them. Dr. Howard smiled at Dawn. "Your boyfriends seem very protective."

"Oh, they're not mine. I mean, I'm not dating either of

them. Someone's been trying to hurt me, and they're protecting me."

"Forgive me, but judging by this scrape, I'm not sure how great of a job they're doing."

Dawn breathed a laugh, then hissed at the pain. "Considering a car was racing toward me and this was all I got, I think Walker saved my life."

"I'm sorry. That's... I forget my manners sometimes. I apologize."

Dawn shook her head. "You're fine. It's a weird situation altogether. But they're nice men I've only met a few times, so getting naked in front of them is a little uncomfortable."

"Totally understand," Dr. Howard said. "I'll have a nurse come in and help you, and I'll be back with some supplies to clean you up. We'll go from there with the rest of the tests."

"Thank you, doctor."

Dr. Howard nodded and left the room. She closed the door, her muffled voice right outside the door. A minute later, a nurse came in and helped Dawn change before the doctor returned.

Cleaning her wound was painful and required a few swear words. Dawn rejected the offer of pain meds, explaining why and grateful when no one pushed her to go back on her choice.

When she was bandaged and resting, Zeke and Walker came back into her room with Captain Patrick right behind them.

"Ms. Patterson, I'm sorry for what happened today," Captain Patrick said.

"Thanks. I'm guessing you need to hear my side of things."

"Please. If you're up to it."

Dawn nodded and recounted what she remembered.

The men in the room were quiet while she spoke, none of them interrupting her except to ask questions for clarification.

When she was done, Captain Patrick asked if he could get in touch with Gage. "I understand you didn't want to call him earlier, but he'll need to help you change the dressing on your wound."

Dawn nodded. "I know. I just didn't want to worry him. I... Yes, you can call him."

Captain Patrick nodded and let himself out of the room.

Zeke and Walker sat in the hard plastic chairs in her room. The doctor did bloodwork and was keeping her until it came back, so the three of them sat in silence.

"Are you both going to stay here? I'm sure you have other things to do," Dawn said.

Walker and Zeke exchanged a glance.

"Right now, you're our priority," Zeke said.

Dawn nodded, knowing arguing wouldn't get her anywhere.

The men scrolled through their phones, and Dawn stared at the ceiling. When another knock brought their attention to the door, an irrational wave of panic swept over her.

Until Gage walked in.

His gaze washed over the two men before landing on her. He ignored them and hurried to her bedside. "Are you okay?" he breathed.

All the moments of the day rushed back to her and brought up her fear. Her throat seized up, stopping any words from coming out. She shook her head and reached for him.

He pulled her into his embrace, holding her close. He

positioned himself on the edge of the bed with her and wrapped her up while she cried.

"I'm so sorry, Dawn. So sorry," he whispered over and over again.

She just laid there, vaguely aware of Zeke and Walker leaving the room. She let all her terror out, leaning into Gage as she cried.

Gage didn't pull back or try to get her to calm down. He let her cry, and when her breathing slowed and she began to fade, he let her.

WHEN MARCUS TOLD Gage that Dawn had been attacked, he wanted to go out and find Trevor and rip his fucking head off. How could he? How could Trevor go after Dawn?

Instead of pretending he could actually do something to Trevor if he did find him, Gage went to Dawn. He needed to see her, to know she was okay. Even though they weren't in a great spot, he cared about her.

No, he loved her. Hearing she was hurt solidified that truth for him. His heart didn't beat until he saw her in that bed and knew she was okay.

And when she reached for him, it started again.

He laid there, not caring that the metal frame of the bed was digging into his hip and he was going to have a bruise. All that mattered was Dawn.

She finally slept, something the doctor said was okay when she came in a while later. She whispered Dawn had had an ordeal and was likely exhausted. So Gage held her and let her rest.

When Dawn stirred hours later, the sun was nearly set, and the room was quiet. Their guards were likely still outside the door and Dr. Howard was likely off-shift, but none of that mattered when Dawn opened her eyes and looked up at Gage.

"I'm sorry about yesterday."

Gage nodded. "Me, too. I know Savannah is important to you. She's everything. And I never want you to feel like you have to choose between me and her. She wins, every time, without question."

Dawn nodded. "Thank you."

"Of course. How are you feeling?"

"Like I was almost run over by a car."

Gage snorted. "I guess that's how you should be feeling."

She shifted, stretching in the too-small-for-two-people bed.

Gage rolled off the edge, giving her space to move and get comfortable.

She reached for him. "Are you leaving?"

He shook his head. "Not until you are."

Dawn nodded. "What did the doctor say?"

"She said you needed your rest."

"What about the police?"

"I don't know. We can ask your bodyguards, though."

'They're still here?"

Gage nodded. "Are you ready for me to let them back in?"

Dawn pulled the blankets up so they covered her gown and kept her decent, then nodded.

Gage let the two men into the room, telling them Dawn was awake.

Both men walked inside and smiled at Dawn.

Walker went to her side. "You look better. The rest was good for you. How's your head?"

"It hurts, but I'll survive."

"Good."

"Are you ready to talk next steps?" Zeke asked.

"Next steps?" Dawn asked.

Gage moved to stand next to her. She reached for his hand and squeezed it.

"We want to put you in protective custody. Around the clock," Zeke said.

"No," Dawn said. She shook her head. "No. I can't do that. I won't."

"Ms. Patterson," Zeke started.

"No. Listen, I know you're trying to do what's right for me, but I need to be able to live my life. I have a kid, a company to run. I can't run and hide and leave everyone else exposed. I'm the one he's after. He's proven he knows where I live and where I'm working, both before and now. He is finding out everything. Locking me up and throwing away the key isn't going to change that. It's only going to mean I can't do what I can to stop him."

"Ms. Patterson," Zeke tried again.

"I'm not doing it," Dawn said, adding a glare and yanking her hand from Gage's to cross her arms.

Gage looked at the other men in the room and recognized the acceptance and astonishment in their eyes.

"Okay," Walker said. "We will say okay, for now. But we reserve the right to change our minds at any moment."

Dawn looked at Walker and nodded. "Agreed."

20

———

Gage didn't like Dawn's decision, but he had already learned there was no way he'd change her mind about something she was so committed to. And he respected her for choosing not to risk anyone else.

The doctor gave Dawn something to help her sleep, telling her she needed it when Dawn tried to argue. The doctor insisted there were no narcotics in the medicine, and only then did Dawn agree.

While she slept, Gage tried to be okay with the events that happened. He didn't like fighting with her. And he liked even less knowing she'd almost been hurt a lot worse than a few stitches and a bump on the head. If he went back to insisting she let him drive her everywhere, he wasn't sure she would react any better than when Walker and Zeke said they wanted her in protective custody.

There was no good option left.

Gage drifted off in the recliner the nurses rolled in for him and slept like shit, but he slept, so he figured that was better than nothing. When the sun filtered through the blinds, he stirred and woke, finding Dawn still asleep.

Gage used the attached bathroom and tried to clean himself up a little, knowing he'd need to go home and shower at some point before he went to work. He had a few meetings that day and didn't want to cancel them, if possible.

He scrolled through emails while his stomach growled, reminding him he never had dinner the night before.

Dawn woke up with a start, sitting up straight in the bed.

"You're safe," Gage said, drawing her attention.

She looked at him, then sighed heavily. "I had a dream Trevor was standing over me."

Gage shook his head and moved toward her, standing next to her bed and taking her hand. "You're okay."

Dawn nodded, letting his words sink in and her body relax. The monitors next to her beeped the rhythm of her heart, slowing as she calmed down.

"I hate this," she whispered.

"I know."

"Do you think I made the right decision?"

Before Gage could answer, there was a knock on the door. They didn't get a chance to say anything before the door was opening and Lorelei stuck her head in.

"You're up. Good."

Dawn sighed again, the beeping of the machines once more slowing down after a scare. "What can I do for you?"

"I want to give you a detail."

"What does that mean?" Dawn asked.

"It means I finally have the authority to assign protection to you."

"What was Rose Protection Agency doing?" Gage asked.

Lorelei shrugged. "A favor, really. They weren't getting paid, but Montgomery understands how important this case is. He agreed to eat the costs if we couldn't find a way to pay for it."

"I already told them I'm not going into protective custody," Dawn said.

"I've heard. I think that's a mistake, but I'm giving you a bodyguard."

"I don't want another stranger invading my life," Dawn growled.

Lorelei didn't flinch at the tone of Dawn's voice. Lorelei took a minute, nodding and moving closer. "I don't think leaving you unprotected is a great idea."

"And I don't think the protection I got from your team was all that effective," Dawn snapped.

The two women faced off. Gage resisted the urge to laugh. It wasn't funny, but the big, bad federal agent was getting her ass handed to her by a single mom lying in a hospital bed wearing the ugliest hospital gown ever. It was kind of comical.

"Will you approve Rose Protection Agency being your protection? I can get that authorized."

Dawn released a breath that hinted at a growl and nodded. "Fine."

Lorelei nodded once. She turned to go, then stopped. She faced Dawn and met her gaze. "I am sorry. Leaving you unprotected never should have happened. It wasn't fair to you that it did. I know you don't trust me, and you have no reason to, but I want you to know I want to nail this asshole just as badly as you do."

Dawn held Lorelei's gaze for a long moment. Finally, Dawn said, "Thank you. I appreciate your apology."

Lorelei nodded and pressed her lips into a smile, then left the room.

Gage watched as Dawn thought through what just

happened. He could see the relief on her face that she'd actually gotten an apology from the agent.

"Are you okay?" he asked.

Dawn nodded. "I'm better now. Knowing she didn't mean to leave me exposed. I know... She said it before, but I was too angry and scared to accept it. It felt hollow then."

"And now?"

"She meant it. I'm still not willing to have her people watching me, but it's better."

"Good."

Not long later, a nurse brought in a breakfast menu for Dawn to order something. Gage went to the foyer to find food and brought it up to Dawn's room just as her breakfast was delivered. They sat and ate and waited for the doctor.

The doctor came in mid-morning and said she'd already signed Dawn's release paperwork. Gage helped her dress in her own clothes, the ripped ones from the day before because he didn't think to go home and get her clean things. He gave her his suit coat to wear out of the hospital and pulled his SUV around while a nurse wheeled Dawn to the exit.

"Mr. Stevens!" someone called out as Gage was about to get into his SUV.

He turned and saw Zeke hurrying across the lot toward him. Gage waited for Zeke to catch up. "Morning."

"Are you taking her home?"

Gage shook his head. "She wants to go to work. We're going to go back to my place so we can shower and change, but I have meetings today."

"Do you want us to take her to work?"

"You and I both know you need to ask her that question."

Zeke chuckled. "Good point. Walker's with her now. She seems to like him."

"He saved her life. I like him, too."

Zeke grinned. "He's a good guy. One of us will be with her all day."

"Thank you."

Zeke nodded.

"Do you have a ride here?"

Zeke pointed to a black SUV a few spots from Gage's vehicle. "I saw you walking out and wanted to find out what you were doing today. Montgomery talked to Lorelei Sloane. She said Ms. Patterson wants us instead of them."

Gage nodded. "She doesn't trust the FBI after the way things went last time they were supposed to be watching her."

"Don't blame her. I wouldn't be too thrilled with that, either. For now, Walker and I are on her case and will likely be together for most of it. We might have another team take the night shift, but we can talk about that. If you're at your house, we might just turn things over to the team watching the house."

Gage nodded. "Thanks. We can all talk later and see what Dawn thinks."

"Sounds good. Thanks. We'll be right behind you to your place and will wait until you two are ready to go. Since her vehicle is still at Davis Developments, we'll see if she's open to riding with us and go from there."

"Thanks, Zeke."

"Happy to help."

Gage got in his SUV and drove around to the door. Dawn was laughing at something Walker said, the nurse smiling at both of them. Gage parked and got out to help

Dawn get into the SUV. Between him and Walker, they guided her steps and got her settled in the front seat.

The nurse told them to have a good day.

Walker jumped in with Zeke, and they all went toward Gage's house.

"Walker and Zeke are going to stay with you all day. They offered to drive you to Davis Developments since they're going to stay there."

"That works. I've put you out enough."

"Never. Not even a little."

"Thanks."

Zeke and Walker insisted on clearing the house before Gage and Dawn went inside, even though the alarms hadn't shown any activity. The two men stayed downstairs while Gage and Dawn went upstairs to shower and change.

Dawn needed help getting changed and in the shower. Seeing her naked had his erection thickening, but with the first hiss of pain, he found it easier to fight his desire.

It took longer than usual, but they got dressed and were out the door again with Zeke and Walker. Dawn kissed Gage before leaving, promising she'd be safe.

Gage had never been so worried about another person's safety in his life. It was not his favorite feeling.

GOING BACK to Davis Developments was harder than Dawn thought it would be. She didn't think about it until Zeke pulled up to the curb and she realized she had to get out and make the same walk she tried to make the day before.

"I'll go with you," Walker said, not hesitating at all. He opened his door, then opened hers, offering his hand to help her out of the large vehicle.

Dawn smiled up at him, hoping the look construed how grateful she was.

He tucked her against his side, putting her on the side opposite of any possible traffic, and waited for her to take the first step.

Dawn drew a deep breath and focused on the door. She couldn't let Trevor stop her from living her life. If she was going to do that, she could have just gone into protection. She refused because she needed to be free.

Dawn took her first step, just far enough for Zeke to pull away from the curb. The sound of the vehicle moving put tension back into Dawn, but Walker's solid presence helped.

He didn't rush her, and he didn't say anything. He let her lead, let her go at her own pace.

Every step brought her closer to the door and farther from the spot she never made it past the day before. When they got to the door, Walker opened it for her and let her go in ahead of him.

Dawn shook uncontrollably without him holding her up. She nearly collapsed, but his strong presence was right beside her again, half-carrying her to the security desk.

"How are you today, Ms. Patterson?" Keith asked.

"It's not easy to be here, but I want to be."

Keith nodded, unlocking the gate for them to go in.

Again, Walker released her to let her go in first and the tremors had her panicking.

Walker was right back at her side, leading her down the hallway toward Tabitha's office. As soon as they made it inside, he closed the door and guided Dawn to the couch off to the side.

"Did something else happen?" Tabitha asked, out of her seat and rushing to Dawn as soon as she saw her.

Dawn shivered and tried to shake her head, but nothing seemed to be working correctly.

"Adrenaline," Walker said. "It happens to a lot of people when they return to where they were attacked. And being only a day later, it's a pretty strong reaction. I figured she felt safe inside, and it was better to get her here instead of having her sit in it outside."

Dawn nodded, or tried to, grateful Walker understood what was happening and believed it was a normal reaction.

Zeke joined them a minute later, and the three of them stared at Dawn while she tried to calm herself down. She'd never experienced anything like that before. But she'd also never been almost run over before.

"I'm fine," she finally whispered.

Zeke thrust a bottle of water under her nose.

Dawn took it, twisted the cap off, and drained the bottle. Walker handed her a candy bar, which she also took gratefully and devoured instantly.

After a minute, the sugar flooded her system and cleared her head.

"Better?" Walker asked.

Dawn nodded, finally feeling like she was being honest with her answer. "Thank you both."

The men nodded and moved to the door. They left the room, leaving Dawn alone with Tabitha.

"At least you brought the eye-candy with you," Tabitha teased.

Dawn snorted. "Only you would make a joke of this."

"You're a strong woman, Dawn. It's a true honor to have you as our leader."

"I think that panic attack proved I'm not as strong as you think."

Tabitha shook her head and breathed a laugh. "That's

exactly why I said it. Most people would run and hide after a panic attack. Or never have come back here anyway."

"I'm not letting that fucker win."

"Good. Then let's close this last loop. I think we finally found it."

"No shit."

Tabitha nodded. "I was about to do it when you walked in. I'll let you have the honor."

Dawn stood from the couch, wobbled a bit, then righted herself. She moved to the desk and saw what Tabitha had been working on. "What an asshole."

Trevor was using their benevolence and pension funds to route his money. Two places that didn't get a lot of attention because contributions and withdrawals were mostly automatic. Somehow, he set up an account for himself to withdraw funds from both. At a fifteen percent bump from what he was putting into each fund to funnel money and avoid detection.

Dawn followed Tabitha's directions and severed the connection Trevor had to those two funds. The last two.

"He's out?" Dawn asked.

Tabitha nodded. "He's out. And he can't get back in the same way. He's done pulling money out of this company."

Dawn burst into tears.

"Oh, my God! Are you okay?" Tabitha asked.

Zeke and Walker rushed into the room, guns drawn and eyes scanning.

"Whoa! Gentlemen, we're good. Guns away," Tabitha barked.

"What happened?" Zeke asked as he holstered his gun.

Walker was a little slower to put his gun away, searching the room and going into the bathroom before he was confident nothing had happened.

"I... I don't know," Tabitha said.

The three of them looked at Dawn and waited.

She hiccuped and sobbed, but worked to calm herself down. "I'm relieved. Happy. I didn't mean to scare everyone. It... We locked him out of our systems and it feels like a huge victory."

"He was in your systems?" Walker asked. "How?"

Tabitha explained the whole thing to him, from finding money flowing out to the deep dive they went through to find every place Trevor was siphoning money from Davis Developments.

"What else did he have access to?" Zeke asked.

"I don't... know. Why?" Tabitha asked.

"Because if he was in your accounts, he could also know what projects you're working on and could be using properties to hide or to move his product or any number of things. And if he was inside everything, we might be able to use the accounts he was pushing money to to track him. Find out where he is."

"You can do that?" Tabitha asked.

Zeke nodded. "We can. We need to get the FBI here now."

Tabitha and Dawn exchanged a look as Zeke made a phone call. In less than twenty minutes, an FBI post was set up in Tabitha's office with a tech expert digging through every transaction that had gone through Davis Developments in the last few weeks.

Dawn struggled to hope it could all be over soon, but there was a part of her that wondered if it was really as easy as this. If it was possible to find Trevor and put an end to all of this with a few keystrokes and some digging.

"Should we have called the FBI?" Tabitha asked.

Dawn shrugged. "It never occurred to me."

"Me either. Did we screw up?"

"No. We were doing what we thought was best. We weren't trying to hide anything. They'll find him. They have to."

By the end of the day, the team was on the way out and Lorelei was barking orders to everyone. They had a few locations to check and a few bank accounts to shut down.

"Thank you for letting us in here today," Lorelei said. "Every day we're closer, but this was a huge help."

"We didn't realize it would help. We should have called before."

Lorelei shook her head. "Not at all. We have this information now. We'll get him. I'm not giving up until we do."

"Thank you," Dawn told her.

Lorelei nodded and led her team out of the office. Without the bustle of the FBI, the office was quiet.

"I think we need a drink," Tabitha said.

Dawn snorted. "Have one for me. Pain meds and alcohol are a bad idea."

Tabitha nodded. "I can definitely do that. And when all of this is really over, I'll buy you a good drink."

"I'm up for that."

Tabitha smiled and packed up her things to head home to her son. She waved to Dawn and the others, hurrying before she missed the chance to be there for dinner with her kid.

"Are you ready?" Walker asked Dawn.

Dawn nodded. She collected her things and was about to walk out the door when her phone rang.

She groaned when she saw Owen's name. She hadn't heard from him since she forgot to get Savannah. Dawn tensed before she even answered.

"Is everything okay?" she asked.

"Okay? No. You were attacked? You spent the night in the hospital? And you didn't call us? Savannah is panicking over here. What the hell, Dawn?"

"How did you find out about that?"

"It was all over the news. The new CEO of Davis Developments was nearly killed in a hit and run. Anyone with any information is asked to call the FBI. What the hell is going on?"

"Shit," Dawn breathed.

"That's not an answer. What happened?"

Dawn sank to a chair and told Owen the whole story. He knew there was a conflict with Trevor, but not the details. As she shared everything, he said all the right things. And then he said the best thing ever.

"Savannah wants to see you. She saw the news, and she wants to have dinner. Tomorrow?"

Dawn couldn't stop her smile. Maybe there was a silver lining to the whole thing. "Yeah, I can do that."

21

———

Dawn sat across the table from Savannah and smiled. It was really good to see her kid, even if she had to almost die for it to happen. Savannah wanted to know everything about the attack. She was worried. Which was nice after being indifferent for so long.

"You're sure you're okay?" Savannah's hazel eyes were lit with emotion.

Dawn nodded. "Yeah. I'll be okay. It was a close call, but the people who are protecting me are amazing and really good at what they do."

"Normal people don't need bodyguards, Mom," Savannah said, eyeing Walker and Zeke, sitting at a table not far from them and trying to blend in. Trying and failing.

Dawn forced a smile. She didn't want Savannah to worry more than she already was. "I know. And when all of this is over, I won't need them. It's temporary."

Savannah scowled into her dinner.

"What?" Dawn asked.

Savannah shook her head. Not a good sign.

"I want you to talk to me, Savannah. I want us to have a relationship again."

"Do you, though?"

Dawn startled at the venom in her daughter's voice. "Why would I not want that?"

"You always told me actions speak louder than words, Mom. That was what you said. And your actions don't tell me you want a relationship with me."

"I'm sorry for that," Dawn said, lowering her voice in hopes Savannah would do the same. "I am not the person I was eighteen months ago."

"Are you sure?"

A slap would have hurt less. "How can you ask me that?"

Savannah shook her head. Tears shone in her eyes. She swiped at one as it fell. She rolled her lips in, avoiding Dawn's gaze.

"Why do you think I haven't changed?" Dawn asked, hating how desperate she was for the answer. She'd worked hard to not be the person she was when she overdosed and almost died. She never wanted to be that way again. Savannah was her motivation for all of it. Not just making up for what Savannah had to go through, but wanting to build something with Savannah. Wanting to regain her trust.

"Have you, Mom? Really, have you?"

"Well, I think so. I went to rehab. I worked to help others. I stayed away from people who could influence me in that way."

"Just not from people who want to kill you," Savannah snapped.

"How can you say that's my fault?"

"You chose this. You told Dad you knew it was danger-ous. But you chose it anyway. You decided to do this.

You're not different. It's the same thing over and over again."

"Savannah," Dawn started, but she trailed off. Was it true? Did she accept the money because she couldn't resist the risk?

"Why didn't you say no?" Savannah asked.

Dawn took a minute before she answered. In the moment, it was the right choice. But if she knew then what she knew now, would she have made the same decision?

Dawn knew she would have. She knew she couldn't let Trevor, or anyone else, intimidate her and convince her to walk away from the people she'd met. They didn't deserve to be at the end of his wrath anymore than she did.

"The man who left me all of this, Mr. Davis, was a patient of mine. He was kind and thoughtful. He never once made me feel like I wasn't good enough. He saw me for all of me."

"You sound like you're in love with him," Savannah said with a scowl.

Dawn shook her head. "There are many different kinds of love, and a part of me did love him. He was like a father to me at a time when I didn't think I needed that. Mr. Davis knew everything. He knew about my mistakes. And he still decided I was good enough to run his company and save it from his son."

"So you blame me?"

"What? No. When did I say that?"

"You said he thinks you're good enough, implying you think I don't."

Dawn shook her head, wondering how in the world the conversation went so far off the rails. "No. That's not what I meant at all. I didn't think I was good enough. I didn't think I deserved anything. He left me a letter asking me to help, asking me to do this. He had no one else. One son was dead, his wife was dead, and his living son is obviously not a great person."

"Obviously."

"I knew there was a risk, but I didn't know it would be like this. I thought he'd be angry."

"Angry enough to try to kill you," Savannah breathed, her emotions coming through in her words.

Dawn nodded, choosing not to tell her daughter that Trevor did kill others. Savannah didn't need to know that. "There are a lot of people looking for him."

"What if he comes after you again?"

"That's why Zeke and Walker are with me. They're part of a whole team of people that are watching out for me. It's what they do."

Savannah was quiet for a minute. She pushed her food around on her plate, not eating.

Dawn waited her out. Her stomach was in knots waiting for what Savannah was going to ask next. What bomb her daughter was going to drop.

"Is that why you didn't pick me up the other day? Because someone was after you? Dad said you were at work."

It was an out. A chance to repair a tiny bit of their relationship. But it wasn't the truth. Dawn debated for half a second, but she couldn't lie to Savannah. "No. I was at work. I was in the middle of something and completely forgot."

Savannah's hopeful expression crumbled. She looked down at her lap and picked at her fingers.

Dawn waited. She wanted the chance to apologize to Savannah that day and didn't get it. She had to take it.

"I'm sorry I forgot. That I left you there. I had every

intention of getting you. I have no excuse and no explanation, but I am sorry."

Savannah shrugged, feigning indifference. "I don't know why I would expect anything else."

"Savannah."

"Mom, don't. I've never been the most important person in your life. I'm a burden, an inconvenience. I always knew it, but you're showing me over and over again. And now you have all this money and this big job and this danger, and I'm still last in line."

"Savannah."

"No," Savannah said, sweeping tears from her cheeks. "Don't try to tell me I'm wrong. I know it's the truth. If I was important, you wouldn't have left me there. If I mattered, you wouldn't have gotten so high you almost died. I had to give you CPR. Do you know how terrifying that was? To think I wasn't going to be good enough? That I was going to be the reason you died? I still have nightmares about that, and now you're involved with someone who wants you dead and you have bodyguards and you're telling me you care about me. But you don't. You don't. You just don't."

"That's not true, Savannah."

Savannah threw her napkin on the table and stood. She shook her head and rushed off.

Zeke was right behind her. Dawn told Owen they would bring Savannah home, and Zeke was likely doing just that.

Dawn didn't move. She wasn't sure she could. She felt bruised and broken. Because Savannah wasn't wrong. Dawn made a lot of choices that meant Savannah wasn't first. She never put Savannah first.

And it was going to cost her any chance at a relationship with her daughter.

Something had to change.

Gage waited up for Dawn to come home after her dinner with Savannah. He checked the clock for the tenth time in the last five minutes. He thought Dawn would be home already, but he hadn't heard from her.

Headlights flashed across the living room. The lights pointed at the house for another minute. Someone was in the driveway. The footsteps outside were no more subtle than the bright lights on his house, telling Gage whoever was there was not trying to be sneaky.

The door opened, and Dawn moved to the alarm panel to disarm then arm the alarm system. She turned, jumping when she saw Gage on the couch.

"How was dinner?" he asked, getting up and moving toward her in the hallway.

Dawn breathed a laugh that didn't sound like it was humorous.

"Did something happen?"

"Savannah thinks I'm a horrible mother."

"What? She's wrong. You're amazing."

Dawn was already shaking her head. "No, she's not wrong. I've put myself ahead of her so many times I've lost count. What kind of parent does that? What kind of parent chooses their own shit over their kid?"

"A real one," Gage said. He gripped her arms, waiting for her to look at him. "No parent is perfect. And sometimes you have to do what you think is right long term instead of short term."

"You don't have kids. You don't get it," Dawn said.

Gage inhaled sharply and stepped back. People had said the same thing to him so many times he was surprised it still bothered him, but it did.

"I didn't mean—"

"Yes, you did," he interrupted. "But you're right. I'm not allowed to have an opinion because I don't have kids."

"Don't be an ass," she spat.

Gage let his breath out slowly, counting to ten as he exhaled. He didn't want to blow up at her, but it was getting harder to keep his emotions in check.

"Savannah was pissed, and I'm... I don't know. I'm just not in a great mood right now. She's not wrong about the things she said. I almost died, and she had to save me. I chose to do what Robert asked, even though I knew there were risks. Hell, I forgot to pick my kid up from school and left her there alone. Not to mention the hundred times I didn't put her first. When I didn't try harder with my marriage, when I let Owen take the lead with Savannah, when I got involved with a man who was wrong for me and let him be around her. There are so many examples, so many times I didn't do the right thing. And I'm paying for it now. I'm going to lose her, and I deserve it."

"How can you say that?"

"Because it's true! Because we don't get a million chances with people. I might not survive tomorrow, and my daughter will live the rest of her life thinking I didn't care. That I didn't care enough."

"She knows you love her."

"You've never met her. You have no idea what she knows."

Gage stifled the growl in his throat.

"I need to put Savannah first. I need to change the way I've been living my life."

"What does that mean?"

Dawn looked around the room, not meeting his gaze, and he knew what her next words were going to be.

"I need to go back to my place. I need to stand on my own and do what is right for my family. For my kid. I need to... I can't be with you."

She whispered the last sentence like it hurt her as much to say as it hurt Gage to hear, but that wasn't possible. She couldn't possibly feel like her heart was torn from her chest and stomped on. She was the one doing the stomping, not him. She was the one choosing to end things.

But he had to let her. He promised her Savannah would always come first. He meant those words, and if she thought the only way to do that was to end things with him, he would let her.

"Okay," he said without any argument or emotion.

She sucked in a breath, like she expected him to say something else and was surprised by his easy acceptance.

"Do you want me to take you back tonight or tomorrow?"

"I have my own vehicle," she said.

Gage nodded, understanding she wanted nothing else from him.

"Is it okay if I stay here again tonight, though? I can have Walker and Zeke put a security system in at my apartment tomorrow. Or I can go to a hotel or something."

"No," Gage said, more forcefully than he intended. "You can stay here. Stay safe with the alarm and the cameras. We can figure out the rest tomorrow. You can, I mean."

Dawn nodded. "Thank you."

Gage didn't know what else he could say, so he said nothing.

Dawn stared at him for a minute, then pressed her lips into a small smile and went for the stairs.

Gage waited until she was at the top before he sat down again. He leaned forward and dropped his head into his hands, wishing things were different for them. Her life was complicated and dangerous, but he was willing to wade in. He'd never been willing before. Not with any of his exes. He'd kept them at arm's length during their entire relationship and told himself it wasn't right.

But with Dawn, it was right. He couldn't explain how he felt, but listening to her upstairs, getting ready for bed and knowing he wouldn't be pulling her close and sliding into her, made him want to tear his skin off.

It would have been less painful than watching her walk away.

The bedroom door closed, and the bed creaked when she sat down. Gage sighed and stood. He turned off the lights and confirmed the alarm was set and the door was locked, then he went upstairs and got ready for bed. Alone.

TREVOR GOT out of the SUV and walked down the street. It was dark, quiet. No one was out, and no one was awake.

Perfect.

He moved up the driveway, past the fancy new vehicle that bitch who stole his inheritance bought with his money. She would pay for what she did.

But first, he needed to get back into the accounts. Get access back so he could make his money. She was going to regret cutting off his funnel.

Trevor nudged the window he unlocked when he was at the lawyer's house looking for the will. He was careful not to touch a thing in the small dining room off the kitchen. It looked like a room no one used much, and the fact that the window was still open told him he was right.

He had Plan B, but he liked the element of surprise.

Letting himself in the front door and turning off the alarm would send up flags and probably put his face in front of that group of idiots that called themselves professionals.

Professionals his ass. They were barely better than amateurs. Not only did they not lock the window, but they put the alarm panel within full view of the street out front. Anyone with a good enough camera could watch the code as it was entered to disarm the alarm system.

"Fucking morons," Trevor whispered to himself.

The window slid open with no resistance, and no sound. It was a bit of a stretch to get into it, but the boss liked acrobatics in bed, and wherever else she let him take her, so Trevor was working out. Anything to make sure she stayed happy.

Trevor pulled himself up easily enough and got his upper body through the window. He had to maneuver a little to fit through the window, but he made it work and landed inside with little more than a thud that no one was likely to hear.

Just in case, he stilled and waited to make sure the house stayed silent.

After a minute of nothing, Trevor moved through the house, leaving the window open in case he needed to make a quick escape.

The kitchen was spotless, as it had been on his first visit. The lawyer was a bit of a neat freak, or he never ate at home. Trevor didn't care. The point was to leave no trace, except the trace he wanted to leave.

The bathroom door was open, and the space was dark. The living room was lit from the streetlights out front, but no one was in the space. Trevor glanced at the alarm panel and debated turning it off, but touching it could alert the company that something different was going on. Best the leave that for later.

He crept up the stairs, his knife in his gloved hand and ready to use. Trevor knew the lawyer and the fat nurse were fucking. Had seen the lights come on in the bedroom in the back but nothing in the front. He would take his time with her when he had the chance, but first, he needed to get to her.

And get rid of the lawyer.

Trevor made it to the top of the stairs. He remembered the first time he broke into a house to kill someone. His heart pounded hard with every step. But he wasn't a fucking pussy, and he slit the man's throat without a second thought. And threw up down the street. But no one knew that. And no one ever would.

Trevor was no longer that scared dipshit kid. His hands didn't shake. His heart didn't pound. Murder was part of his job. And he was good at it. One slice and the lawyer would never tell a soul he was there.

Trevor took a step toward the bedroom. It was less than three feet away. The door was partially open. He could only see one person in the bed, but it wouldn't take him long to figure out which side of the bed was the lawyer's.

He pushed the door open just enough to see the whole bed when he heard a sound behind him.

A door.

The bed only had one lump. Which meant.

"Gage!"

The lump sat upright, his gaze searching before it landed on Trevor.

"Dawn, run!" he shouted, scrambling out of bed and rushing toward Trevor.

The door slammed behind him, but Trevor didn't care. He'd get her after he was done with the lawyer.

The lawyer came for him. The weight of his blade was reassuring in his hand. Solid. Steady.

Trevor waited until the lawyer was close, then slashed.

A hiss told Trevor the blow landed.

He struck out again, but the lawyer dodged that one.

The lawyer moved forward, like he had a chance in the fight.

Trevor swung, and the lawyer blocked it, then swung his fist.

The punch caught Trevor off-guard. He took a step back.

And found air.

He was falling.

Down the stairs.

His hand hit the wall. The knife clattered to the wooden steps, bouncing with Trevor's body down, down, down. Until both came to rest at the bottom.

22

———

"Is he dead?" Dawn breathed. She opened her door when she heard someone fall down the stairs. The relief she felt when she saw Gage standing at the top was unmeasurable.

Gage shook his head. "I don't think so. We need to call the police."

"They're on the way."

"Did you call Marcus or nine-one-one?"

"Nine-one-one. Mackenzie answered. She was going to send someone on duty and let Marcus know."

Gage stared down the stairs and nodded. "Good. Thank you."

"Are you okay?" Dawn asked, moving closer.

Gage swayed, like he was having a hard time staying upright. When he stumbled and nearly fell down the stairs himself, Dawn gasped.

"Are you hurt? Gage!"

"Get my phone. There's an alert button on the app for the alarm. It'll bring that team here, too."

"Not until you let me help you."

Gage looked up at her, his eyes dark and glassy. He was hurt worse than she realized. When he nodded, she knew it was bad.

Dawn positioned herself under his arm, but when he winced, she moved to the other side. He let her drape his arm over her shoulder, and he worked to stand upright instead of the severe lean against the wall.

He shuffled his feet slowly, barely supporting his own weight. Dawn tried not to panic at the amount of his weight she was carrying. It meant he was weak. Losing blood, most likely. Fast.

Dawn got him to his bed and lifted his shirt. A deep gash on his side had already soaked the sheets under his body. "Oh, God."

He grunted, not offering much in terms of aid or words.

Dawn ran to the bathroom and grabbed a clean towel from the cabinet. She hurried back to the bedroom and pressed the towel against his side as she heard the first sirens.

"Thank God," she whispered. Tears filled her vision, but she knew they were going to be okay.

Someone pounded on the door, but Dawn couldn't leave Gage to let them in. They would have to let themselves in somehow.

A second later, the splinter of wood told her they'd done exactly that.

"Police Department!"

"Upstairs!" Dawn yelled back. "He needs an ambulance!"

Footsteps rushed toward her. A man came into view, but in the dark she had no idea what he looked like.

"Is anyone else here?"

"Not upstairs. The man at the bottom of the stairs

attacked us. He got in somehow. I got up to use the bathroom and saw him coming in here. Gage told me to run, so I went back into the other bedroom and Gage fought with him, but Gage is hurt. He needs a doctor."

The police officer listened and checked the closet and bathroom before moving to her room while she spoke. When he came back in, his gun was in the holster. "An ambulance is on the way."

"Is Trevor dead?"

"I thought you said his name was Gage?"

Dawn nodded to Gage. "He's Gage. The man at the bottom of the stairs is Trevor Davis."

More footsteps sounded on the stairs, and the cop turned to see his partner.

"House is clear."

"Thank God he didn't bring anyone else."

"Who didn't? Did you attack this man?" the second cop said.

"No! He's... No. Why would I do that? The man at the bottom of the stairs did this. He broke in and tried to kill Gage. Probably me, too."

The officers exchanged a look. The second one shook his head, and the first turned to her. "Ma'am, I'm sorry, but we have no idea what you're talking about. There was no man at the bottom of the stairs when we came in."

"What?" Dawn breathed.

"The only people in the house are you and the man who's bleeding. And us."

"No," Dawn whispered.

Before anyone could say anything else, the alarm screeched, telling all of them and half the neighborhood there was an intruder.

Gage's phone rang, but Dawn ignored it. Rose Protection

Agency would be there soon, and so would Marcus and the FBI and half the city. But until that happened, Dawn needed to make sure Gage didn't lose anymore blood.

"Where's the ambulance?" Dawn snapped.

Just as she asked, someone else appeared on the stairs. This one was a paramedic.

"What happened? And can we turn that alarm off?"

Dawn explained what happened and let the paramedic push her out of the way. Dawn went downstairs to silence the alarm with the cops on her heels as a second paramedic hurried upstairs.

"You can't leave, ma'am," one said.

"I'm trying to get the alarm to stop screaming," Dawn said, punching in the code and not getting anything to work. She tried again, and it finally fell silent.

Except for the ringing.

Dawn moved toward the stairs to get Gage's phone, but one of the cops pulled a gun on her.

"Stop!" he shouted. "Hands up!"

Dawn froze. Her eyes went wide. She stared at the cop, her gaze locked on his gun.

"You need to stay away from the man upstairs."

"Do you think I stabbed him? I told you it was Trevor Davis!"

"No one else was in the house, ma'am."

Dawn moved toward where Trevor had ended up, a spot she stepped over. All the lights were still off, which made it hard to see anything.

"Freeze!" the cop shouted again.

Dawn's emotions boiled up and over. She was scared and angry and being accused of trying to kill the man she loved instead of helping him. All she was doing was trying to survive, and instead of helping her, the police officers were accusing her of the worst thing imaginable.

"Are you going to shoot me? You really think I did this? Who called nine-one-one? I was helping him! Why would I have a towel pressed to his side if I was the one who stabbed him? Huh? What is wrong with you? You're going to kill me because you can't pull your head out of your fucking ass and look for evidence!"

"What's going on here?" another voice boomed.

Everyone turned to see Captain Marcus Patrick, followed by Agents Lorelei Sloane and Adam Johnson. Not far behind them were Walker and Zeke.

"Thank God," Dawn whispered, then she sank to the ground, all her fight leaving her.

The cop heard her fall and pointed his gun at her again.

Dawn didn't have the strength to fight him. If he was going to shoot her, she was going to just have to die.

"Officer! Holster your weapon!" Marcus shouted.

The cop looked between Dawn and Marcus.

"Now!"

The cop finally put his gun away, and Marcus grabbed him by the collar. "You pulled your gun on an innocent civilian? What were you thinking?"

"She said there was another man in the house, but we didn't find any evidence of that."

The light in the hallway came on, illuminating the entire space. Including the blood on the floor.

"You mean like that evidence?" Adam asked with a sneer.

"We... I..." the officer said.

Marcus grabbed the other officer and dragged both of them out of the house.

Adam moved toward Dawn and offered her a hand. "Is Gage okay?"

Dawn shook her head, tears falling freely. "He's upstairs. Trevor was here. He got in somehow. He stabbed Gage, and Gage pushed him down the stairs. I... I thought he was dead."

Lorelei took off up the stairs, announcing herself to the paramedics and offering assistance.

"They'll take care of him. Are you okay?"

Dawn nodded. "Gage told me to run. I couldn't really go anywhere, but I went into my room and called the police."

"That was all you could do."

Lorelei and the paramedics stomped down the stairs, with Gage strapped onto a backboard.

"Oh, my God," Dawn breathed.

"He's alive. Meet us at the hospital," Lorelei said, directing her words to Adam.

Adam nodded.

"You might want to change before you leave here," Lorelei told Dawn.

Dawn looked down at her clothes and realized she was still in the tiny shorts and see-through tank top she'd slept in, and both were covered in blood. She moved to cover herself with her arms, but Adam gave her his jacket.

"Thanks."

"If it helps, I didn't notice until Lorelei said something."

Dawn pressed her lips into a smile.

Lorelei and the paramedics left, and Zeke and Walker came in.

"What did you find?" Adam asked them.

"Window into the dining room was open. He must have gotten in through there. Wasn't broken so I'm guessing it was unlocked." Zeke looked at Dawn. "Do you remember locking it?"

Dawn shook her head. "I think I've been in there once since I came here."

"He could have left it unlocked the last time he was here. Just waiting," Zeke said.

"That's a scary thought," Dawn said.

Zeke nodded. "It is. But he's gone now."

"Yeah, but she can't stay here. The cops kicked in the door. It's not secure," Walker said.

"I know. We'll get you in a safe house for the night and go from there," Zeke said.

"I want to see Gage," Dawn said.

The three men exchanged a look. One that said they were all going to try to talk her out of that idea.

"We all know Trevor was here for me. Gage was protecting me. I'm not going to let him lay in a hospital bed alone. Not when it's my fault," Dawn insisted.

Zeke and Walker shrugged.

Adam nodded. "Fine, but Lorelei's going to be pissed."

"I don't care what she thinks," Dawn said.

"She's a good agent," Adam said. "Best partner I've ever worked with. I know that protection detail getting pulled was a major fuck-up, but she got her ass handed to her for ordering them to watch you in the first place."

"Why?"

"Because it wasn't allowed. She didn't care. Our boss ripped her a new one, and when Dr. Walden's body ended up on your doorstep, she had the restraint to not tell him *I told you so*. She wanted to, but she knew that wouldn't get you the protection you needed. She is on your side," Adam said.

"I guess that's good."

"Go change. Then we'll all go to the hospital. She did tell you to meet her there."

"I thought she was telling you that," Dawn said.

Adam shrugged. "Not real clear. We can play dumb."

Dawn snorted and knew none of those men were anywhere close to dumb, but she appreciated the idea.

GAGE SCOWLED at everyone who came into his room. He did not want to be in the hospital. He knew he lost a lot of blood and was lucky, but he felt fine after they gave him blood and fluids and stitched up the gash on his side.

The pain killers probably helped, too.

There were a lot of conversations happening without his involvement, and that pissed him off more than anything else. He didn't like people making decisions for him. Ever.

Marcus finally walked into the room. Gage scowled, but he was at least grateful to see a friendly face.

"How are you feeling?"

"Pissed off. What the hell is going on out there without my input?"

Marcus sighed. "We're putting you into protective custody. Around the clock."

Gage shook his head. "No. Not happening."

"You no longer have a choice. You're injured, and you're in danger."

"He's not after me, and we all know it."

"Actually, we don't," Marcus said.

"What the hell are you talking about?"

"Rose Protection Agency said he got in through a window in the dining room. Unless you're in the habit of leaving that window unlocked, we believe he left it unlocked when he was at your house a month ago."

"Are you kidding me?"

"No. Which is why we think he might be after you, too. At that point, Dawn wasn't staying with you. There was no reason for him to plan to come back to your house except for you."

"Fuck."

"Rose Protection Agency is already working on where they're going to take you guys. They're going to be in charge, and Lorelei is the only one who's going to know where you will be."

"I fucking hate this," Gage said. "Wait? You guys? Dawn agreed to this?"

"Lorelei and Adam are talking to her right now."

"She's not going to go for it. She ended things with me last night. Said she needs to focus on her kid. There's no way she'll be okay with going into hiding. Especially not with me."

"I don't think she's going to get a choice. This is no longer an optional thing."

Gage sighed. On the one hand, he was happy to have more time with her. On the other, she was going to be mad. And he didn't blame her.

But he'd rather she was mad than dead.

"I'll do whatever I need to do," Gage said.

TREVOR SAT behind the wheel of the SUV and waited in line. He fucking hated waiting. Almost as much as he hated that bitch and the fucking lawyer.

He wished he'd killed them both. Instead, he barely

made it out of the house before the cops arrived. His head still fucking hurt four days later. If he went to a doctor, they were sure to tell him he had a concussion, but he wasn't going to a doctor.

A car pulled away, and he eased forward. He studied all the kids walking out. Talking, laughing, living their boring fucking lives. By the time he was their age, he'd already learned about the reality of the world. Kill or be killed. That was how things worked.

A horn behind him had him ready to jump out of the SUV and beat the fucker to a bloody fucking pulp, but then he saw her.

If he hadn't been studying her picture, he still would have recognized her. He rolled down the window and waved to get her attention.

She looked over at him, then at her friends. The other two girls shook their heads.

"Savannah!" Trevor shouted, forcing a smile to his face.

She stopped in the middle of the sidewalk. Her eyes widened.

"How does he know your name?" one of the girls asked.

Savannah shook her head. "I don't know."

"I work with your mom," Trevor said. "Didn't she tell you about the protection she has now?"

"Rose Protection Agency?" Savannah asked, stepping closer to the SUV.

Trevor nodded. "Yeah. She asked me to get you."

"Why?"

"She's stuck at work again. You know how she is. Sorry, kid."

Savannah shook her head. "She wasn't supposed to pick me up. My dad is."

"Oh, that. Your dad got tied up with something. He

called your mom in a panic. He didn't want to because he knows she's not all that reliable, but she knew I wouldn't forget to grab you."

"Do you know him?" one friend asked.

Savannah shook her head.

"Maybe you should call your mom," one girl said.

"Or your dad," the other said.

"You can come home with me," the first one said.

Another horn blasted behind Trevor. He looked up in the rearview mirror but kept the nasty words inside. If she was suspicious at all, she wouldn't get in the SUV. And he needed her to get in the SUV. Kidnapping was much easier when no one knew it was happening right in front of their stupid fucking faces.

"Savannah, come on," the second one said.

"It's fine," Savannah said. "My mom has this group she's working with. Their SUVs are like this one. And look." She turned her phone around to show the text Trevor sent from her dad's phone. "My dad texted me and said Mom would be getting me, so this isn't a shock."

"Your mom is the worst," friend two said.

"I wish you had someone better," friend one agreed.

Savannah shrugged. "We don't get to choose our parents."

The girls grunted.

Another horn almost had Trevor reaching for his gun, but the girls turned to the vehicle and made faces at them. Trevor watched the driver throw their hands up. The girls flipped them off, and the driver returned the gesture.

"We should go before that lady loses her shit," friend two said. "Call me later."

Savannah hugged friend two and nodded. "Of course." She turned to friend one and hugged her. "Me, too."

"Bye hun!" the girls said before walking down the line toward the other vehicles.

Savannah opened the passenger door and got in, shoving her backpack at her feet. She buckled her seatbelt and settled into the seat.

Trevor pulled out of line and rolled up the windows, sealing them inside from the world around them. He turned onto the main road and headed toward his compound. The one the police searched the week before. They were so dumb. They went down the list in numerical order. Like he wouldn't figure out exactly where they were going.

He loved stupid cops. Made his job easier.

"Where are we going?" Savannah asked.

"To get your mom," Trevor said.

"Oh, okay." She pulled her phone out of her bag and unlocked it. "Oh, what's your name? I forgot to ask."

"Trevor."

She stilled, the name meaning something to her.

Trevor grinned.

"Trevor?" she breathed.

He looked over at her and nodded. "Trevor Davis. Nice to meet you, Savannah. Time for a nap."

He swung before she could react, knocking her out with one punch. Such a sweet sound.

23

─────────

"Are you fucking kidding me? How in the hell did that happen? No. No. Why do you think that's a good idea? No. You're fucking nuts. There's no way I can keep that from her. It's wrong. I don't fucking care what you say. How would you feel—? Yeah, I know, and that's why I'm saying that. I don't agree with it. Fine. Fine!"

Dawn hated being treated like she wasn't capable of making her own decisions. Like she was a charity case or a child or something.

It had been three days since she and Gage left the hospital and were whisked away to a safe house. Three days since she'd been allowed to contact anyone. Not that she was allowed to do so before they took her from the hospital like she was a criminal and not the victim.

She hated that fucking word, and the longer she stayed inside the house, being watched like she was going to go off the rails at any moment, the more she hated the word victim.

She wasn't a victim. And she wasn't going to let Trevor do any more damage than he'd already done.

Which meant finding out what in the hell was going on.

Zeke was standing in the kitchen of the house they'd all been sharing for three days. Being alone with three men should have been something fun, but it was the farthest thing from fun. The mood around the place was strained, and not just between Dawn and Gage. Zeke and Walker were off, too. Everyone was off. Because they all knew this wasn't the answer. Not forever.

"Who was that?" Dawn asked, not making her presence known to Zeke before she spoke. She wanted to catch him off-guard and get him to be honest with her before he came up with a story that was bullshit.

"Montgomery."

"What does he want you to keep from me?"

Zeke looked up at Dawn. The battle waged in his gaze. Pain and regret were clear, and both gave Dawn an insight into the man who seemed like he didn't have emotions. Not that Zeke was cold, but he wasn't overly friendly. Not the same way Walker had been with her.

Of course, everyone said that was different for Walker, so what the hell did Dawn know?

"Savannah is missing."

"What?" Dawn screeched. "My daughter? How in the fuck did he think you could keep that from me?"

"Getting emotional leads to unnecessary risk." His voice was devoid of emotion, and his gaze held the weight of something Dawn didn't know anything about. But he knew what he was talking about.

Tears streamed down her cheeks. She shook her head. "We're talking about my child. My blood. The person I would do anything for. Of course I'm emotional."

"Which is dangerous."

"What's dangerous?" Gage asked from behind Dawn. He

was still weak and groggy from the blood loss, but he looked better every day.

"Trevor has Savannah," Dawn said.

"What?" Gage barked. He glared at Zeke. "How in the hell did you let that happen?"

Zeke shook his head. "I only just found out. I don't have all the information yet, but he attacked your ex-husband and tied him up. Then he went to school and told your daughter you sent him there because your ex called and asked you to help and you were busy."

"It sounds like you know a lot," Dawn said, sucking in a ragged breath and trying to stop the tears that fell freely.

"She was with two friends when she left with Trevor."

"When was this?" Gage asked.

"This afternoon. He picked her up from school today," Zeke said.

"Why are we sitting around here talking about this and not out looking for her?" Gage asked.

"Because we know he's using Savannah to get to Dawn," Zeke said.

"So let me go. Let me trade myself for her," Dawn said.

Zeke shook his head. "We can't do that. Trading one life for another—"

"She's my daughter! I'm not going to stand here and let him torture and kill her. He will..." Fear overwhelmed Dawn. She sank to the floor and sobbed. She didn't want to think about the things Trevor would do to her daughter. She knew enough about the man to know it would be bad. Very bad.

"We will find her," Zeke said.

"How?"

"He sent a video," Zeke said.

"What? Show me," Dawn demanded.

"I don't—"

"Show me the fucking video now," Dawn growled at him. She didn't care that he was bigger and stronger and had all the power. She could lift a car if she needed to. Her daughter was missing, and the one piece of evidence they had was in his hand.

Zeke looked between Dawn and Gage, then unlocked his phone. A few seconds later, he flipped it around so Dawn could see the screen.

Her throat closed up. Savannah was unconscious. A large bruise covered the side of her face. Her eye was swollen. Dawn clapped a hand over her mouth to keep from screaming.

Then he spoke.

"You had your chances to back off. To stop what you were doing. I have been patient. But the time for patience is done. You will come to me, alone. You will restore my access to my money, to what I earned with a lifetime of kissing that old man's ass. He got what he deserved when I put a pillow over his face and watched him die. Your daughter will get what she deserves if you don't do what I say."

Trevor reached out and slapped Savannah right on top of her bruise. She startled and blinked her eyes open. Fear immediately filled them. She tried to scream, but a gag was slipped over her mouth from behind. Her shoulders moved, but her hands were tied somewhere below the view of the camera. Tears fell from her eyes.

"Say hi to your mom, Savannah. Maybe you'll see her again. But we both know how unreliable she is, so you might just get to spend your last days with me. We can have so much fun together." He trailed a finger down her throat. It disappeared below the screen.

Savannah screamed against the gag and tried to get away from him. Then the screen went dark.

"I have to go," Dawn said.

"He'll kill you," Zeke said.

"Do you think I care about myself? Do you really fucking think I care? That sick monster has my daughter. She's fourteen! I will trade my life for hers in a second."

"He'll probably kill you both," Zeke said.

"I won't let him."

"It's not an option, Dawn. I'm sorry, but I'm not letting you out of this house."

Dawn stared at the man she thought was there to help her. She hated him in that moment. As much as she hated Trevor. Because Zeke was keeping her from saving her daughter. And that was not okay.

GAGE WATCHED as Dawn ran down the hallway away from Zeke. She slammed the door to the bedroom she'd been staying in.

Zeke sighed heavily. "I know she doesn't understand, but if we let her go, we lose them both."

"There's no way she's ever going to be okay with that. You know what he's capable of."

Zeke nodded. "I know. Montgomery didn't want her to know about this at all. He knew this would be her reaction."

"Then why did you tell her?"

"She overheard my call with him. She knew something was going on."

"And you didn't do that on purpose? You didn't have that conversation in a common area of this house with the thought that maybe she'd overhear it?"

Zeke glared at Gage. "Montgomery's sister disappeared more than a decade ago. She was... she was family to me, too. I was at their house the night she left. There was a lot going on at that time, but I saw her trying to sneak out. I knew she did it a lot. She always came back, but that night she didn't. No one's seen her since. She vanished, like a ghost."

"I had no idea."

Zeke shook his head. "He doesn't talk about it. He blames himself. Thinks there was more he could have done or should have done. He never once blamed me, even though I could have stopped her. But losing someone like that, someone who you love so much that you'd give your life for theirs... I knew keeping it from Dawn wouldn't make the outcome any easier."

"What would you have done? If you could have traded yourself for his sister? Would you have done it?"

"In a heartbeat." His answer was immediate, and the pain in his eyes said she was more than just a sister to him.

"You loved her."

Zeke held Gage's gaze but didn't answer. "It was my fault. I should have stopped her from leaving."

"And you know that's how Dawn's feeling right now. So help her."

"I can't. She's my job. To keep her from leaving. I'm not going to make the same mistake twice. To watch another woman walk out the door and know she's never coming back."

His words hit Gage square in the chest. Letting Dawn go... He'd never see her again. But she'd never forgive herself if Savannah died.

Savannah was innocent. Just like Gage's mother. Wrong

place, wrong time. She got in the middle of something she had no influence on. She was unlucky.

And she was going to die for it.

"I'm going to go talk to her," Gage said. "See if I can talk her down."

Zeke nodded. "Thanks. I know you love her. I know you understand how I feel. She'll understand one day that this was the only option."

"Do you know where Trevor is?"

Zeke shook his head. "No. But it must be somewhere he thinks Dawn would know if he's asking her to meet him."

Gage nodded, thinking through the possible options. There weren't many.

"Tell her I'm sorry," Zeke said.

Gage smiled at the man and almost felt guilty for what he was going to do. But not guilty enough. "I will."

Gage shuffled back to the bedrooms and knocked on the door to Dawn's bedroom.

"What?" she shouted.

"Can I come in?"

She barked a mirthless laugh. "It's not like I have a lot of choices about anything right now."

Gage opened the door and walked in. He closed the door again and leaned against it so he would hear if anyone got close to the bedroom door. "What's your plan?"

"Why? So you can rat me out?"

Gage shook his head. "No, so I can help you get out of here without them knowing."

"You're going to help me?"

"I told you Savannah always comes first. Always. I know Trevor's going to try to kill you, probably both of you, but I know you'll never survive if she dies because you didn't go to her."

"Gage." Dawn broke, collapsing onto the floor again.

Gage moved to her and sat down next to her. He ached to hold her. He put his hand on her back so she knew he was there, and was surprised when she crawled onto his lap and buried her face in his neck.

"I can't let him hurt her. I just keep thinking she's going to die alone and he's going to do horrible things to her before he kills her."

"No. Don't go there. You need to be able to think clearly. First, you need to figure out where he is. Did it look familiar at all?"

"No. Why would I know where he is?"

"He sent that video to you. I'm guessing he sent it to your phone. You were the one who needed to see it. He told you to come to him alone. Do you have any idea where he would be?"

"No, he... He has to be at the office. At Davis Developments. That's the only place I would have access to the accounts. He said he wants his money. It has to be that."

"Okay, good. I'm not sure exactly where we are, but you're probably at least ten miles from there. You don't want to walk that far."

"There's an SUV in the garage."

"Yeah, but they'll hear you if you go there. Do you know how to hot-wire a car?"

She snorted. "Who do you think I am?"

"Is that a yes or a no?"

"Uh, that's a no. Got any other ideas?"

Gage shook his head. "I guess I'll have to distract them long enough for you to flee in the SUV in the garage."

"Why are you doing this?"

"Because I love you. And because if I could have saved my mom, I would have. I don't want to lose you, Dawn, but if

Savannah is killed, you're going to blame yourself. You already blame yourself for her being kidnapped. You won't survive if she doesn't."

More tears fell down her cheeks. "You love me?"

Gage nodded. "I know you don't want to be with me, and I respect that, but I want you to know I love you. Before you walk out that door and I never see you again, I need you to know I love you. You are amazing. You are strong and smart and caring, and I wish I could spend the rest of my life with you. I'll settle for loving you the rest of my life and wishing we'd met under very different circumstances."

Dawn looked up at him, still curled up in his lap. She wrapped her arms around his neck and brought his lips down to hers. She kissed him the way she did the first time they made love. Rushed and patient. All in and tentative. Gage wanted to hold her in that moment and never let go. Never let her walk away.

He knew he'd never see her again. He knew she was walking to her death. He knew Trevor would never let her go.

It broke Gage's heart, but he couldn't stop her. If he could go with her, he would, but he was still too injured to be of much help, and someone needed to distract their protectors.

"I love you, Gage," Dawn whispered against his lips.

"You don't have to say that," he argued.

She shook her head, their noses bumping. "I'm not just saying it. It's the truth. You scare me. You have since we met. I wanted you the first time I saw you, but we don't make sense. You're smart and successful, and I'm an addict with a target on my back. I wish we could have met a different way, but I will love you until I die. If things were different, I would love you a whole lot longer than I have."

Gage sucked in a breath, the reality hitting him hard. "Do everything possible to come back to me. Please."

She nodded. "I will. I promise."

"Okay, now, how are we getting you out of here?"

DAWN WATCHED Gage slip out of her room and prayed it wouldn't be the last time she saw him. She was scared. She knew what she was doing was dangerous, but she couldn't leave Savannah with that madman.

Gage was going to distract Zeke long enough for Dawn to get to the garage. Walker was sleeping, so she only needed to get past Zeke to get out of there. Dawn felt guilty for leaving, but she couldn't hide and hope someone else saved her daughter. Trevor wanted Dawn. So he'd get Dawn.

Footsteps passed by the bedroom. A door closed and Dawn opened her door. No one was in the hallway and the bathroom door was closed. She pulled her bedroom door closed silently, twisting the knob to close the door and hoping it was quiet enough to get away.

The keys for the SUV were on a hook by the door, since Zeke and Walker both needed access. Dawn grabbed the keys and opened the garage door. She closed it quietly and tiptoed to the vehicle.

The interior lit up when she opened the door, so she got in quickly, being careful not to slam the door. Zeke would only stay in the bathroom looking at the fake leak Gage was telling him about for so long. Even though he wouldn't know she was gone, he'd hear the garage door and know what was going on.

Dawn put her foot on the brake and pressed the ignition button at the same time she hit the button to open the garage. She stared at the door leading to the house, waiting for someone to come flying through it. She glanced in the mirror, hoping the garage door was faster than Zeke.

As soon as the garage looked high enough for the SUV to clear it, she put the vehicle into reverse and started out the garage. Slow wasn't an option when they'd be after her any second. She hit the button to close the garage door and hit the gas to back down the short driveway fast.

Dawn backed out onto the quiet street just as the front door opened. Zeke ran outside, yelling at her to stop.

Dawn ignored him and took off. She had to save her daughter. No matter the consequences.

24

———

"WHAT IN THE HELL IS WRONG WITH YOU?" ZEKE YELLED AT Gage. "You let her go? You encouraged this?"

"You know she'd never forgive herself. How can you blame me?"

"Because you love her. Why would you let her do this, help her do this, if you love her?"

"It's because I love her! Because she'll never be the woman I love if she sits here and does nothing while her daughter is raped and beaten and murdered by that sick fuck. So stop being mad at me and do your fucking job and help her."

Zeke glared at Gage. He ran a hand over his head and shook his head. "She's not coming back."

"I know. And she knows. But she's willing to take that chance."

Zeke ran a hand down his face. He closed his eyes.

"You're former military, right?"

Zeke nodded.

"You would have given your life for strangers, for people

you've never met. You have to understand she would do the same for her child."

Zeke nodded. "I do understand, but I don't want her to end up dead."

"Then help her. There was no way you would have been able to stop her, so help her. Get your team there. Fix this."

"She knows where he is?" Zeke asked.

Gage shrugged. "She has a guess. The only place that makes sense."

Zeke narrowed his eyes for a second, then sighed when he figured it out. "Davis Developments. Where she can give him access."

Gage nodded. "That's what we figured."

"And that's where she's headed."

"It is. But you can't stop her."

"Stop who? What's going on?" Walker asked, rubbing his eyes and taking in the room.

Zeke was standing on the front porch, the door wide open. Gage was right behind him, inside but exposed.

"What the hell are you two doing? A rookie could pick you off without a second thought," Walker barked. He yanked Gage back, then reached for Zeke.

Zeke walked in and closed the door. "Dawn's gone."

"What the hell do you mean, she's gone?"

"She took the SUV and fled. Trevor has her kid."

"What? How the fuck did that happen?" Walker snapped.

Zeke walked away from the door and laid the whole story out for Walker. By the end, Walker was pacing like a caged animal ready for a snack.

"Why the hell are we still standing here?" Walker asked.

"Because she needs time to get there," Gage said.

"I thought you cared about her. Why the fuck are we giving her time to get to a crazy son-of-a-bitch?"

"Because she has to. She made this choice. It's no different than joining up and serving our country," Zeke said.

"Fuck that. This is all kinds of different. How many times did you go into hostile territory alone? How many missions did you go on without your team? Without backup and backup for your backup? Or training or communication or someone knowing every fucking thing you were about to do? This isn't the same thing. Don't try to lie to make yourself feel better. You let her go. You're to blame if he kills her." Walker turned his glare on Gage. "So are you. When you love someone, you do everything you can to protect them. Even if it means protecting them from themselves or from someone they love. You don't let her go off on her own to face a psycho."

"Don't tell me I don't love her. I'd do anything for her. Including helping her save her daughter," Gage snarled at Walker.

"You have a twisted fucking way of showing that," Walker snapped back.

Zeke stepped between the two of them as they each took a step toward the other.

Gage knew Walker could lay him out with one hit, but he was willing to take it. He loved Dawn. He would have given his life for her. But she was the only one who could save Savannah. So Gage did what he could to help her get there.

"Stop fucking fighting and let's go. We know where she's going," Zeke said.

Walker glared at Gage again, then turned his look toward Zeke. "Did you at least let Montgomery know?"

"Yeah. He's reaching out to Marcus and sending a team to get us. Since we don't have a ride."

"Let's get ready. We have no idea what we'll be walking in to."

A BLACK SUV was in the parking lot of Davis Developments when Dawn arrived. The windows were dark, making it impossible for her to see if someone was in the vehicle or not. It didn't matter. She knew where she had to go.

The front door was unlocked, something that didn't surprise her and told her she was in the right place. Dawn swiped her badge at the desk and the gate beeped, then whooshed open for her to enter.

It wasn't hard to guess where Trevor was. His father's old office. The one Tabitha insisted Dawn use for her own. Dawn hadn't set it up yet, but she had her computer there. And a picture of Savannah on the desk. That was as far as she went toward personalizing the space she didn't feel was hers.

Dawn made it to the door and saw Savannah tied to a chair in the corner. One of the plastic chairs from the conference room next door, not a chair that was normally in the office. Trevor sat in Dawn's chair, staring at the pictures on the wall, left over from his father.

"I always thought this would be my office one day," Trevor said. "When I was young, it was exciting to think about coming here and building something like he did."

"What changed?" Dawn asked.

Savannah looked up at Dawn. Savannah's eyes went wide and tears fell freely from them, soaking into the already drenched fabric tied around her mouth. "Mom," she tried to say.

Dawn moved toward Savannah, but Trevor spun in his chair and pointed his gun at Savannah.

"You don't need to go over there. Sit down right here." He pointed to the chair on the other side of the desk. When Dawn didn't move, he cocked the gun.

Savannah squealed, and Dawn hurried forward.

"I'm sitting. Leave her out of this. She has nothing to do with it."

Trevor chuckled. "She has everything to do with this. Don't you get it? She's your heir. This will all be hers one day. At least, that's how these things are supposed to work." He focused over Dawn's shoulder at Savannah. "Unless someone sneaks in and steals what belongs to you, Savannah. It's like your mom never learned about sharing or being a good person. You know what I'm talking about."

Savannah whimpered again, but Dawn didn't look back at her.

"I never asked for this. I didn't know your father had so much until after he died."

"It doesn't really matter, though. Because you benefited from it. You got what was supposed to be mine. You got my money, and then you cut off the access my father gave me to move money through the company. Everything was fine until you took over."

"He never would have done that," Dawn said.

Trevor snorted. "Oh, he did. He wanted to make sure I didn't hurt anyone. That whore you meet with all the time? Tabitha went and tattled on me like a little bitch. If it wasn't for her, dear old dead dad wouldn't have had to give me access. And you're going to give it back to me."

"After you let Savannah go," Dawn said.

Trevor looked at Savannah, then Dawn, then shook his head. "Nah. She stays."

"I'm not going to do anything until you let her go. You have me. You don't need her."

"You don't think so?" Trevor stood. He held Dawn's gaze as he walked across the room.

Dawn turned to watch him.

He stopped in front of Savannah and tilted her chin up. "We've had fun together. She's a feisty one." He pressed the tip of his gun to her chest. He dragged it down, exposing the edge of her bra. "But she learned it's better to do what I say. Right, beautiful?"

Savannah cried and tried to move away from him, but Trevor grabbed her hair and yanked her up. Her hands kept her bound to the chair.

"Stop!" Dawn shouted. She was out of her chair and moving toward them when Trevor swung the gun around to her.

"If you don't sit down and do what I say, one of you gets a bullet. I don't really care who gets one first, but you're more valuable to me, so I'm leaning toward putting one in her pretty chest. Right between these plump tits." He nudged one of Savannah's breasts with the edge of the gun.

"Get away from her, and I'll do whatever you want me to do."

Trevor grinned. "Perfect. That's all I'm asking for."

He took a step away from Savannah, and Dawn breathed for the first time since he got up. He walked toward Dawn and pointed to the chair he vacated with the gun. "You need to be at the controls."

Dawn stood and walked around her desk. She sat down at the chair and logged in. "Why did you kill your father?"

"Because he told me he gave everything I earned to someone else."

"How did you earn it?" Dawn opened her email so she could send a message to someone, but she wasn't sure who to send an email to. She didn't have Gage's email, and he wouldn't be checking, anyway. She didn't know how to contact Rose Protection Agency or the FBI or anyone. She was alone.

"What the fuck are you doing?" Trevor barked.

"What? Nothing?" Dawn stammered. She closed the email and went to the accounts.

"Why do you care how I earned my money? Why are you stalling? I told you to come alone!" He was out of his seat and pressing the gun to Savannah's head again.

"I did! I did! No one is here."

"Then why are you stalling?"

"Because I figured if I'm going to die, I want to know why."

Trevor glared at her. "You want to know the whole story? How your favorite patient was such a horrible man, and an even worse father?"

"I don't believe that."

"Yeah, well, he was." Trevor took the gun from Savannah's head and sat down again. He looked over Dawn's shoulder at one of the pictures. "My mother was the most amazing person in the world. She always watched out for my brother and me. When she died, we lost both our parents. Dad put everything into this place. He worked long hours and barely spoke to us when he came home. My brother and I learned to fend for ourselves. Clyde took to stealing. Got caught by the wrong person and ended up getting involved with Damon Street."

Dawn gasped.

"I see you know the name?"

Dawn nodded. "I've heard it."

"Everyone has. But not everyone knows that Damon murdered my brother. When he did, I decided I'd get my revenge. It took me a lot of years, but I got my revenge. I took the one thing Damon wanted. His position of power. Because I had something he never did. A rich daddy."

"And the money helped you get ahead."

"It's still helping me. See, my boss needs this money. Needs the access to funnel our funds. If it's gone, I'm no longer as useful. That's not an option for me."

"And when your dad said he gave it to someone else, you killed him because you were angry. Why not just talk to him?"

"I'm a man of action. Speaking of action." Trevor stood and went to Savannah again. "Quit stalling and return my access. Pension fund, benevolence fund, city maintenance, and Davis Investments. I want in on all of it."

"I can't do that," Dawn said.

He cocked the gun again and pointed it at Savannah's head. "Try again."

"No! No! I don't have access to all of that. I can do the pension and benevolence, but the investment fund isn't something I've ever accessed."

"Fine. Do those. And the maintenance fund."

Dawn nodded. Her stomach turned as she reversed the work she and Tabitha did to cut him out of their system. They could do it again, but he wouldn't stop. He would keep coming back.

"Where is the money going?"

"Do you think I'm dumb enough to tell you that?"

"If you kill me, this will all be erased tomorrow. Everyone knows what you've been doing. Tabitha and the rest of the executive team will revert all these privileges in a day."

"They wouldn't dare."

"Why not? Why would they let you ruin this company? You might hate your father, but these people don't. These people loved him. He gave everything he had to them. He was like a father to them. A grandfather. He treated them like family. Giving everything he had to them. Making sure they knew how much they were valued and appreciated."

"Like he never did to me. Is that what you're trying to say? Get me upset. Make me emotional and angry. Do you really think I care? That the old man's thoughts are news to me? He was a shitty father. He never put me first. I'm guessing that's why he left everything to you. Because he knows you're the same as he was. Another parent who couldn't care less about their kid. I mean, do you know how easy it was for me to talk Savannah into my vehicle? Do you have any idea? All I had to tell her was that you were stuck at work and sent me. It happened so many times that she didn't even think twice about it being a lie." He turned back to Savannah and smiled. "Isn't that right?"

Savannah pleaded and apologized to Dawn with her eyes.

Dawn smiled at her daughter. She would always have things to make up for, but getting Savannah caught in the middle of this because she wasn't a good enough parent was something she could never forgive herself for.

"You're right," Dawn said. "Your father thought of me as his daughter. He thought of me as the child he always wanted but never had. Who could blame him after two disappointments like you and Clyde? I mean, really, did you think all of this was going to make things better? That you could steal his money and feel like you got what you deserved? I know you think he did, but he was dying anyway. And one of his last actions when he was alive was to make sure you knew exactly what he thought of you. Exactly how much you meant to him."

"Shut up, you stupid bitch. You don't know anything!" Trevor came at her.

Dawn grabbed the letter opener from her desk and stabbed Trevor with it. She hit his thigh, so it wouldn't kill him, but it was enough to send him to his knees.

Dawn scrambled the other way around the desk and grabbed Savannah. She was heavy, especially in the chair, but Dawn used the adrenaline coursing through her and half-dragged-half-carried Savannah out of the office.

Dawn went into the conference room next door, even though she knew Trevor wouldn't stay down for long.

She pulled the gag from Savannah's mouth.

"Mom! He's going to kill us."

"Shh! I know. But I had to try to get you away from him." She ducked her head to work on the ties holding Savannah to the chair and heard Trevor stand in the room. Something fell off her desk, or was thrown.

He shouted, his footsteps heavy as he tried to follow them.

Dawn got Savannah's hands free, and they both untied one of her ankles. She wasn't tied very tight or very well, which made it easy to free her.

"Mom?" Savannah whispered.

"Stay behind me. No matter what. Do you understand me?"

Savannah nodded.

"I love you."

"I love you, Mom."

Dawn heard Trevor outside the door. His steps carried

him past the conference room. He was going for the front door.

Dawn crept out of their hiding place. She held the letter opener in her hand, wishing she had a gun. She picked up a stapler from the table. It was better than nothing.

As soon as Dawn stepped into the hallway, Trevor turned.

He raised his arm.

A spark lit the air.

A blast rang out.

Then pain like Dawn had never felt sliced through her thigh.

"Mom!" Savannah shouted.

Dawn caught herself on the doorframe. The pain made her feel sick. Her leg gave out, and she fell to the floor.

Trevor came forward, his gun still pointed at them.

Then all hell broke loose.

"Hands up, Trevor Davis! You're under arrest," a voice shouted from the doorway.

Dawn swallowed her sob. They were safe.

"I'm not going down like this," Trevor yelled back.

Trevor fired again, the bullets zipping past Dawn and Savannah. Savannah screamed. Dawn shoved her to the floor.

A door slammed, and the gunfire stopped.

People rushed in, dressed in bulletproof vests and dark clothes, with their agencies written across the front. Police, FBI, SWAT, F-BOMB, Rose. They were all there.

Lorelei Sloane was at the front of the pack. She met Dawn's gaze, assessing quickly where she needed to focus her attention.

Dawn gave Lorelei a thumbs up so the agent would know she and Savannah were okay. All things considered.

Lorelei and three others surrounded the door Trevor went through. She shouted for him to come out, but Dawn didn't pay attention to what he said.

"Mom!" Savannah screamed.

Adam rushed to Dawn's side, followed by Zeke and Walker.

"Savannah?" Adam asked.

Savannah nodded.

"Are you hurt?"

Savannah shook her head. "Help my mom. She saved me. She got me out of there before he could do anything. He said... He was going to hurt me if she didn't come."

"We'll take her," Zeke said, reaching for Savannah.

She went willingly into his familiar embrace. "Zeke."

"Hey, kid. Your dad's at the hospital, and your mom will be there soon. Want to ride with us?" Zeke asked.

Savannah nodded. "Can I ride with my mom?"

Zeke looked at Dawn and nodded. "Yeah. We can wait for her."

Adam did a quick exam of Dawn's gunshot wound. "You were lucky, but it looks like you opened your stitches from last week. They're going to want to fix that, and stitch this up."

"Did they get him?" Dawn asked.

Adam nodded. "He's in custody. Lorelei wanted him alive."

"Good," Dawn whispered.

Adam breathed a laugh and shook his head. "You're just like the rest of them."

"The rest of who?"

"The Curvy Vigilantes. I have a feeling they're going to be at the hospital when we get there. They're going to be pissed you didn't call them for help," Adam said.

"I barely know them."

"Doesn't matter. You're all in this together. You're part of the group now, whether you like it or not."

Dawn didn't know what that meant, but she couldn't

worry about that while she was bleeding all over her office. Adam helped get her on a stretcher and into the back of an ambulance. Zeke and Savannah rode with her to the hospital, with Walker and Adam right behind in their vehicles.

The hospital was a zoo. Cameras and visitors and half the law enforcement in the area were all there. Zeke shielded Dawn and Savannah from the attention, but it was clearly useless as the reporters called them by name.

Inside the hospital, Dawn saw Frannie and Raina first. They rushed to her side, Raina ignoring her fiancé to grab Dawn's hand.

"Are you okay?" Raina asked.

Dawn nodded. "I'll be fine." She forced her lips into a smile for the woman who was barely more than a stranger.

"You should have called us," Frannie said.

"I... Why?" Dawn asked.

Frannie pulled out a black mask and pressed it into Dawn's hand. "Because we would have been there for you so you didn't have to face him alone. We would have helped."

"Why would you help me?"

"Because you've been helping us this whole time. You're a good person, Dawn Patterson. And we protect our own," Frannie said.

"I..." Dawn didn't know what to say. She'd never had women she felt close to. Women she could trust.

"Mom?" Savannah said.

"It's okay, hun. I'll be okay." Dawn smiled at her daughter and hoped Savannah would forgive her one day.

"You're a hero, Mom. Thank you for saving me."

Dawn's throat tightened. "I would do anything for you, Savannah. I know I haven't always shown you that, but—"

"You're not the same person you were before, Mom. I'm sorry I held it against you."

"It's not always easy to let go," Mackenzie said from behind Savannah.

Savannah turned. "Do I know you?"

Mackenzie nodded. "We're never met, but we spoke on the phone. You're a brave girl, Savannah."

"You helped me that night. You taught me how to save her," Savannah whispered. She cried and threw herself into Mackenzie's arms.

Mackenzie smiled at Dawn. "I got her. You go get fixed up. We'll be there soon."

Dawn nodded and let the hospital staff wheel her away. Adam and Raina stayed with Dawn, leaving Frannie, Walker, and Zeke with Savannah and Mackenzie. Dawn knew they'd protect her with their lives.

WHAT GAGE DID WASN'T illegal, but it wasn't exactly smart, either. He rode to Davis Developments with the men from Rose Protection Agency, even though they threatened to leave him behind. When they arrived, Zeke handed Gage over to Marcus with a scowl and a warning of what Gage did.

Marcus smirked at him. Gage knew Marcus would have done the same thing. But that didn't mean it was smart.

Even worse, Dawn was shot. Something that could have been prevented. But Dawn and Savannah were alive, and that was the most important part of the night.

Gage sat in the hospital waiting room, hoping someone would give him information about Dawn. He wasn't family, so whenever he asked, he was told they couldn't give him details, but he didn't want to leave.

A woman strode by with purpose, stopping at the desk

before heading toward the elevators. She was almost out of sight before Gage recognized her.

"Lorelei!" Gage shouted.

She turned and spotted him. She waited, her foot tapping with impatience.

"Is she okay?" Gage asked.

"No one's told you?" Lorelei asked.

Gage's heart sank. "No one will tell me anything."

"Come on. Let's go see her." She looked at the man behind the desk and flashed her badge. "He's with me."

The man nodded.

Lorelei hit the button for the elevator. It opened almost immediately, and they stepped inside.

"Is she alive?"

"She's fine. The bullet grazed her leg. Her other stitches opened up, so they want to keep her for a day or two. Trevor is in federal custody, being booked tonight. He'll be in jail until a trial. We have enough evidence to hold him without bail."

"What about Savannah?"

"Not a scratch. She has a nasty bruise on the side of her face, but she said he didn't touch her other than that. She'll have some bruising on her wrists and ankles where he tied her to a chair, but she was lucky. It would have been worse if Dawn hadn't gone there."

"So, she did the right thing?"

Lorelei snorted. "I'm not going to say that. I wish she would have called me and told me what she thought. We were narrowing down the options and would have figured it out and been able to save her from what she went through, but—"

"It all worked out," Gage said.

Lorelei smiled as the elevator opened. "Thankfully, yeah."

Lorelei led the way down the hallway. She flashed her badge to two guards outside a room and told them Gage was okay to come in. The men stepped aside, and Gage got his first look at Dawn since she snuck out of the safe house.

The breath he hadn't realized he was holding whooshed out of him so fast he got lightheaded. He hurried to her side, ignoring the others in the room. "Are you okay? How bad is it?"

Dawn smiled and reached for him. She pulled him down for a kiss. "Thank you for helping me flee."

"I'm so sorry you were hurt. I shouldn't have let you go alone."

"He was going to kill me if anyone else showed up," the teenager who looked far too much like Dawn to be anyone but Savannah said. "She saved my life. You did, too. You're Gage, right?"

Gage straightened and looked at her. "I am. I'm guessing you're Savannah."

She stood and walked around Dawn's bed. When she walked straight into his arms, Gage breathed another shaky exhale.

"I'm so happy you're safe."

"Thank you for helping my mom."

"I'm happy you're both safe."

Savannah released him and returned to the other side of the bed. The man there put his arm around her and kissed the top of her head.

"Dawn was telling us about you. I'm Owen. And I'm really appreciative Dawn's had you to help her the last few weeks. I couldn't see how much she's changed."

"She's an amazing woman," Gage said.

Owen nodded. "She is. And she's an amazing mom."

Dawn sniffed, drawing all their attention. Tears trickled down her cheeks. "I never thought we'd all be in the same room talking positively about me."

Owen and Gage chuckled.

"There are a lot of positive things to say about you," Gage said. He leaned down to kiss her again, lingering for a second.

Dawn yawned. "I'm so sorry. They loaded me up on something that's going to make me tired."

"We'll go so you can rest," Owen said.

Gage started to follow them, but Dawn grabbed his hand.

"Will you stay?"

Gage nodded. "Absolutely." He turned to Owen and Savannah. "Nice meeting you both. I hope we see a lot more of each other."

They nodded, and Owen said, "We hope so, too."

Lorelei followed them out of the hospital room, leaving Dawn and Gage alone.

"Thank you," she whispered. "I can't tell you how scared I was, but I'm so grateful I was there."

"It looks like things are better between you two," Gage said.

Dawn chuckled. "It's funny how saving someone's life makes them forgive you for all the shit you did in the past."

"That and she loves you," Gage said.

"Mm hm," Dawn mumbled, sleep claiming her.

Gage sat in the chair next to her bed and watched her sleep. She was okay. Savannah was okay. And Trevor was going away. Everything was how it should be.

THE BOSS TAPPED her screen to call her new number two. Third one in a year. Her father would have her ass. If she hadn't taken care of him years ago.

"Yeah?"

"Trevor's compromised. He needs to be eliminated."

"And you want me to do it?"

She rolled her eyes. "I don't really give a fuck as long as he'd dead by morning. He can't talk."

"I'll take care of it."

"Good. One more thing."

"Yeah?"

"The FBI got too close. They know more than I want them to know. You need to interrogate the agent and find out everything."

"Done. Who's the agent?"

"Lorelei Sloane."

"I NOW PRONOUNCE you man and wife. You may kiss the bride," the minister said. He smiled and stepped back for the couple to have their moment.

Dawn couldn't hear what Adam whispered to Raina, but the look on her face said it was something scandalous. Dawn's lips curled up with Raina's before Adam sealed his lips over his bride's.

Cheers echoed all around celebrating the newly married couple. Dawn clapped with everyone else, feeling out of place at the wedding of two people she still didn't know well. But they insisted she and Gage come. And that they not bring a gift.

Raina went out of her way to make sure Dawn knew she wasn't being invited because she had money. She was being invited because Raina felt a connection to her. A bond that couldn't be broken.

Dawn was working on letting the Curvy Vigilantes in. It wasn't easy since she'd always been a private person, but when they all shared their stories, Dawn knew they understood what she'd been through in a way no one else ever would.

"That was a beautiful ceremony," Gage whispered in her ear, kissing her neck in a way that make her tingle all the way to her toes.

"It was. They're really in love."

Gage nodded. "They are. It's nice to see something good come out of all this madness."

"Hopefully the madness is over now."

Gage nodded, but the look on his face said he didn't believe that anymore than Dawn did.

Trevor didn't last twenty-four hours in jail before he was killed. Not that Dawn felt sorry for him in the least, but she knew he answered to someone, and that someone was still out there. Still pulling the strings and hurting others.

Lorelei hadn't stopped looking for connections, but she told Dawn at the rehearsal dinner she was frustrated because every lead she had went cold before she could get any new information.

"Are you ready for the reception?" Gage asked.

Dawn nodded, sliding her hand over his arm and letting him lead her out of the church.

The wedding was well-attended. Adam's entire extended family had come in from Vermont, and Raina's parents were there. Both had a few friends, including the Curvy Vigilantes and their significant others and kids. Rose Protection Agency attended, and so did all of F-BOMB since Adam's cousin was one of the owners.

Dawn hadn't felt so safe in public since before she'd learned about Trevor Davis.

Dawn's injuries were mostly healed. Her stitches were all out, and her bruises had faded, but the fear lingered at times.

The reception was loud and happy, two things Dawn hadn't experienced much of lately. She was looking forward to letting her guard down for a little while and celebrating the love of two people she was starting to think of as friends.

They danced and laughed and ate and drank, the night passing by in a rush of fun and happiness. Dawn downed a glass of water and let Mackenzie pull her away to the bathroom, since none of them were going anywhere alone.

"How's Savannah doing?" Mackenzie asked as they were washing their hands.

"She's doing well. I think it would have been worse if he'd done anything to her, but she was lucky."

"She's lucky to have you for a mom. You saved her."

Dawn smiled. She had a hard time thinking of herself as saving Savannah. If it wasn't for her, Savannah never would have been in that situation. "Thanks."

"She's right," Lorelei said from a stall. She flushed the toilet and walked out. "Sorry for the eavesdropping, but Mackenzie's right. It's not easy to accept that you saved her when you're blaming yourself for her being there in the first place, but you saved her."

Dawn inhaled deep and nodded. "Thank you. Both of you. It isn't easy, especially because I don't want to think about her being vulnerable like that again."

"She won't be. You have your safe words now. It's something I recommend to all parents," Lorelei said.

"That's such a great idea," Mackenzie said.

Lorelei nodded and looked at her watch. Her face pinched in frustration.

"Everything okay?" Mackenzie asked.

Lorelei looked up and shook her head. "A contact needs to talk to me." Lorelei headed for the door.

"Now?" Mackenzie asked, following Lorelei out the door. Dawn was right behind them.

"Yeah. I'll be right back."

"Do you want us to go with you?" Mackenzie asked.

Lorelei waved her off. "I'll be fine. I'll see you guys in a little bit."

Mackenzie chewed on her lip. "I know she's an agent and all, but I worry about her."

Dawn didn't like it anymore than Mackenzie did, but Dawn knew there was nothing they could do to stop Lorelei. "She'll be fine. She'll be back soon."

Mackenzie and Dawn stared at the door until the ball-room door opened behind them, noise pouring out.

"What are you doing out here?" Raina asked. "Come dance with me!"

Mackenzie and Dawn smiled at each other, then let Raina pull them inside and onto the dance floor.

Dawn danced until her feet hurt and her side and thigh ached. She fell onto her chair and let Gage pull her feet to his lap. He pressed hard on her arches, and she groaned.

"Feel good?"

She nodded, moaning. "Don't stop."

"You say that a lot," Gage teased.

"And I always mean it."

Gage chuckled low, the sound vibrating through Dawn and settling low in her belly.

"I love you."

"I love you." He was quiet, his fingers working the pain from her feet. "Do you want to get married again someday?"

Dawn looked up at him. "I hope that's not a proposal."

Gage shook his head. "It's not. Just a question."

Dawn shrugged. "I don't know. I never really thought about it. I'm not opposed to marriage just because mine didn't work out. If I ever got married again, I'd do things differently."

"How so?"

"I'd make sure we knew each other well and were compatible before we got married. Probably live together for a while. Share all our secrets and know if we could survive the good and the bad."

"Makes sense. Are we talking bad like kidnapping and gunshots, or bad like canceled flights and shitty hotels?"

Dawn snorted a laugh. "I'm hoping the latter because I never want to experience the former again."

"Works for me."

Dawn settled in her seat again, wondering about marrying Gage. She didn't hate the idea, even though they hadn't known each other long. Maybe one day he'd ask. And she was pretty sure she'd say yes.

"Have you guys seen Lorelei?" Adam asked, stopping at their table.

"Nope," Gage said.

"I saw her earlier in the bathroom. She said she was meeting a contact," Dawn said.

"When was this?" Adam asked.

Dawn shrugged. She looked at Raina. "Before you saw Mackenzie and me in the hallway."

Raina looked at Adam. "At least two hours."

Adam swore and took off.

"What's going on?" Dawn asked.

"Lorelei's gone."

FRACTURE IS COMING JULY 5...

Lorelei wakes up in her old apartment with a vaguely familiar man standing over her. Beaten, bloody, but breathing, she doesn't remember how she got there, or the details of her life. But the stranger, Vinnie, says he's there to help. Help her heal, help her remember, and help her put an end to the evil she was chasing. An evil that isn't willing to let Lorelei remember what she already forgot.

PREORDER **FRACTURE** TODAY!

Everyone deserves justice. Even when they're no one.

Witnessing a murder was not on Frannie's bucket list.
Marcus had to find out what the curvy dancer knew.
They made a deal. She would help him, and he would find
the murderers. No one would know she was involved. She
hoped.

**Frannie and Marcus's story is available only to
subscribers.**
Sign up at https://dl.bookfunnel.com/y9ms2k2dq8 to get
FORSAKEN now.

Turn the page to read chapter one of FRACTURE.

FRACTURE
CHAPTER 1

Vinnie Morgan ignored the buzz of the phone on his hip and continued on his path. Something wasn't right. His gut told him he needed to investigate, and he never ignored his gut. Not when it was so loud.

Three days. It had been three days since anyone had heard from Lorelei Sloane. The badass woman who was in charge of the investigation hadn't been out of touch with her team since she established her team.

Going missing at her partner's wedding wasn't more of a comfort. Especially when he heard she was meeting with a contact. Not that it surprised Vinnie she would take off during a social event for work.

In Vinnie's line of work, people didn't go missing. Not when they were on a case. Not without someone knowing where they were. Sure, the gorgeous woman in charge could have shacked up with someone after the wedding, but that didn't feel right to Vinnie. He'd seen her in action. He knew her type. The type that would stop at nothing to get the job done and put the bad guys away.

He was the same type. It was why he was plucked from

the force and invited to join SWAT. A decision he never once second guessed.

Vinnie's heart pounded as he drew closer to the door. If he broke in, he could surprise a woman who was perfectly fine. If he ignored that fear, he could find anything.

No one was in the hallway. Not a sound came from behind any of the doors. Either they were expertly sound-proofed or no one was home. A high-end place like that could have been either. But it made Vinnie aware of every creak the floor made as he moved toward Lorelei Sloane's apartment.

The door was closed. It didn't appear to have been forced open at any point. The trim was intact and the door wasn't damaged. But something still wasn't right.

Vinnie tried the knob. Locked. He jiggled it a little and could tell the deadbolt wasn't engaged. A single woman living alone in a big city would never lock her doorknob only. Especially not one with her training.

He knocked softly, hoping he was wrong about every-thing and Ms. Sloane would open the door and tell him he was being paranoid and a creep. He waited, holding his breath so he didn't miss a sound from the other side of the door. None came, and Vinnie pulled out his lock-picking kit.

Less than ten seconds later, he had the door open and knew he wasn't being paranoid. Lorelei Sloane laid on her couch in the living room. She'd been badly beaten. Her beautiful face was marked with cuts and bruises. Her clothing was all in place. But she was not okay. She was far from okay.

She was barely alive.

Vinnie pulled out his phone just as the buzzing started up again. He swiped to answer, not caring who was calling him. "What?"

"Where the hell are you?" his boss barked.

Yeah, Vinnie sort of skipped town. Against orders. He would be lucky if he wasn't fired. Except he had good news. Sort of.

"I found her."

"Who?" Damien asked. Vinnie had his boss's attention now.

"Lorelei Sloane. She's in her apartment in Boston. We need an ambulance here now. Head trauma, bodily injury." Vinnie swallowed roughly as he took in the bloody clothes and bruises appearing on Lorelei's dark skin. He knew if he could see them, they were worse than they appeared. And so was she.

Noises in the background told Vinnie Damien was notifying everyone that Lorelei Sloane was alive and where she was. Vinnie set his phone down, putting it on speaker so he could hear if Damien asked more questions.

Vinnie probed her skull, checking for fractures.

She groaned and opened her eyes.

"You're safe now," Vinnie whispered to her.

She appeared to nod, then drifted off again.

"Hey, wake up. Stay with me."

Her eyes blinked open again, slowly like it was taking all her effort to open them.

"There you go. Do you know who you are?"

The pinch between her brows said she either thought he was insane or she had no idea who she was. Either was possible. She opened her mouth, then winced and slammed her eyes shut again.

"Lorelei, look at me. I need you to stay with me. Help is on the way."

She drew a breath, one that stopped in the middle with another wince.

Vinnie laid her head back on the couch and ran his hands over her sides. At least a few broken ribs. She wormed away from his touch, telling him where she hurt the worst. He held his breath and slid his hands over her hips to her legs. She didn't fight him until he touched her right ankle, which he realized was bent at an awkward angle.

"Fuck," Vinnie whispered.

"Paramedics and police should be there any minute," Damien said.

Vinnie sucked in a breath and looked back up at the woman he'd been watching for months. The woman who led a multi-agency group without any hesitation. She was strong and smart and capable.

And she was broken.

She opened her mouth again, a whisper of a word coming out.

Vinnie moved back to her head again and saw the marks around her throat. It could have been hands or it could have been something more. It didn't matter what it was, she was going to have a hard time talking for a while.

"I'm not going to let anyone else hurt you, Lorelei. You're safe now."

She nodded, the move jerky like it hurt. Her eyes filled with tears.

All Vinnie wanted to do was scoop her up and hold her, but he didn't know what other injuries she had. That and they'd never actually spoken, so him being in her apartment was more than a little fucked up.

Voices outside grew louder, then the squawk of a radio echoed in the hallway.

"In here," Vinnie said, drawing the attention of the

people working toward them. "I haven't cleared the apartment."

Two officers walked in first, guns drawn. They nodded to Vinnie, then spread out to search the place. Both called out clear and came back into the living room as the paramedics entered.

"Can you tell us what happened here, Mr. Morgan?" one of the cops asked, clearly getting the brief rundown from Damien.

Vinnie shook his head and watched the paramedics work. "I wish I could. I showed up and found her like this. She's been missing for three days. People were here two days ago, but there was no sign of her. She's an FBI Agent."

"It's pretty clear someone wanted her dead."

"Yeah. The people she's been investigating. We just don't know who that is."

"We'll get a crime lab out here. Hopefully we'll find something. Are you local?"

Vinnie shook his head. "No, sir. I live in Niagara Falls, New York. Where she's been for the last few months, running the investigation."

"That's a long way from here."

"Yeah. These people are smart."

"Too smart."

Vinnie nodded. Unfortunately, that was accurate.

"Your name is Lorelei Sloane. You are an FBI Agent," the woman said.

Lorelei nodded, the small movement making her brain feel like it was full of eggs. Raw ones that had no shape and would make you sick.

Which was how she'd spent the last day.

"Okay," Lorelei whispered. It was the best she could do with the damage to her throat.

"Do you remember anything about who attacked you?"

Lorelei groaned, sending a bolt of pain through her throat. She jerked at the feel and send more pain through the rest of her body. Tears welled up in her eyes, but she refused to let them fall. She was not going to show her pain.

"Do you need more meds?" the menacing man in the corner asked. He was up and out of his seat, hurrying to her side.

The nurses said his name was Vinnie and he came in with her, but Lorelei didn't remember him. Not that it was a shock since she didn't remember any damn thing.

"I'm fine," she hissed.

She was being a bitch to everyone. She fucking hated feeling like she was incapable of doing something, and at the moment, she was incapable of doing everything. She couldn't go to the bathroom alone. She couldn't sit up. She could speak or think or remember anything.

All she wanted to do was cry and scream and remember who she was and what happened to her.

"Maybe we should do this another time," Vinnie suggested.

The woman sighed heavily. She glared at Vinnie, but he didn't blink. She looked back at Lorelei and flipped her tablet closed. "Fine. I'll be back tomorrow."

"Thanks," Vinnie said in a tone that suggested he was less than grateful.

Lorelei watched the woman walk out of the room. She knew there was a reason she was there, but everything was so mixed up that she had no idea. "Who was that?"

Vinnie moved to the chair next to the bed. "That was

Alexis Waterford. She's an FBI Agent in your old office. She said you didn't work together so you only met a handful of times, but she is the one trying to find whoever attacked you."

Lorelei nodded, trying to pretend she followed any of that. She'd been told over and over again that she was an FBI Agent, but she wasn't even sure what that really meant. Since she woke up the day before with Vinnie hovering over her, she hadn't recognized anyone or anything. It was all foreign to her, including the woman in the mirror.

The doctors said it was because of the assault. She'd been beaten so badly she didn't recognize herself, but shouldn't she recognize something? Her eyes, her hair? Something?

For all Lorelei knew, it was a stranger staring back at her.

The only thing she was sure of was that Vinnie was one of the good guys. She couldn't explain how she knew that, but she did. He saved her. He protected her. He hadn't left her side since she woke up.

A knock on the door made Vinnie tense. He moved around the bed to check whoever was at the door before opening it.

"Vinnie Morgan?" a man asked.

"Yes, sir. I'm sorry—Oof," Vinnie said.

Lorelei panicked. Someone hit him or did something to knock the words out of Vinnie.

"Thank you," the other man whispered.

What did that mean?

"Happy I made it in time, sir," Vinnie said.

Who the hell—?

The curtain separating Lorelei from the men slid to the side and they both stepped back into view. Lorelei's gaze slid down Vinnie, cataloging him to make sure he wasn't harmed.

Satisfied her protector was okay, she looked at the other man. Blond hair, blue eyes. White. There was something familiar about him, but Lorelei wasn't sure what it was.

"Holy fuck. Are you okay?" He moved toward her quickly, crossing the space before Lorelei could say anything.

She recoiled when he reached out to touch her, and he pulled back.

"Sorry. I should have asked where your injuries are. I was just going to touch your hand," the blond man said.

"Who..." She looked from him to Vinnie, then back to the blond man.

"This is Adam Johnson. He's your partner. At the FBI," Vinnie said.

Lorelei looked at the man.

He held her gaze for a moment, then turned his eyes to Vinnie. "Why are you telling her who I am?"

"She doesn't remember anything. Who took her, from where, where she was held. And she doesn't remember who she is. You're the first one to show up that she should know, but clearly she doesn't know you either."

Adam looked at her, his face going soft.

"Nope," Lorelei said. "No pity. Fuck that. Get out if you're going to look at me like that."

Adam snorted. "Well they didn't knock your personality out. We just have to help you remember everything else."

"We?" Lorelei asked.

Adam nodded. "Raina is here. My wife. You were at our wedding when you went missing. And your cousin, Karli, is here with her boyfriend, Cole."

"Cousin?"

Adam nodded and looked at Vinnie. "Is it okay if the others come in?"

Vinnie nodded. "As long as everyone gives her space and time to process. Maybe start with her cousin."

"Okay. Thanks."

"I'm here, too, you know," Lorelei snapped at them. She didn't like people making decisions for her.

"You are, but if you don't know me, chances are you're not sure what the doctors have said about visitors and recovery. I'm asking the person in the room who has an intact memory."

Lorelei scowled at both men. She wanted to be indignant, but they weren't wrong.

Adam walked out, saying something to someone in the hallway before coming right back in. He held the shoulders of a Black woman with dark hair like Lorelei's, same tight curls and dark brown eyes. She had full lips and red circles around her eyes.

"Oh, my God," she whispered as she moved toward Lorelei. "I'm so happy you're alive."

"Me too," Lorelei said. She stared at the woman she knew was her cousin and tried to remember her. Just like Adam, she was familiar, but her mind wasn't letting her access any of her memories.

"Adam said you don't remember anything."

Lorelei looked at Adam, once more trying to place him. She kept scanning the room and found Vinnie. "I remember Vinnie."

Karli looked at the man who'd been Lorelei's one and only memory and smiled. "I don't remember Vinnie. Have we met?"

Vinnie shook his head. "No, ma'am. I'm on the SWAT

Team that's been called in a few times. I heard about your cousin's disappearance and couldn't let it go."

"Wait, we didn't know each other before?" Lorelei asked.

Vinnie shook his head. "No. Not well. We've met, but we've never spoken until yesterday."

"Well, shit. I thought I remembered you." Lorelei looked at the man who said he was her partner. "Wait. How do I know you're all here to keep me safe and not to hurt me again?"

"Look at me, Lorelei," Vinnie said. He sat down in the chair next to her bed. "You know I'm not going to let anything happen to you. You know I'm here to protect you and help you and keep you safe. You might not know me, but you know that."

Lorelei looked at the man and nodded slowly. The beeping of her heart rate monitor slowed as she stared at him.

He was right. She wasn't afraid of him. He wasn't a threat. He was the one who saved her. And he was protecting her in ways she didn't even realize. Making sure she was given time to rest and not pressured to reveal things she didn't know.

He was her guardian angel.

"Wow," Karli whispered from Lorelei's other side. "I've never seen you calm down that quickly."

"Same. You're good for her, Vinnie," Adam said.

Vinnie didn't look away from Lorelei as he spoke. "She's good for all of us. I'm just lucky that I get to be around her for a little while."

Lorelei's body tingled at his words. Desire? Maybe. Appreciation? Definitely. "Thank you."

Vinnie nodded at her. "I'm not leaving unless you tell me

you want me to. And if you do, I'll be right outside making sure no one ever hurts you again. I promise you that."

Lorelei sucked in a breath. She might not remember anything about her life before she woke up, but she knew, without a doubt, no man had ever made her a promise like that. And no man had ever made her feel like she didn't have to do it all. Like she could lean on someone else and know she wouldn't fall.

It was a damn good feeling. Because with Vinnie by her side, Lorelei knew she'd find answers. All the answers.

PREORDER **FRACTURE** TODAY!

ABOUT THE AUTHOR

USA TODAY Bestselling Author Mary E Thompson spent most of her childhood wishing she had a few less curves. She hid in the pages of books because her favorite characters never cared what size her clothes were. Now, neither does Mary, and she writes stories that celebrate women like her. Real women who have curves, chase dreams, and find love, because we should all be happy, no matter our dress size.

Mary spends her non-writing time with her husband and two kids, watching too much TV, cheering for her hometown football team (Go Bills!), and hiding chocolate from her family.

Visit https://MaryEThompson.com/ to sign up for Mary's newsletter, **Romancing the Curves**. Subscribers get free ebooks and other fun stuff, like exclusive, members only content and giveaways, plus are the first to know about new releases and sales!

9 781953 879455